ALSO BY RICHARD LAN

Dan and Frankie se

Dan and Frankie Save the

Non-fiction

How to Not Die (According to Movies)

DAN AND FRANKIE AND THE END OF EVERYTHING

By

Richard Langridge

A Dan and Frankie novel

(#2)

DAN AND FRANKIE AND THE END OF EVERYTHING

First edition February 2017

ISBN: 978-1542770835

www.richardlangridgeauthor.com

FOREWORD

Dear Reader,

I would like to apologise in advance for the things you are about to read—all of which may or may not be true, depending on the strength of your bullshit detector. And before you descend upon me like a pack of rabid, sex-starved flying monkeys, please note I am only as responsible for the things portrayed in this book as a mentally ill person is for the feces he smears along the walls of his padded cell. We can't help playing with our shit—it's just what we do.

That being said, I hope you enjoy.

(Just don't say you weren't warned.)

—Rich

October 10th 2016

PROLOGUE

"Most gods throw dice, but Fate plays chess, and you don't find out til too late that he's been playing with two queens all along."

— **Terry Pratchett**

PART 1
AMERSTOW'S MOST WANTED

INTERLUDE—PART 1

DR PETER NATHANIEL LAKE was an average-looking man. He was my height, maybe an inch taller, with short, neatly trimmed hair the exact shade and colour of an overcast sky right before rain. I put him around early fifties. He wore a shit-brown corduroy jacket, with elbow patches that looked like they had been hand-sewn by small fingers — for reasons I could not explain. The word *nondescript* came to mind. He was the kind of man that could walk through a crowded room without a single person noticing. I thought he would have made for a brilliant spy.

'So tell me, Mr Pratt,' he said after a long pause, leaning back in his chair to better regard me over his clasped fingers. 'What exactly is it I can do for you today?'

I took a moment to observe my surroundings. Lake's office was a single room on the third floor of a dingy little building near downtown. Like Lake himself, there was very little of note. It had a large desk near the back by the window, possibly but not necessarily oak, behind which Lake himself sat, me on the other side. All along the walls hung dozens of framed certificates and diplomas that I had the feeling were probably of things very respectable and important. By the desk to my right stood a plant of whose name I did not know, and next to it, sitting dumped on the desk like some kind of huge, elaborate paperweight, was a rack of little silver balls — a metronome.

I wasn't sure exactly what I'd been expecting the guy's office to look like. More of those long psychiatrist's chairs, for sure. Whatever you call those. But the guy didn't have a single one. I wondered exactly how well being a psychiatrist paid, if it would have been rude to ask.

Lake must have caught my hesitation, because he suddenly tilted his head.

'Mr Pratt?'

I took a steadying breath.

Here goes nothing.

'Do you believe in curses, doc?'

'*Curses?*'

'Yeah. You know, like how some people seem doomed to have the same bad shit happen to them over and over again?'

'You mean fate.'

I shrugged. 'Fate, curse. Whatever you want to call it.'

He took a lot longer answering than I would have liked.

'Do you believe *you* are cursed, Daniel?'

'I dunno. It's just that, even from when I was little, weird things have always seemed to happen to me.'

He raised an eyebrow. 'How so?'

Well, there was that whole "alien invasion" thing that one time. Not to mention that other thing that happened recently...

I shook my head. 'Just... *weird*. You know — *not normal.*'

'You feel you're an outlier.'

I fidgeted in my chair. On the desk before me, the metronome continued to clack away. Man, who knew therapy would be this hard?

I sighed. 'Have you ever seen *Titanic*, doc?'

'Of course. It's a very famous movie.'

'Right, well, for most people, they see it as a love story. An example of how love conquers all, even in the most impossible of circumstances.'

He nodded. 'That's right. It was very moving, if I recall.'

I leaned forward. 'Want to know how I see it, doc?'

He held his hands out to the sides. 'Of course.'

'*It's a horror movie.* Think about it; the fear, the devastation, all those countless lives lost. Those that don't drown immediately quickly freeze to death in the Atlantic's icy waters. Tell me that isn't a horror story — *and it's like I'm the only one who sees it.*'

'Well, I guess that's one way to look at it —'

'And don't even get me *started* on that fucking floating door.'

Lake was silent a moment as he considered this.

'You feel as though you're different from most people — that you've been singled out?'

'*Yes!*'

Man, this guy's good.

'*By whom?* God? The universe? Because if what you say is true, that would mean somebody must be behind it — the architect of your misery, so to speak.'

Actually, doc, she goes by many names. Nidreth. Khavhu. Yithyla. They say to look upon her is to go mad.

I shrugged. 'I dunno.'

There was another long pause. They were starting to piss me off.

'I sense there's something you're not telling me, Mr Pratt,' he said, when the silence had finally run its course. 'Therapy only works if all

5

parties fully commit to the healing process.' He smiled faintly, in a way that wasn't patronising at all, and leaned forward in his chair—a chair I suddenly noticed looked a lot more expensive and comfortable than mine. '*Please*. You're safe here. Tell me what's really on your mind.'

I sighed.

Fuck it. You want to know what's really on my mind, doc? You got it.

I leaned back in my seat. 'So I guess it all started that day over at Lake Fairburn...'

ONE

IF THERE'S ONE THING you need to know about Amerstow, it's that Amerstow is not like your ordinary city.

We have a funny name—that's the first thing. We're bigger than a town, but smaller than a city, though the "powers that be" supposedly had to call us something, and thought "city" was the most fitting. We have more missing persons per square foot than any other city in the state—and that's without taking into account all the countless homeless people that disappear annually, too, but that nobody seems to care about, because they're homeless. Unemployment is a real issue. We're a city that is famous for having literally nothing famous happen here in all the hundred and fifty years of its existence.

Of course, then there's that "other" stuff.

If you've lived here for any amount of time, you'll have probably already heard the whispers. In the waiting room at the doctor's office. The local cafes. Hushed chatter from people of various ages and walks of life, all of strange things happening the instant the sun goes down. Things stirring in the darkness. People disappearing, always under suspicious circumstances, never to be heard from again. Of course, if you were to ask anybody outright, they'd deny any knowledge of it. As a people, it's not something we like to openly talk about.

Let me give you some examples.

So remember that time Ronald Reagan was almost assassinated? Well, a week leading up to it, the residents of our fair city were inundated one night with phone calls from, and I quote, "wheezy sounding men", who warned them that somebody was going to make an attempt on the president's life, and that he or she needed to be stopped. This went on for approximately four hours, until, as inexplicably as they'd begun, the phone calls suddenly ceased, leaving everybody dumbfounded as to exactly what the hell was going on.

Then there was that time it rained popcorn for a solid week.

Yes, you heard me. *Fucking popcorn* — salted caramel, to be exact. It started on the Monday and ended on the Friday, leaving the streets looking like the morning after at a frat party that had included lots of popcorn for some reason — not that you'll find any record of this anywhere. Like I said, as a city, we really don't care to talk about it.

To say that weird shit happens here is an understatement.

So with all this in mind, I really shouldn't have been surprised then, when, slipping behind the wheel of my Accord whilst on my way to work one Monday morning, I found my burrito stalker sitting on my backseat waiting for me.

A little backstory:

It had all started in those first couple months following the whole Belmont Grove incident. *Burritos.* I'd find them in weird places — my shoes, my chair, sitting on my desk at work. Wherever I went, they were always there, fresh and piping hot and delicious. At first I thought little of it, that it was probably just one of my coworkers playing a prank. Ha-ha. Very funny, *Ted.*

But then I'd started finding them in other places — on my doorstep, shoved through my mailbox, or sitting on the front seat of my Accord.

Suddenly things hadn't seemed so funny anymore.

Then, just as I was beginning to think I had a genuine burrito-stalker on my hands, the offerings (if that's what they were) suddenly stopped, leaving me confused and angry and scratching my head as to what the purpose of it all had been.

That had been weeks ago.

Now, I'm not sure whether I saw the burrito lying on the dash first, or whether I just got the feeling that something here was about to go terribly wrong.

All I know is, one moment I was reaching for my keys, preparing to slip them into the ignition like I'd done on a countless number of mornings before, the next strong hands were gripping me by the ears, pulling on them with such manic force I thought they were going to tear them clean off my head.

I jolted in surprise, sending the coffee I'd been juggling between my knees spilling all over my crotch and a wave of hot agony searing through my loins, effectively making what was already a bad situation even worse.

I tried to spin around —

Something cold and hard pushed itself up against the side of my head.

I suddenly went very, very still.

'Listen,' I said, my voice coming out in a register I would have to misremember later if I wanted to maintain my dignity. 'I don't have any money, but if you want, I can —'

My head rocked jarringly to the side as whoever holding the gun suddenly bitch-slapped me like a disobedient hooker — which, all things aside, is one hell of a way to start your day.

'*Ow!*'

'Now, are you going to be a good little boy and sit still, or do you need me to slap you some more?'

I shot a glance up into the rearview.

He looked a lot less like a car-jacker than I had been expecting.

Handsome guy. Slicked-back hair. Cheekbones so sharp you could have cut light with them. He had his eyes narrowed to slits, like someone had just blown smoke into his face, and he really didn't appreciate that a whole bunch. A coat like the type detectives always used to wear in movies back before they realised how impractical and ridiculous they were concealed his frame from view.

I blinked.

I'm getting car-jacked by Columbo. Holy shit.

'But I—'

He nudged the gun into my temple—which actually wasn't a gun, I saw now, but rather a block of what looked like very old wood, carved into the rough shape of one.

So that wasn't strange at all.

'*Ah-ah.* No more talking. Just listen. Understand?'

Slowly, I nodded.

'Attaboy. Now, pay attention, Mr Pratt, because I'm only going to say this once. *A war is coming.* The darkness has found its way past the light. The defences have been overwhelmed. You've been dragging your heels for too long now. If you're going to stop what's coming, you're going to need to be on your A-game.'

Ah, that sensation again. That feeling of reality shifting around you, warping before your very eyes like when you look into those mirrors they always have at the fair where everything's all twisted and ugly and not as it should be. The feeling of everything you've ever known—or *thought* you knew—going screaming out the window, and you not having a damn thing to say on the matter.

Somebody really needs to come up with a name for that.

'But I don't want to stop what's coming,' I said. '*And who the hell are you, anyway? How did you get in my car?*'

He frowned. Holy shit, those cheekbones, man. '*Didn't you get my burritos?*' He shook his head. '*Huh.* Guess they must not mean the same thing here.'

Here?

The man leaned forward. 'Never mind that. Who I am isn't important. What's important is that you prepare yourself.'

'Prepare myself—*for what*? What the hell are you talking about?' I thought it over a moment. 'Wait—do you mean the Phonies?'

"Phonies" is the term Frankie and I use for the body-snatching aliens currently running round putting slugs into people's brains. Think of them like your everyday house-slug, only bigger, and uglier, and with an agenda to take over the world. Did I mention they were slugs? Yeah—they're pretty gross.

I shook my head. 'But... we *beat* them. They're gone now. We haven't heard from them in months.'

This was true. After the whole incident back over in Belmont Grove, we hadn't heard a single peep out of them. I was hoping they'd all just gotten bored and gone away.

The guy actually laughed. '*Beat* them? *Seriously?* Do you honestly believe the O'tsaris would simply let slide the fact you killed one of their best men?'

'Well, since you put it like *that*—'

He held up a hand. '*No,* Mr Pratt. We've been watching over you. Keeping you safe. Think of us like your guardian angels. You've kept us pretty busy these last few months. These guys really want you dead.'

At least that explains why everything's been so quiet on the Phony-front lately...

'But—*why*?' I said. 'Why would you do that?' A man carrying a leather satchel made as if to walk past the car, took one look at what was going on inside, and backed slowly away again. 'What's it to you?'

He rubbed his face with his hand and sighed. I noticed suddenly how tired he looked.

Who the fuck is this guy?

'Look, it's complicated, all right?' he said. 'Let's just say there are certain parties out there invested in your continued existence.'

'That makes no sense,' I said. 'Like, literally, none at all.'

He pulled the not-gun away from my temple and leaned back.

He clapped me on the shoulder. 'So long, Mr Pratt. Stay safe. And remember—we're all counting on you.'

'Wait—*what*?'

But he was already on his way out the door.

There was the familiar *clunk* of metal as the rear driver's side door quickly slammed shut behind him.

Trench Coat stepped up to my window.

He gave me a thumbs-up.

Good luck!

Then he vanished into the many shadows that comprised my building's underground parking facility, his trench coat billowing out behind him like a cape, despite there not being any wind in order for it to do so.

I sat there for a good five minutes, breathing heavily, hot coffee pooling in my lap like so much diarrhea as the heat from the burrito on my dash quickly fogged the windshield.

Then, when my hands had finally stopped shaking, I slipped the key into the slot and went to work.

**

Back in high school there'd been this physics teacher, Mr Philtrum. He'd been a tall man, with horn-rimmed glasses and that constant five o'clock shadow all teachers who aren't women seem to have.

As far as teachers went, he wasn't too bad — he never tried to make me climb rope, for example, and he never once fingered me — but he had taken his physics very seriously.

So one morning we go in there and he's got this physics conundrum set out on the blackboard for us. Something to do with mass versus velocity... I forget. Anyway, nobody in my class had been able to solve it. Because, you know — *physics*. That shit's complicated.

As I've gotten older, I've thought about that physics question of which I can't remember more and more, and what I've come up with is this: all of reality is based upon a certain set of principles. Call them rules. A person cannot simply float off into outer space because of gravity, for instance. That's one rule. There're probably a lot more.

Sometimes, though, things happen that go against these principles, that violate these rules to which we must all adhere in order to maintain balance in the universe.

Which brings me, squarely, to Steve.

I found him in his office, standing on his desk and stabbing at an AC unit with what looked like a stapler. Steve was the Office Manager, and unlike my last boss, a thoroughly nice guy. He was also human, which helped. Still, there was something about him I just didn't trust. I knew it was possible I was simply being paranoid — and what with my recent history with managers, you could hardly blame me. But I couldn't help it.

He was just so... *nice*.

'Oh! Hi, Dan!' he chirruped as I stepped into his office.

He was a short slender man in bifocals with a goatee of the style that just screamed pedophile. Today he was wearing tweed trousers and a white sleeveless work shirt that had what looked like flecks of old coffee stained all down the front of it. From his neck hung a tie bearing a picture of Big Bird from *Sesame Street*, posed in a thumbs-up, or whatever the equivalent was when you had wings for arms.

It actually summed Steve up pretty well.

He gestured at the AC with the stapler. 'Don't mind me — just doing a little DIY. Damn thing won't turn off. It's nine below outside, and this stupid machine wants to blow cold air down on my head! Technology, am I right?'

'Sure, Steve.'

'So what can I do for you?' he said, hopping down from the desk in what was a surprisingly graceful little soubresaut. 'Would you like a drink? A coffee, perhaps? Some lemon water?'

'Actually I just —'

'How about a mint?' He handed the bowl out to me. Looked like Mentos.

I took a closer look.

They were Mentos.

Bastard.

I shook my head. 'No, thanks — look, I was just wondering if I'd be able to take next week off. Tonight's the night I'm supposed to do that thing with Abby, see, and if things go well I want to take her away somewhere. Maybe Atlantic City. Or Vegas. Somewhere with lights.' I hesitated. 'I, uh, know it's late notice and all, but —'

Steve held up his hands. 'Nope, say no more. Consider it all arranged — shoot, why don't you take the rest of the day off, too?'

I frowned.

Even for Steve, this was unusually nice.

'*Seriously?*'

'Absolutely! Endeavours of the heart are no laughing matter, Dan. When something like love is presented before you, you must grip it with an iron fist, lest it slip out of your grasp forever. Believe me — I know.'

I looked at his Big Bird tie and tweed pants again.

He did.

'Right. So... we're good, then?' I said.

'We sure are.' He reached across the desk and thrust out his hand. 'Now fist me, partner.'

'Uh, I think you mean "fist bump", Steve.'

'Yes. Right. Of course.'

We bumped our fists together. It felt dirty and wrong, like a lingering kiss on the mouth from a close relative. I mean, unless you're from the South. Then it's just called "Saturday".

'Now go get her, tiger.'

'Okay, well, thanks —'

'Because as George Sand once said,' he went on, ' "there is only one happiness in life, to love and be loved".' He was facing the window now, gazing out of it with his hands on his hips and his mind set firmly in the past, the sheer injustice of it all.

'I really have to go now, Steve.'

'Yes. *Go*. Plant your flag in love's fertile soil, my friend!'

I got the fuck out of there.

***

It wasn't until I got back to my cubicle that I realised I had mail.

It was sent to my personal account, from an address I didn't recognise. The subject heading was two words.

READ ME!!!

I frowned.

For most people, receiving an email is not a cause for alarm. People get emails all the time. Big deal.

Unfortunately for me, however, I am not most people.

Like the burritos, it had started in those first few weeks following the Belmont Grove incident. Little things at first. Random late-night phone calls from private phone numbers, emails from bloggers and media websites requesting my take on what had really gone down that day. Then later had come the stalkings, the spontaneous visits, the ambush tactics whenever I went to the store to buy groceries, or, as in most cases, beer.

I don't know how they found out about us, or our involvement. It's not like we put out an ad, or anything. I only know that since then, I am very wary whenever opening mail — of the digital kind or no.

To this day, I still have no idea why I even bothered opening that email. I mean, sure, we humans are curious creatures, and so I guess that probably had something to do with it. Or perhaps it was something more sinister, like sadism, like how sometimes when you pick at a scab, even though you know you should leave it alone and let the damn thing heal already. Really, I should have deleted it at once. Surely nothing good could ever come from an email with that amount of unnecessary exclamation points.

But like the idiot that I am, I didn't do that.

Instead I grabbed the mouse, manoeuvred the cursor over, finger already clicking away —

My breath caught.

It was a photograph, taken from the website of an insurance company whose name I knew only too well. Inside the photograph was the face of a man—one I recognised instantly, not least of which because I'd been the one who killed him (although, in my defence, he was already dead at the time, so "killed" may be a bit strong).

Below the photo, in bold red font, the words **I KNOW** glared back at me like the very angry, all-knowing eyes of justice itself—along with yet more unnecessary exclamation points.

Time stopped. I realised suddenly I wasn't breathing, and forced myself to take a breath.

Was it true? Was it really possible somebody had found out about what Frankie and I did, and was now using said information against me in order to, what... *blackmail me? Torment me?* How was that even possible? We'd been so careful.

At the bottom of the email was an address and a time.

I didn't think.

I grabbed my things from my desk and left.

TWO

TWO STRANGE THINGS HAPPENED whilst on route to the meeting with my new mysterious blackmailer.

The first was that my Accord wouldn't start — which was actually not that strange, given the state of it. The electrics failed constantly, and the footwell was always wet for some reason. Also, the blinker only worked when it wanted to. It really was a piece of shit, now that I think about it.

The second thing that was strange was the thing I saw whilst strolling past the Rolling Falls shopping centre on East and 29th — or, I should say, "things".

To put it into some kind of perspective, it is not unusual to occasionally see the odd military vehicle driving past when out and about in town — especially considering the Pennyfield Air Force Base lies only a couple miles outside the city limits. On more than one occasion I myself had watched in star-spangled awe as a military vehicle of some indistinguishable make or another had shot past, showering me in its fleeting, authoritarian superiority. One time as a child, a kid on my street—Jimmy Howser—had told me he'd even seen a Hummer (though to be fair, he also thought "chow mein" was a breed of dog, so—you know. Take that as you will).

But what was strange about the vehicles I saw whilst on the way to my meeting that afternoon was the sheer number of them. I counted twenty, in all. A genuine convoy of them—all driving at speeds that would have put Vin Diesel to shame.

I reached the Wendy's twenty minutes later, stepping though the doors under a bluster of snow-laden wind.

The Wendy's itself was pretty empty, given what time of day it was, and that it was a Wendy's. Aside from myself, there were only a handful of other customers, all spread out as far away from each other as they could get, in what was the universally agreed upon distance whenever you found yourself in a chain restaurant with little to no customers. Guy in a Yankees cap and paint-stained overalls by the front, head buried in a newspaper. A young couple in not-quite-matching outfits over by the back, sipping milkshakes whilst staring deep into each other's eyes.

Not knowing what else to do, I found myself a table and began going over what I knew so far of this guy.

Though I wasn't entirely convinced whoever had left me that email had any proof I had murdered the manager from my old place of work, Baxter & Klein, what was beyond doubt was the guy knew *something*—at least enough to taunt me. The question was—*how*? And why? Why contact me at all? Why not go to the police? Wasn't that what you were supposed to do in situations like these? It just didn't make any sense. Unless he or she didn't know anything, of course, and were just bluffing—which was somehow even *weirder*.

I was still procrastinating over these things when a man the size of a small car flumped down into the seat directly across from mine, startling me and causing me to cry out in surprise.

He was a heavy-set guy. Possibly Latino, or maybe just really tanned. He had long raven-black hair that he had gelled back on his head, giving his entire head a shiny look, like he'd just stepped out of the shower, or the ocean maybe. Covering his rotund belly was a battered and stained Ramones shirt that I knew without having to ask had been a hand-me-down—from an older sibling, or a cousin, perhaps. Along his forearms were tattoos of things like anarchy symbols and words like **TRUTH** and **MONEY IS THE ROOT OF ALL EVIL**—which may have gone some way to explaining why the guy looked as if he really didn't have any.

He smiled at my obvious discomfort as he went about wedging himself into a seat. 'Mr Pratt. Good of you to come. I'm Wesley Chang. I'll be your blackmailer this evening.' He extended his hand and waited for me to shake it. When I didn't, he grinned. 'So. You probably have some questions for me,' he said, leaning forward against the table—or at least, as forward as his stomach would allow. I caught a whiff of something that smelled suspiciously like Brute. Of course it did.

'You could say that,' I said.

He nodded. 'As I thought. And, seeing as you're probably a busy guy, let me just get straight to it.' He reached into a satchel hanging from one meaty shoulder that I hadn't even registered yet and pulled out a plastic file.

He flipped it open.

It was another photograph, like the one the email I'd received earlier had contained—only this time the quality was far, far worse. It was that kind of *grainy*, indecipherable quality, like something filmed on a turn-of-the-century cellphone, or a potato. There was no mistaking the origin — this was surveillance footage.

'The hell's this?' I said.

'Oh — you mean you don't recognise it? *Take a closer look.*'

I returned my eyes to the photograph. I didn't see anything, however. It was just some car, one that, on second glance, actually looked kind of familiar. Funny; it almost reminded me of —

I suddenly went very still.

No. Fucking. Way.

'Aaaand here's a photograph from the station's other cam,' said Chang. 'As I'm sure you'll agree, the quality here is much better.'

It's a very particular sensation, having your world collapse beneath you. All of a sudden, I couldn't speak. Like all the air had been knocked from my lungs. Suddenly the lights seemed too bright, the walls too close. I wondered if I was about to pass out. I'd never passed out in a Wendy's before.

The photograph was of my own face.

I slumped back against the booth's plastic seating like a deflated balloon.

So right here you're probably wondering why a simple photograph had such a profound effect on me. And the truth is there's no easy answer to that. Well, I mean... *technically*, there is, but if I'm honest it doesn't paint me in the best light. The long and short of it is that I really had no business being behind the wheel of that car — not least because it had the decapitated body of my now ex-boss in the trunk (who was neither dead *nor* my boss, seeing as we're on the subject). Yeah — don't even. In my defence, though, he totally deserved what happened to him. And all the things we may or may not have done later, the details of which shall remain vague.

Whole "body-snatcher" thing aside, the guy was kind of a douche.

'I mean, don't get me wrong, I get the compulsion,' Chang went on. 'Murdering one's boss, and all. Hell, I've had a few bosses myself I'd have liked to have seen put under the ground — if you take my meaning. It was a good plan, too. It was the stopping for gas where you really screwed the pooch — *see the time stamp there*?' He cupped a hand round one side of his mouth and leaned forward. 'And, not to be a dick or anything, but that was honestly pretty retarded of you. I mean, taking a joyride in the car of the person you just murdered — and on the very night of his "disappearance", no less?'

He gave a disapproving shake of his head.

When some semblance of reality returned, I pushed myself up in my seat. 'What do you want, Chang?'

'Not justice, if that's what you're worried about. I could care less about the people you may or may not have killed.'

'Then what *do* you want? Why am I here, and not locked up in some prison cell somewhere?'

Probably having all sorts of unsavory things shoved up in my fun-zone, too...

'Well, see now, that's simple. You have something *I* want. And I have something *you* want. Ergo, what I propose is a trade.'

'*A trade?*'

He leaned forward again, his face now all stern and serious. Well, *serious*, anyway. It's hard to make anything firm when your body is ninety per cent gelatin. 'I know you were there, Mr Pratt. You and your accomplices. At Belmont Grove. And before you start, I already know it wasn't any gas leak, or terrorist attack, or whatever else they're saying it was now, so don't waste my time — and, more importantly, your freedom — by pretending otherwise. What I want is the *real* story. I want to know what really went down that day.' He pointed a plump finger in my direction. 'And you, my intellectually challenged friend, are going to give it to me.'

Suddenly, everything clicked into place. It was so obvious. How hadn't I realised this before?

I almost burst out laughing — the guy was a fucking journalist.

'You want an *interview*?' I scoffed.

And here I thought I was supposed to be the intellectually challenged one.

'An *exclusive* interview,' he corrected me.

'But I —'

He held up a hand. 'No — don't answer now. You've had a nasty shock. You're not thinking clearly. It'd be foolish to make a decision in your current state of mind.' He pried himself loose from the table and stood. 'You have one week. If you haven't made a decision by then, I'm going to the cops.'

He flipped a little white card down onto the table — his phone number.

Then, without so much as another word on the subject, he suddenly turned and waddled himself over toward the exit, leaving me staring dumbfounded after him and wondering absently if my life could possibly get any worse.

I had no fucking idea.

***

Abby's work had a Christmas party, so that's how I got to know Eric.

Eric worked part-time at the juice bar where Abby and her gaggle of new friends worked — a little, hidden away place down at the Rolling Falls shopping mall, aptly named "Juice Bar".

He was a handsome-enough guy — providing, of course, your definition of "handsome" is a man with a face the *literal equivalent* of a smashed-in ham. I think he must have played football in college or something. It was really startling.

And yet, despite this, the ladies loved him. Sure, the fact he'd just returned home from the Middle East after having successfully taught poor, orphaned children how to read might have had something to do with it. Personally, I like to think — and often do — that they were all simply humouring him; the same way doctors humour patients' families about their loved ones' chances of survival, even though deep down they know they're fucking doomed.

Whichever the case was, one thing that could not be denied of Eric, was that the guy was a goddamn magnet when it came to women.

Naturally, I hated him.

'I just can't believe how unsympathetic some people are, you know?' he was saying as I struggled to hear him over my own startling lack of interest.

We were at a bar down on 23rd and Wesson called the Quivering Lips — which I thought was a sex-thing, but apparently wasn't. The people all wore suits, the men with their ties pulled loose, the women with the buttons of their blouses undone, revealing more boob than a Kardashian home video. The music was too loud, and everybody seemed to be having a great time — everybody except for me, that was. What was worse, the surface of the bar — and granted every other surface I'd touched thus far this evening — had not so much as a splash of spilled alcohol on it.

This was definitely not my kind of place.

'Uh-huh,' I said.

'I mean, the kids are our *future*, Dan — only it's like nobody cares,' he went on, ignoring the fact I had so obviously quit listening to him months ago.

'Yeah. Fuck those kids, Eric.'

'I just don't understand it, you know? And don't even get me *started* on global warming...'

I stole a quick glance around the bar for Abby. Last I'd seen her, she'd been heading off to grab drinks. That had been decades ago. Where the hell had she gotten to? Should I have gone looking for her? Exactly what kind of name was the Quivering Lips for a bar, anyway?

Just as I was thinking this, a hand fell on my arm.

I looked back.

Abby.

So you know how all parents think their baby is the cutest, even though in most cases said baby looks more like a battered cabbage somebody has for some reason kicked repeatedly up against a garage door? Well, that was how I felt about Abby. Not that she was a baby, of course. Or a cabbage, for that matter. Christ, that would have been weird. But there was no denying that—to my eye, at least—Abby was without a doubt the most attractive girl in the room. Granted, the fact that she occasionally let me do things to her lady parts may have left me slightly biased.

Hey—it was what it was.

'Here. I brought beer,' she said, holding out a glass to me.

I'd decided against telling her of my meeting with my new, sweaty friend, Wesley Chang—not because I thought she couldn't handle it, or anything. I'm not a misogynist. Truthfully, I was worried she might go kill the guy if I did—and I don't mean "kill" like "have a stern talking-to", like how when your girlfriend says it about so-and-so having stood her up again or whatever. I mean *literally* kill him, like with a knife, in the head. And I just wasn't sure having another dead body on our hands would have helped our current situation any.

'Can you believe Sandra's pregnant?' she said, as I quickly took the beer from her. 'Isn't that crazy?' Tonight she was dressed in a jeans and jacket combination that, despite how little effort it had taken her to put on, still left her looking the most dazzling woman here. Or maybe it was just that bias at work again. Never underestimate the power of the vagina, folks.

'Sure is.'

She eyed me curiously. 'What's wrong?'

'You left me,' I said. '*With Eric.*'

'So? What's wrong with Eric?'

'There's just something not right about that guy. Nobody's that dreamy. He's definitely up to something.'

She grinned. 'Is somebody jealous?'

I let out a long sigh. 'He's a Phony, Abby.'

'He is not a Phony, Dan.'

'He *could* be a Phony. We should probably take care of him. Just to be safe.'

She laughed and kissed me, even though I was being serious. Around us, well-dressed strangers grinded furiously against one another like they didn't know what discretion was.

'You're adorable, you know that?'

'No, I'm not. I'm very manly.'

She put her arms around my waist and squeezed, pinning my arms to my sides. If we'd been boxing, I'd have been fucking screwed.

In case I haven't mentioned it already, Abby is my girlfriend. We had met during the whole Belmont Grove fiasco three months ago. I'd like to say it was love at first sight, but if I'm honest there had been far too much dick-punching for that. Yeah, turns out she's kind of a ninja. And a spy.

But, just like a tumour, I had eventually grown on her. Now I guessed she was stuck with me.

I fought my way free and took her by the hand. 'Hey, you want to get out of here?'

She looked at me sideways a moment. 'Somebody's feeling pretty sure of themselves.'

'Come on. Let's take a walk.'

I led Abby out onto the sidewalk, where the final vestiges of last night's snowfall still lay in evidence on the ground.

Now, I'm not exactly the most proactive of guys when it comes to romance, but there's no denying the fact there's something magical about freshly fallen snow. And from where we were walking along the sidewalk, the streetlights above us burning fierce amber down on our heads like fallout and painting everything it touched a warm orange, it was almost beautiful. I thought it would have made for a great postcard.

'So...' I said, boots crunching as they fought their way through thick ice and snow. Despite the cold, I was dripping with sweat. It was seriously ball-soup down there. I didn't think I'd ever been so sweaty in my whole life.

'*So?*'

'We've been together a while now, wouldn't you say?'

She grabbed my arm, stopping me. God, she was so strong. 'What's this all about, Dan? You're acting all weird again. I hate it when you act weird.'

I took a deep breath.

Well. Now or never.

I reached a hand into my pocket, began to bend down —

'Oh, wait, my phone's ringing,' said Abby.

I watched as she turned away from me to answer it, leaving me half-mast and feeling like literally the biggest asshole in the world.

Good job, Danny boy. Fucking great work there. Way to seal the deal.

'*What the hell?*'

I looked up to see Abby frowning.

'Who is it?' I said.

'I don't know. But this area code — it's from Fort Larsen.'

Fort Larsen: the small, no-nothing farming town in Texas where Abby had grown up — that was, before a certain "incident" there had seen her run out of town faster than Frankenstein's monster on a jet ski. And by "incident" I mean she had killed her boyfriend at the time, Jeff, who was meant to have been a pretty big deal. Something about football, yadda yadda. In her defence, though, the guy had been a Phony at the time, so "killed" was probably stretching it a little. But whatever.

From what I knew, it had been years since she had last spoken to anybody from her hometown.

I waited for her to answer, then when she didn't, I said, 'You going to answer it?'

She hesitated a moment longer, then slowly raised the phone to her ear.

After only a short moment, she lowered it again.

'*Well?*' I said, not wanting to be an ass, but unable to help myself. I was freezing, and I still had yet to recover from looking like a complete jackass a moment ago. It's not often said, but a man's pride is like his life force. What the East (possibly) refer to as "Chi". It's what fuels us, gives us the strength and wilful ignorance to continue on doing the stupid shit we're so renowned for, because we're men, and that's just what we do. Women have their sex appeal. Men have their pride. Take that away, and you might as well put a bullet through our brains. It's biology, really. Christ, it was a miracle I was still alive. 'You going to tell me who it was, or not?'

Nothing. Just silence.

'*Abby?*'

'That... that was my Aunt Cassie,' she said. 'I think my dad's dying.'

Shit.

I stood very still for a moment. Across the street, late night revelers stumbled drunkenly through the snow. 'Are... you okay?'

Abby and her father had always had a complicated relationship — even more so after he had let the townsfolk effectively shun her from the community. She never really talked about him, but on the odd occasions that she did, it was never in a, shall we say, "positive" manner.

She shook her head. 'I don't know. I just honestly don't know.'

'Are you going to go see him?'

'*Do you think I should?*'

'Well... he's still your dad, right?'

Even if he is a steaming pile of rhino diarrhea.

'This... this is all just — I need to go home, Dan. *Right now.*'

And so we left the Quivering Lips, marching through the snow back the way we'd come as drunkards and late-evening Christmas shoppers encumbered with store bags battled not to fall down.

Merry fucking Christmas.

***

Six hours later, and I was standing in the check-in aisle inside Amerstow International Airport, an anxious Abby on one side, several hundred irrelevant other people on the other.

'Are you sure this is what you want?' I said, having to shout a little to be heard over the white-noise hiss of chatter around us.

I've never liked airports. I'm not sure why. I suspect it's something to do with the nature of them—how they're never the place you're trying to go, only the place you have to go through to get to your destination. There's just something so dishonest about that, I find.

From beside me, Abby nodded. There were tears in her eyes and her make-up was smudged. I'd never seen her look so frail and un-ninja-like before. It was fucking terrifying.

'Because you know you don't *have* to go,' I said. 'You can stay here. *With me*. You don't have to go, Abby.'

It was the first time since becoming a couple that we had ever been apart, and I was feeling insecure. But it was more than that. Though I didn't often like to admit it, Abby was in a lot of ways my protector. For whatever reason, God had seen fit to put me under her protection. I was the frail duckling, unfit for life on my own, an easy target for any nearby foraging animals looking for a quick and easy meal. She was the caring mother duck, bravely warding off the riff-raff looking to put me kicking and screaming into their bellies. Really, what it came down to was trust; the trust between mother and child, of not letting that child get fucking eaten to death. Her getting on that plane broke that trust. As far as I was concerned, now she was just being a terrible mother.

She took a deep breath and sighed. 'Yes. Yes, I do.'

I nodded. She did.

We watched the line jostle along for a while, every shoe-squeak like knives in my ears.

'Are you going to be okay?' she asked, when we were finally nearing the front.

I thought again of my new friend, Wesley Chang. I should have told her about him, of course. It was the only responsible thing to do. But I had put a lot of energy into Abby's "rehabilitation". I didn't want to jeopardise all the progress she'd made, simply because some sweaty, overweight dude in a Ramones T-shirt had decided now was a good time to try and blackmail me.

It had been hard, in the beginning. Having spent the majority of her life as a lethal killing machine, reassimilating into a normal way of living had proved no easy task. There had been incidents. Fights. Some sneaking out at night. More than the one shouted expletive. As it turns out, one does not just simply quit hunting extra-terrestrials. You have to wean yourself off these sorts of things.

Six weeks ago she'd landed her first real job at Juice Bar, and so far things had been going great.

I wasn't about to ruin that for anything.

'Of course,' I lied.

'You'll call me, won't you? If something weird should happen, like with that thing the other day that I know you don't like to talk about, but that you really need to —'

I put a finger to her lips.

'*Shush*. Relax. I'll be fine. I'm very brave, Abby.'

'No, Dan. No, you're not.'

I stood aside and waited whilst the attendant checked Abby in, wondering if I looked overly like a terrorist, if there was a way to tell.

When she was done, Abby and I turned to each other.

Some things were said. Mushy things. I don't want to go into it. It was like that one scene they always have in movies where the happy couple are forced to part ways for some stupid reason or another. The guy gets drafted and has to go to war, leaving his beloved to sit at home pining for him whilst he tries his best to dodge bullets like some kind of limber, death-shy acrobat — which is kind of sexist, actually, if you think about it. I didn't want to go to war.

'And remember to take Frankie out,' she went on. 'You know how he gets when he doesn't go out.'

Ugh.

After a final hug, she grabbed her little suitcase-thing by the handle and sighed. 'Okay. Here I go. Wish me luck!'

'Good luck!'

PLEASE DON'T GO.

I watched as she dragged her little suitcase-thing across the foyer towards departures, listening to its wheels squeaking and wishing there was a baby somewhere close-by crying its fucking eyes out, because it felt like one of those moments. But there wasn't—which was a shame, but not exactly a surprise.

At the barrier, she turned back.

I saw her lips move.

Hate your face.

Then she was gone.

Of course, if I could have known what was about to happen, I probably would have gone with her—I certainly would have worn better shoes.

But that's the thing about hindsight, isn't it?

Man, hindsight's a bitch.

THREE

BELIEFS ARE A FRAGILE thing. It's something we never really think about. They're like those little china dolls you always find at yard sales—sure, they may *feel* solid to the touch, but you know that any real bit of pressure and they'd crack and fall to pieces like Oscar Pistorius' defence case, and then you'd have all those little fucking flakes of china everywhere and a dead girlfriend. And nobody wants that.

It had been my belief, for example, that all the craziness of the last few months was finally behind me, that I was done with conspiracies and spies and things of an extra-terrestrial nature.

But as I was soon to discover, just like the mankini, I was very, very wrong.

I found Frankie on the couch, head pressed so close to the laptop screen in front of him it was like he was trying to meld with it.

It was the day after taking Abby to the airport. He had a bottle of Jack Daniels in one hand, a crumpled sheet of photocopy paper that looked to have started life as an origami swan in the other, but that in all honesty now looked more like something a child molester might show to small children in an attempt to frighten them into keeping quiet. On the TV before me, a man with an unconvincing toupee and what I assumed to be some sort of vitamin deficiency assured me of the value of life insurance.

Frankie saw me enter and his eyes widened. 'Oh, Dan, you're back! Finally! Check it out!'

Frankie was my best friend, and what some might consider a lodger, only this lodger didn't pay rent. A bad lodger, then. Today he was wearing an amalgamation of different clothing, none of which matched. I don't want to go into it. Let's just say he looked like someone who required constant monitoring by a qualified adult and leave it at that.

He turned the laptop to face me.

It was then I noticed all the open textbooks lying spread out on the carpet around him. Covers with titles like *Demonology For Dummies* and *Stargazing: The Hunt For Extra-Terrestrial Life*.

Following the events of three months ago, Frankie had convinced himself that the whole fiasco with the Phonies was just the tip of the iceberg, that there were other things out there. And up until the incident with that "thing of which we do not speak", I thought it was all just hogwash—fantasies from basement-dwelling MMO players with no girlfriends and nothing better to do.

Now, though... now I wasn't so sure.

Not that I'd tell Frankie that, of course.

What was more, in an effort to connect with other people across the globe and "share their collective knowledge", he had even started up a blog. He called it **THE WATCHPOST**. I, on the other hand, called it by its actual name—a **GIANT WASTE OF TIME**. Which it was.

Still, the emails kept on coming. So that was awesome.

I peered at the screen. 'What's that?'

'Email from an old acquaintance of mine. Says some "thing" crashed in the field next to where the old steelworks used to be. He thinks it might be alien.'

'Sounds serious,' I said.

He nodded. 'Uh-huh. He even took pictures. Look—'

I shot up my hands. 'Uh-uh. Nope. I'm not doing this with you again, Frankie.'

He frowned. 'Do what?'

'*This.* This... obsession of yours, or whatever it is. I'm not getting sucked into another one of your flights of fancy. Count me out.'

He looked crestfallen. 'But... what if there's something really cool out there nobody's ever seen before?' he went on, completely disregarding everything I'd just said. 'Like maybe some kind of weird, gross thing that shoots fire out of its ass or whatever. Imagine it, Dan. It'd be awesome.'

'Why would it shoot fire out of its ass?'

He sighed. 'It's a *defence mechanism*, Dan? You know, like how when an octopus—'

He caught the look on my face and frowned. 'Wait, hold on—this is about Abby again, isn't it?'

I blinked. 'What? *Abby?*'

'Come on, *Dan*. Since she dumped you, all you've done is mope around the apartment like a little lost puppy.'

'She didn't dump me. Her dad's sick. I told you.'

'Whatever. I'm just saying, you need to snap out of it is all. Get back on the, uh...'

I waited. *'Horse?'*

He grinned. 'That's the spirit, Dan! You need to mount that bitch, homie. Seabiscuit that shit.'

'I'm not mounting anything. I'm grabbing some water and going to bed.'

Frankie nodded as if that was just the answer he'd been expecting. 'Sure thing, Dan — whatever you say.' He turned back to the laptop.

It was then I noted the sudden, mischievous look in his eye.

Looking back now, this is probably the part where I should have realised Frankie was up to something. Frankie would never be so easily deterred from an adventure, especially when the prospect of something alien or ridiculous was involved.

But like the asshole that I was, I didn't.

And nothing was ever the same again.

***

They say that inside of every man is a small child just waiting to get out.

I'm pretty sure it's a metaphor — some faux-cute narrative on our secret, inherent desire to go grab a pack of bubblegum and roll around naked on the front yard for all the neighbours to see. Jesus, that was a crazy weekend. Unless, that is, they mean it *literally*, which — let's be honest here — is a logistical nightmare if I've ever heard one, but also very creepy.

Either way, it was this metaphor that came to mind as I awoke with a start, slumped on the passenger seat of my Accord, screaming like I was six again and kicking out with my limbs in a spastic imitation of a man straddling a live electrical wire.

'WHAT'S GOING ON? WHERE AM I? WHY AM I — ?'

A hand fell on my shoulder.

'*Shush.* It's okay. You're fine. Everything's fine. Now go back to sleep.'

I looked round.

Frankie. In the driver's seat.

My driver's seat.

'Frankie? *What? Why are you —?*' I gasped as the obvious dawned. 'Wait — *did you kidnap me?*'

'If by "kidnap" you mean did I carry your unconscious body down to your car, load you in, then drive away with you passed out in the passenger seat, then... yes.'

'THAT'S KIDNAPPING.'

And while we're on the subject, care to explain exactly how he managed to do all that without you waking, Dan? Are you really that heavy of a sleeper?

Frankie sighed. 'See? This is why I didn't tell you, Dan. I knew you'd get mad. Look how mad you are.'

'YOU FUCKING KIDNAPPED ME.'

'I *did not* kidnap you. Jeez, you're so dramatic.' He nodded through the windshield. 'Besides, we're almost there.'

I followed his gaze.

It was some dirt road. I saw trees. A collection of collapsed wood-pieces that looked like somebody's poor attempt at a perimeter fence. All covered under a blanket of inch-thick snow.

I tilted my head to look at him, incredulity turning all the skin on my face lax. 'You didn't...' I said.

But he had. He really, really had.

He nodded. 'You're damn right I did, mister. Someone's got to pull you out of this slump you're in. You can't hold on to anger, Dan. Holding onto anger is like holding onto a hot coal — the only one who gets burned is you.'

'*Did you just quote Ghandi at me?*'

'*Face it,* Dan. You're on the edge. You're treading water. Sooner or later you're going to have to let somebody in. And seeing as you really don't have any other friends, that somebody's going to be me.'

'I have other friends,' I said.

'Oh really? Name one friend you have besides me.'

'I have... Doug.'

'*The racist from downstairs?*'

Doug was the guy from the apartment below mine. Doug was a supervillain. Or maybe not, but he had an Eastern European accent, and really what other job opportunities are there in America for somebody with that kind of handicap? He was a tall, wiry man with liver spots and sagging skin, and he always seemed to be wearing a robe, regardless of what time of day it was. He was like a poor man's Hugh Hefner.

He was also super racist.

I nodded. 'We're very close.'

'Oh yeah? What's his cat's name?'

I thought it over. 'Doug Junior?'

'He doesn't have a cat, Dan.'

Balls.

'And besides, if he did have a cat, he most definitely would have eaten it by now.'

Because all Eastern Europeans are pet-eaters, apparently...

The Accord's headlights arced suddenly to the right as we turned onto yet another country lane, this one narrower, and even less maintained than the one we had just left. I saw fresh tyre tracks in the snow up ahead. From the looks of them, more than one pair. Above our heads, branches reached for us in the growing dark, their gnarled limbs beckoning to us like the crooked, skeletal fingers of Death himself. Needless to say, it was spooky as hell.

Slumping into the passenger seat, I let out a groan.

Great. Trust Frankie to try and cure my depression by taking me to the one place in the world I'd least like to go. Goddamnit.

When we finally emerged at Lake Fairburn, full-dark had fallen.

For reasons that have never been made clear to me, Lake Fairburn has always been a magnet for teenagers. I suspected a lot of the reason was due to its seclusion. You had to *really want* to come to Lake Fairburn in order to drive all that way through miles upon miles of treacherous, unkempt country road—not that this stopped the teenagers, of course, who took it all in their stride like the relentless, sex-hungry zit-demons they were. Every once in a while the cops would swing by, pay Lake Fairburn a visit, break up whatever nefarious activities the teenagers currently hanging out there happened to be engaging in. Mostly, though, they left it alone.

I spotted the first of the group, moving awkwardly by the back of an open-bed truck, in a fashion the more cultured amongst us might interpret as dancing. She was a young girl; probably seventeen or eighteen, with curly golden hair, not unlike Abby's. Despite the bitter cold that held the evening, she wore very little in the way of clothing. Just short-shorts and a pink sleeveless tee, cut raggedly to just above her belly button, like she'd suddenly needed to dress a wound, but had nothing else with which to do so.

She must have seen the approach of our headlights, because she suddenly stopped dancing. She turned back to some place I couldn't see and raised her hands to her mouth.

'Hey, Craig, they're here! Those guys are here!'

We pulled up close, and she shakily made her way over to greet us, the faint sound of some generic pop song or another trailing closely after her.

She was actually way younger than I'd initially assumed. Probably closer to sixteen, than twenty. As she stepped up to the driver's side, I noticed suddenly how smooth and toned her stomach was, then made myself look away, because noticing that felt wrong.

'Hey, you're those guys, right? The alien dudes?'

Alien dudes. Christ.

She was very drunk. Her mascara was smeared, and there was spittle forming in frothy clumps on either side of her mouth. Her hair hung tousled over to one side, and one eyelid seemed determined to close itself, leaving her half-lidded and looking more than a little sunshine-bus material. There was something rabid about her.

'That's us,' said Frankie, opening his mouth before I had chance to object. He looked around questioningly. 'Where is it?'

'In Beaner's truck. This way.'

Beaner?

We stepped out of the car and followed her across the snow towards the waiting cluster of vehicles. I'd never been to Lake Fairburn at this time of year before. To my left, the lake's frozen surface lay white and still, like the cataract on some felled giant's eyeball. Above us, stars shone fierce and bright like an endless procession of curious, unblinking eyes. It was pretty, in an irrelevant sort of way.

We stepped up to a gaggle of young men and women, each dressed in what looked to be increasing layers of nudity, crouched around a fire comprised of what I thought was a combination of old pallets and couch-parts. Another thing you should know about Lake Fairburn: it's a dump. Not literally. You weren't supposed to dump shit here, or anything. Regardless, over the years, Lake Fairburn had become the go-to place whenever you had a dresser or couch or any other unwanted household item to get rid of, and because of this there was always plenty of shit on-hand for anybody so inclined to make a fire out of.

As we approached, a man stepped forward from the group. Tall guy. Skinny. Holes in his ears like the ones people always get when they've decided they want to become rock stars, or homeless. Like the others, he was mostly naked—spare, thankfully, for a pair of trendy sports-pants, of whose brand name I was unfamiliar, and a beanie hat approximately three sizes too big for him.

I almost burst out laughing.

Yup—this was Beaner, all right.

'Yo-yo, Frankenstein! My man!' said Beaner, stepping up to Frankie, whom he then promptly embraced in a fierce but totally non-gay man-hug. They shook—one of those elaborate, complicated handshakes, like the ones frat members and cult leaders are always using to signify their mutual love and respect for one another. Frankie has always been way cooler than I am. I stood there like a sore thumb, pretending to be watching the fire, wondering if this "Beaner" was going to try to hug me, too, if handshakes were something you could just up and learn on the fly, even without any formal training.

'Been a long time, Craig,' said Frankie, stepping back. He gestured at me with a thumb. 'This here's my buddy, Dan.'

Beaner turned to face me, seeming to notice my presence there for the very first time. He put his hands on my shoulders and stared hard into my eyes. To say it made me uncomfortable, would have been an understatement. '*Welcome*, Dan. Any friend of Frankie's is a friend of mine.'

Uhh, thanks?

'Though I should mention I go by Beaner, now.' He pointed to his hat, like it wasn't already glaringly obvious. 'But never mind all that.

You fellas have come to see something, ain't ya? Come on—it's this way.'

We let him lead us over to one of the several vehicles parked behind us in a rough horseshoe. As we walked, I took in all the cases of beer, the strewn cans lying everywhere and—*holy shit, is that a keg? Man, teenagers today fucking party.*

We came to a stop beside another pick-up truck, not unlike the one we had seen upon first arriving. In the bed lay a lump of something small and round-shaped, wrapped loosely in a dirty beach towel.

Before I could so much as open my mouth to inquire about it, Beaner grabbed the beach towel by one corner and heaved.

'*Voila!*'

It was a rock—though, granted, not like any rock I had ever seen before. About the size of a basketball, maybe a bit bigger. A spider-web of cracks ran through it from top to bottom, and looking into them I could see what looked like a very faint, yet unmistakable reddish glow. On one side, barely visible in the poor light, was a marking—like a hieroglyph. For no obvious reason I could think of, I was reminded of those signs they always have on the fences at power stations: **WARNING. DANGER OF DEATH. KEEP AWAY**—which, looking back now, is exactly what it was.

Beaner turned back to us, grinning like a Cheshire cat on smack. 'So? What do you guys think? Is this cool, or what?'

'It's a rock,' I said.

'Not just *any* rock. What you're looking at is a genuine, bona fide meteorite.'

'*You brought us here to look at a meteorite?*'

I mean, don't get me wrong, it was better than an alien. But still, talk about an anticlimax.

More of Beaner's crew had gathered around us now, each of them staring silently into the truck-bed with something like genuine awe.

When I was a kid, my Grandma Helen had taken me to see Prince perform. This had been in Atlanta. I remember standing there, in the front row, looking around at all the people's faces standing beside me staring up at him.

The expression on their faces had been the exact same expressions I saw on the faces of Beaner's friends now.

Look at them. They're fucking in love with this thing.

Beaner nodded at one of the group — a short guy with dreadlocks and pockmarked skin.

'Show him.'

Without a word, the guy leaned into the truck, picked up a crowbar I hadn't even registered had been lying there.

Then, before I could hazard a guess as to what he was about to do —

He whacked it.

DONG.

The light from the rock intensified for a moment, then settled.

I blinked, surprised.

Huh. Well there's something you don't see everyday.

'And that's not the only thing,' Beaner went on, as if reading my mind. 'When we first found it, the fucking thing was *singing* at us.'

I looked around the group again, all those chuffed, beaming faces. Whilst I couldn't deny the thing lying in the truck-bed before me was strange, I didn't think it deserved that amount of reverence. Okay, so it glowed — and maybe sung occasionally, too. Whoopty-fucking-do.

I just didn't see what all the fuss was about.

'*How did you even get this?*' I asked, the words tumbling out of my mouth before I could stop them.

'Picked it up right before the army got there,' said Beaner. 'From Ackerman's Field. It was just lying there, in the crater. Bobby here saw it coming down, managed to give us the heads-up. Said it looked like fireworks, only in reverse — didn't you, Bobby?'

He gestured at a fat guy over my shoulder boasting sporadic chest-hair like mould-growth, who nodded eagerly.

I decided I couldn't hold my tongue any longer.

'I'm sorry — *why are you all naked, again?*'

A handful of knowing smiles from around the group.

'This rock,' said Beaner, who I noted was smiling hardest of all. 'It *spoke* to us. Told us things. Wonderful, magical — just *impossible things*. About life and death, the universe. *All* the universes.'

'Did it tell you to take off your clothes, too?'

Frankie threw me an elbow. 'Don't mind him. He's just grouchy cause he got dumped yesterday.'

I groaned. 'For the last time, Frankie, I didn't get — '

Okay, so you know those moments you have sometimes where you suddenly become uniquely aware your life is about to take a drastic turn for the worse? Maybe you receive a bad diagnosis. The neighbour from across the street singles you out for an unbridled hate campaign. Perhaps your dog dies.

These are things that might happen. It's the three or four seconds before your out-of-control semi jack-knifes into a nearby group of nun-led orphans out for their annual — and I guess, last — field trip, whereupon the realisation quickly dawns that no matter what happens next, your life will never, ever again be as it was.

Well, little did I know, but I was about to have one of these moments.

Seriously — fuck my life.

There was the sound of a woman shrieking from behind us.

It was another of Beaner's group. Petite girl. A redhead. She had one hand pressed to her face, eyes wide and staring, the other hand outstretched, pointing at something I couldn't yet see because of all the shoulders currently blocking my view.

Then one of the shoulders shifted, and —

I squinted.

The fuck?

It was a man — or at least, what I *thought* was a man. Technically speaking, he was a man. He had arms and legs and a head — all the usual telltale signs.

And yet, there was something about him that just didn't *feel* right.

He was pale, for one thing. Skin like a porcelain doll's, and equally unblemished. Maybe he was albino, or something. He wore a lush black suit, expertly fitted, and on his head sat a hat of the kind businessmen always used to wear back in the fifties when the fear of getting your hair rained on was a genuine concern. Did I mention he also had no eyebrows? Yeah.

Of all these things, however, the thing I have to admit I found most strange was the truncheon-like staff he held in his hand — which, from what I could make out, was currently busy exploding the little Vietnamese-looking guy I'd noticed earlier upon first arriving.

Vietnamese Guy squealed as the truncheon-like staff pressing up against his chest suddenly crackled.

There was a blinding flash of light. A *pop* like when you accidentally sit on a balloon, then have to go lie down for a little while until your nerves have recovered.

When I looked back, Vietnamese Guy had vanished. All that remained of him now was a twelve-foot-diameter ring of blood and viscera in the place where he had until only seconds ago been standing, staining the ground a blackish-red like the Devil's snow-cone.

He killed Vietnamese Guy! That racist!

There was a moment of deafening silence.

Then everybody was running—Frankie and I included, for reasons I really should not have to point out.

I was a good half a dozen paces, however, before noticing Frankie was going the complete wrong way.

I should explain; Frankie has always had a problem making good decisions. I mean, shit, just look at his life choices. But that wasn't his biggest problem. Really, his biggest problem was his curiosity. Most people, they see a fire, they go call the fire department, or the sheriff's office. Frankie? He'd pull up a chair and watch that thing burn—just on the off-chance something unexpected and amazing should happen.

So it should come as no surprise then when I tell you that Frankie did not split for the treeline, as he so obviously should have—like the rest of us were doing. Instead he ran towards the well-dressed albino man, shouting random expletives, and informing him—in increasingly vivid detail—exactly how he would soon be dining on the flesh of his own pasty nut-sack.

'Frankie! What are you — ?'

He reached into his pockets, pulled out what I for one crazy moment thought was snow, but that I realised all too late was not.

'SURPRISE, DICK-BAG!' he cried as he launched the handful of salt—*my* salt, from my kitchen—directly into Albino Man's face.

He waited for him to melt.

He waited some more.

After a few seconds and no melting, he turned back to me. *'He's not melting, Dan...'*

He was right. Even from as far away as I was standing, I could see Albino Man's face was noticeably un-melted. Hell, it wasn't even singed.

(I should also mention there was a good reason we thought salt would melt him. Yeah, as it turns out, the Phonies aren't the biggest fans of salt. It kind of melts right though them. Yeah — I know. Hey, I didn't make the rules, okay?)

Albino Man stood there motionless a moment, salt dripping from his face and shoulders like dandruff.

He raised the truncheon-thing.

'*Run!*' I cried.

But Frankie was already moving. Across the snow, through the network of parked cars and beer kegs.

I caught up with him moments later next to a burned-out old Ford and crouched low.

'*Did you fucking see that?*' he said, gasping for breath. 'Guy just took a saltshaker's worth to the face, and he didn't melt even a little.'

'I saw it.'

'Do you think they're — ?' He shifted his gaze over my shoulder and his eyes widened. '*Dan!*'

I turned.

It was the girl from before — the one who had so drunkenly greeted us upon first arriving at the lake. She was stumbling over the snow, a few feet from where we knelt, a beer in each hand, seemingly unperturbed by the fact we were currently under attack. I noticed she still didn't have many clothes on.

Oh, goddamnit.

Before I could give myself time to reconsider, I leapt up from my hiding place, grabbed her by the shoulders, and quickly pulled her down with us.

'*Hey!*' she slurred, more upset that I'd spilled her beer than anything.

I turned back to Frankie. 'What's happening now?'

'There're more of them,' he said, peeking up over the Ford's hood. 'Six, by my count—no, make that seven. I think they're searching for something.'

There was another flash. Another deafening bang.

Frankie thought for a moment. 'Make that eight...'

I ran my hands through my hair.

It's happening again. I can't believe it. Oh, man, how can the same shit happen to the same guy twice? Who am I, fucking John McClane?

'This is bad,' I said, my sanity draining swiftly out of me like piss down my leg. 'We need to call someone.'

'No, we don't. We can handle this. Besides, we fought off slugs from another world attempting to take over the president's brain. Trust me—we got this.'

From behind us, Drunk Girl let out a groan. 'Ooh, my stomach. I think my period just came...'

Frankie turned back to me, his face serious. 'We're out of our depth here, Dan. We need help. *Stat.*'

I reached for my phone.

Nothing. Not even a bar of signal.

I groaned.

Are you fucking kidding me right now?

I could hear more pops coming from the other side of the burned-out Ford now. More anguished squeals. More pleas for mercy.

It was a goddamn bloodbath out there.

I flinched as Frankie suddenly grabbed my arm. 'Okay—I think I *may* have an idea,' he said. 'Wait here. I'll be back in a sec.'

'What? What do you mean you'll be—'

He took off running for the treeline.

'Hey!'

Bastard.

I turned my attention back to Drunk Girl, who I noted was now busy dribbling all over herself. Christ, what a mess. 'Don't worry — it'll be fine. He, uh... he knows what he's doing.'

She blinked. *'Who are you again?'*

OH GODDAMNIT.

I'm not sure exactly how long we waited there for. Enough for me to begin to wonder whether or not he was coming back, put it that way.

'All right,' I said, an indeterminate amount of time later. 'Looks like we're going to have to make a run for it. If we're quick, we *should* be able to get to my car without any of those assholes spotting us. Do you think you can run?'

Drunk Girl's shoulders jerked as a fierce hiccup rocked her entire body, almost spilling her over. 'I kissed my cousin once... we were only kids...'

I groaned.

Fuck it. Good enough.

I took her by the hand and pulled her clumsily to her feet. She swayed, tried to sit down. I pulled at her again.

After several minutes of this, we ran.

Well, I say "ran". To be honest, there was far too much falling down to have considered what we were currently doing running. But we were moving. Slowly, sure — so *very, very* slowly. But moving all the same.

One of her arms flung limply over my shoulder, I dragged her over to an old, abandoned trailer half-buried in the snow to our right.

I peeked around the side.

I could just see my Accord, now; its snow-covered hood, maybe fifty or so yards away from where we were standing — within running-distance, in other words.

I leaned back around the side of the trailer. 'All right. Almost there. Just a little further —'

What happened next was like something out of a bad dream.

It emerged suddenly around the side of the dilapidated trailer in a flash of fabric and pasty-white skin. Another albino dude — this one taller, with a large, hooked-nose like a beak.

It all happened so fast. I don't think his legs even moved — like he'd just glided there on invisible rollerblades. I know how that sounds, but I swear, it's the truth.

'*Get down!*' I cried as Albino Boy suddenly raised the truncheon-of-fiery-death in the direction of Drunk Girl's face.

I pushed her to the ground, tried to backpedal out of Albino Boy's reach —

Blue fire enveloped my world as the truncheon struck me directly between the shoulder blades.

I'd never been electrocuted before, but I imagined this was probably how it felt.

Every muscle tensed beyond my control as I began to shake like an epileptic in the grip of a particularly violent seizure. Limbs strained and cramped. I thought I could smell hair burning, then looked down at my arms and saw that, sure enough, the hair there was indeed gone, burned away to nothing.

It only went on for a second or two, but felt like much longer.

Then, just as I was sure I was about to become but another red stain on the snow —

The electrocuting stopped.

I collapsed onto the snow, gasping and moaning, dimly aware of a spreading warmth in my crotch.

Oh, look at that. Peed my pants, too.

There was the crunching of boots on snow.

Albino Boy loomed over me.

'*You...*' it said, its voice all hollow and tinny, like radio-static. 'I know who *you* are. You're — '

Before it could finish, its head went suddenly flying up into the air like the lid on a party-popper.

I screamed; a deep, manly — not-at-all ladylike — scream, as Albino Boy's headless body collapsed onto the snow less than a foot from my face, arms still desperately trying to fend off its unknown attacker.

I looked back to the place he'd been standing.

I groaned.

'YE-AH!' cried Frankie, flailing his arms like one of those kids at Disneyland they're always letting on the rides before you. 'Take that, you pasty fuck! TASTE MY COLD STEEL.'

I looked down at the item in his hand.

I blinked. 'Is that a — ?'

He nodded. 'Yup. Broadsword. Pretty cool, huh?' He held it up to the light and turned it around. 'Of course, it's no *battle-axe*, but...'

'*Where the hell did you get a broadsword?*'

He sighed. 'You really don't go into your trunk that often, do you, Dan?'

I thought about asking him to elaborate on that, then shook my head instead. '*Whatever.* We need to get out of here. Quick — before more of them come.'

He reached down and helped me to my feet. Together, we bent and scooped Drunk Girl from the snow, who I was unsurprised to find had now completely fallen asleep.

Figures.

We booked it for the car.

'Okay, you drive,' I said, once we'd finally reached the door.

From beside me, Frankie frowned. 'What? Why should I be the one to drive? It's *your car.*'

'*You drove us here!*'

'I CAN'T WIELD A BROADSWORD AND DRIVE A CAR, DAN!'

I had to admit, he had a point.

I groaned. 'Give me the keys!'

He tossed them to me, then jogged round to the passenger side, simultaneously leaving me to cope with the burden that was Drunk Girl all by myself.

I propped her up against the Accord's side, went to open the door —

Thud.

I turned back.

Drunk Girl. Lying facedown in the snow.

I stiffened. 'Shit! I'm so sorry!'

'What's taking so long?' shouted Frankie from the passenger seat. 'Broadswords aren't exactly light, you know.'

'But —'

He sighed. 'Seriously, Dan, it's like you've never manhandled an unconscious woman before.'

After a mammoth effort, I finally shoved Drunk Girl into the backseat.

I turned for my door, breathing heavily —

And that was when I saw them.

They came from between the cluster of cars and trailers parked along the bank before us. Black coats and hats. Perhaps a dozen of them, maybe more. All staring in the Accord's direction with faces each as pale as a mannequin's.

I didn't wait around.

I jumped into the front seat, hands fumbling at the ignition like a kid receiving his first touch of boob.

Click-click-click.

'What's wrong?' said Frankie.

I turned the key again. And again.

Nothing.

I shook my head. 'I don't know — it's not starting.'

'Try it again.'

'What the fuck do you think I'm doing?'

'They're almost here, Dan!'

'The engine must have gotten too cold, or something. *It won't start!*'

Faces grew in the windshield, the side windows. A ring of black coats and hats. Closing in fast.

Click-click-click...

'Dan!'

'What the hell do you want me to do, Frankie? It won't — !'

Suddenly, the Pale Men stopped advancing. They tilted their heads and looked past my Accord at the road behind us instead.

It was then that I heard it; a *whining* sound, far off at the moment, but growing louder by the second.

I almost burst out laughing.

Sirens.

The cops! The cops are here! Holy crap, and right on time, too!

The Pale Men looked at each other. I sensed something passing between them, some decision being made.

Then they were receding back into the trees from whence they came, gliding slowly, not hurrying but hurrying all the same.

When they had all gone, Frankie and I turned to each other.

Frankie let out a breath.

'We have a strange life, don't we, Dan?' he said.

I sighed.

FOUR

JOE'S WAS A TAVERN along the less busy part of downtown, and if we're being totally honest here, a complete shithole. It smelled like how I imagined homeless people to smell — like pee and sweat and crushed dreams — and the surface of everything was always sticky with beer, regardless of what time you got there. Not even the rats would come to Joe's — that's how bad it was. And you know a place is filthy when not even the rats are willing to go there.

Still, the beer was cheap.

So that was good.

The owner's name, despite expectations, was Mearl. Mearl liked guns. Big ones, little ones. Those ones you see in movies sometimes, pebble-dashed with so many diamantes it'd put Kim Kardashian's vagina to shame. He was a short man with a wide neck and the kind of flushed face you only get when you're either wind-chaffed or a seasoned alcoholic. Legend had it he'd once shot and killed a man who'd refused to pay-up on his tab, though I get the feeling Mearl might have started that rumour himself to deter potential flakers.

'So...' said Frankie suddenly from across the table from me.

It was later that evening. We had spent the past couple hours answering questions from the local authorities. The woman in charge—a young detective with caramel skin and shoulder-length black hair—had made us sit on the snow like naughty children whilst she rattled off question after question, all the while my poor butt-cheeks cramped with a combination of wet and cold. Questions like who we were, what we were doing there—which, to be fair, we'd been able to mostly answer, though explaining the broadsword had admittedly taken some doing. That kind of thing almost always does.

Then something *strange* had happened—well, strang*er*, anyway.

Right in the middle of our interrogation, the National Guard had shown up (or at least, what I *presumed* was the National Guard). More of those trucks and personnel carriers, like the ones I had witnessed yesterday whilst on route to my meeting with the ever-charming Wesley Chang.

There had been shouting. A lot of finger-wagging and cursing. I got the impression the detective lady really didn't appreciate the National Guard just swooping in and taking over her investigation like that—mostly because she'd said so: *I really don't appreciate you swooping in and taking over my investigation like this.* Like that.

Then she'd left, and we'd been forced to answer a whole other bunch of questions, questions I really didn't think were pertinent to our current situation, but that seemed important all the same.

What high school did you attend?

Do you enjoy your job?

What are your parents' names?

What's your stance on cattle mutilation?

Have you or anyone you know ever been subject to an alien abduction?

He had been your typical military-type. Tall guy. Buzz-cut. Strong jaw. Immaculately groomed, with small, piercing eyes, and an air about him like he was constantly battling against the clock. It's very time-consuming being a soldier. His nametag had read **HAVISHAM**. Although I couldn't see a ranking on his uniform anywhere, I got the feeling he was somebody pretty important.

Then, after an hour of this, had come the clincher:

Do you know of anyone who might currently be harboring knowledge of the whereabouts of any extraterrestrial life-forms?

I got the feeling Frankie and I weren't the only ones crapping in our pants right about now.

'So,' I said.

'What do you think those guys were? The pasty ones, I mean. Because, clearly, they weren't Phonies, Dan. You see that one guy? He didn't melt—not even a *little* bit.'

I'd been wondering that very thing myself. What with the discovery of that "thing of which we do not speak" a few weeks ago, I'd come to accept the fact (albeit reluctantly) that the Phonies were not the only things out there. Yet even with this knowledge, I couldn't deny that the discovery of yet another group of alien douchebags bothered the shit out of me. Because it meant more danger, sure. But mostly cause it was all just so dumb.

'I have no idea.'

'And those army dudes—you saw them, right?' he went on. 'The ones in the black suits? Those were no ordinary military fatigues, Dan. They must be special ops, or something.'

'Yeah.'

'And of course there were those guys in the hazmat suits sealing off everything, too. You bring in that many white-suits for a simple murder scene? Seriously? Tell me that's normal, Dan.'

'I really don't care, Frankie.'

'They must have been looking for this—'

Before I could inquire as to his meaning, Frankie suddenly lifted his jacket.

He didn't. Oh, God, please tell me he didn't...

But he had.

With a grunt, he dropped the rock-thing from the late-Beaner's truck onto the table, making the glasses there rattle and clink.

I stared at him, slack-jawed. *'Dude!'*

So right here you're probably wondering exactly how it was he managed to get the rock-thing into the restaurant without myself or anyone else noticing. And that's a very good question—one I've been asking myself ever since, in fact. But, just as with my manager, Steve, there are certain things about Frankie that defy explanation. I don't know how or why Frankie does the things he does. All I know is that he does them, and that they make me very sad.

'What?' he said.

'You stole it?!'

'Yeah—so?'

'So you can't just—*get that thing the hell out of here before somebody sees!'*

'Like who, Dan? Look around—nobody cares. Here, I'll prove it.'

Before I could stop him, he suddenly got to his feet and lifted the rock above his head. 'Hey, everyone! Look! Alien rock-thing over here! Yoo-hoo! Everybody!'

Nothing. Not so much as a single glance in our direction.

I grabbed his sleeve and pulled him back into his seat. 'Okay, okay, you've made your point. *Ass*—but that still doesn't change the fact that we really shouldn't have this thing. I mean if you're right, and everyone and their mothers really *is* looking for it—hell, are even willing to *kill* for it—do we really want to be the ones standing in their way?'

'I'm sensing hesitation, Dan.'

'Get serious. That thing is bad news. We need to get rid of it.'

'You're right.' He thought it over a moment. '*Or...*'

'Or nothing! It's dangerous!'

'Come on, Dan! *Something strange is going on here.* You know it as well as I do. And whatever it is, I'm betting it has something to do with this rock.'

'All the more reason to get rid of it, then.'

He sighed. 'Oh, please, Dan! Let me keep it. Just this once? Let me keep it and I promise I'll never drag you out on another adventure with me ever again.'

'YOU KIDNAPPED ME.'

'*Please*, Dan? Just this once? Pretty-please?'

He shot me with those big puppy-dog eyes of his. Yeah—like *that* was going to work...

'All right,' I said.

Balls.

'*Yes!*'

'But just this once. And only if you promise you won't go looking into matters any further. I mean it, Frankie. *This shit stops here.* We don't need to go getting ourselves any more involved than we already are.'

He placed a hand over his heart. 'You have my word, Dan. I will not go looking into things any further.'

Even as he said it, though, I could read the lie in his eyes.

I groaned.

Goddamnit.

PART 2
SMALL FUCKING WORM, BIG FUCKING HOOK

Excerpt from the *Amerstow Chronicle*, dated December 9th, 2015, from the article 'Strange lights in sky cause major pile-up':

...however Mayor O'Brian thanked emergency services for their speedy response.

As to the cause of the pile-up, the origin of the lightshow is still currently unknown, with locals claiming everything from space debris to meteorites, to, you guessed it, UFOs.

Whilst an official reason for the lights has yet to be disclosed by local police, in an attempt to quell the number of incoming calls, they have issued a statement stringently denying anything of an "extra-terrestrial" nature.

Expect more updates in the days and weeks to come.

End of excerpt.

INTERLUDE—PART 2

'SO LET ME JUST make sure I've got this straight...' said Dr Lake from across the table.

He was leaning back in his chair again, his clasped hands once more propped just beneath his chin. He looked very wise. Like a yogi, or one of those people that live up in the mountains that are always very dirty and can supposedly talk to God or whatever. Maybe he was even in prayer. Man, psychiatry is so complicated. I had no fucking idea.

'You and your friend found a "mysterious rock" that you say crash-landed in Ackerman's Field?'

'That's right.'

'A rock that "glowed red" and "sang" to you?'

'We, uh, never actually heard it sing. That was all Beaner's group. We only saw the lights.' I hesitated. 'And stuff.'

'And you say it came from outer space?'

It was the most he'd said in a very long time. I knew there was a good chance his silence was nothing more than another of his sneaky psychiatrist-tricks, no doubt allowing me to talk myself into some kind of sudden revelation or whatever, which let's face it would pretty much be me doing his job for him. When you looked at it like that, really he should have been paying me.

I nodded. 'Probably outer space.'

'So—and please correct me if I'm wrong, here—you found a singing, glowing rock, "probably from outer space", and when the appropriate authorities showed up to claim it, *you hid it from them?'*

I cleared my throat.

This was not going how I'd planned.

'I mean, *sure*, it sounds retarded when you say it like *that—'*

He held up a hand. 'If it feels as though I'm doubting your story, Daniel, I apologise. That is not the impression I wish to convey.'

'But you don't believe me?'

'Why, sure, I do.'

I blinked. 'You... *do?'*

'Absolutely—what's not to believe?'

I wondered if this was a trick question.

'You feel your story is... *strange. Unique,'* he continued.

'Well—'

'Would you be surprised if I told you I had heard far stranger stories already this week? For instance, only yesterday I spoke with a man who was convinced he was hearing the voice of his dead mother beckoning to him from his kitchen sink. Now, do I think he's a liar? That he's making it up? *Not at all.* As far as I can tell, he one hundred per cent believes his dead mother has chosen the kitchen sink as a means with which to communicate with him.'

'So you *don't* believe me...'

He sighed. 'The brain cannot differentiate between an experienced event and an imagined one, Daniel. It doesn't have *bias*. The brain receives stimulus — imagined or not — then proceeds to react accordingly, in most cases simply by flooding the body with adrenaline, or endorphins. It's how PTSD works: the body constantly responding to a repetitive — and often negative — thought cycle.'

'*You're saying I have PTSD?!*'

Holy shit. Things were even worse than I thought...

He smiled. '*No*, Daniel. I'm saying *you* believe what happened. Therefore, its existence is beyond refute.'

I stared evenly across the table at him.

'No offence, doc, but I think you should be the one sitting in this chair.'

He laughed. It was a completely genuine laugh, too, from deep in the belly. It caught me off guard. I didn't know psychiatrists were allowed to laugh like that. Hell, I didn't even know they *could* laugh.

'Are you familiar with Pavlov's Dog, Daniel?'

'Is... that a friend of yours?'

'*Not quite.* Ivan Pavlov was a famous physiologist — a pioneer in classical conditioning, you might say. Through years of studies and research, he was able to determine that, by pairing a biologically potent stimulus with a previously neutral one, a mental association can be established — one that has a perceivable effect on the body.'

He might as well have spoken Klingon.

'*Come again?*' I said.

'He rang a bell at dinnertime and his dogs dribbled.'

'Oh.'

Then why didn't you just say that?

'But then, after enough times of this, all he had to do was ring the bell, and the dogs would salivate — do you understand?'

'Yes.'

I did not.

Lake leaned back in his chair and waved his hands. 'Please —
continue with your story.'

I did.

FIVE

THE NEXT FEW DAYS passed like this:

We returned to the apartment.

Almost immediately, Frankie began looking into the events of that evening, despite his solemn vow he would do no such thing. To be fair, though, I always knew that he would. It was just his nature — even if it did really piss me off.

That following morning I awoke to find Frankie sitting slumped over on the couch, surrounded by books he really had no business possessing, face once more deeply buried in the laptop screen in front of him. As he would swiftly go on to tell me (despite my constant urging that he please not do so), these well-dressed albinos, or "men in black", as he called them, were not nearly as much of an unknown quantity as we had at first automatically assumed.

As it turns out, throughout history there have apparently been numerous reports of these "pale suited-men" appearing after a supposed alien-event and harassing people — some even dating back to the early nineteen hundreds.

Now, accounts vary with regards to exact details, but one thing that remains consistent with these reports is an overwhelming sense of dread felt on behalf of the visited. Why that should be an important point, I have no idea. I'm just telling you what was said, goddamnit.

I called Abby every few hours or so to see how her old man was doing, and so far, no change. He had been happy to see her, though, which I guessed was good — even if I admittedly had my reservations about the whole thing. But, whether I liked it or not, the guy was still her father — a fucking asshole, true, but still her father.

As the days went by (and despite knowing better), I eventually found myself becoming fascinated with the rock-thing from the late-Beaner's truck. Even though I knew what a complete and utter hypocrite it made me, I still found myself joining Frankie at the breakfast bar each morning, watching as he poked and prodded at it, all in a desperate attempt to get it to do something. You probably think that makes me kind of an asshole. And you're right. It does. But, seriously — *alien space-rock*? Like you wouldn't have, too.

We tried cursing at it. Belittling it. Setting it on fire. A whole bunch of stuff, really — eventually culminating with us one drunken afternoon dropping the fucking thing off the roof of our apartment building, whereupon it was quickly decided that we should never, ever do that again.

And still — nothing.

Then, that following Friday, after a quick trip to the store, I returned home to find a note waiting for me.

Ordinarily, whenever I returned home I would find Frankie slumped in front of the couch in his underpants, watching TV or playing videogames or doing something else equally unproductive. Since the whole "incident of which we do not speak" a few weeks back, however, he had started going out. A little at first, then more often as the weeks went by. Exactly where he went on these occasions, I had no idea. All I know is, the notes he left continued to baffle me.

Dan,

Had to shoot out for a bit. Morgan's guinea pig got into a fight with a squirrel at the park and we think it might now have rabies. Also, we're out of beer. I hope you don't mind, but I took some cash out of that box you keep under your bed – you know, the one you also keep all those "magazines" in that we don't tell Abby about? I promise I'll pay you back.

Also, Abby, if you're reading this, Dan absolutely doesn't have any porn magazines hidden in a shoebox under his bed. And if he does, they're CERTAINLY not of Asian women.

– Frankie.

P.S. – Can guinea pigs even get rabies? It just seems like it would be a waste on them, you know? Like they're so small, who're they gonna bite?

And so on and so forth.

It was but one of several notes he'd left for me recently. I had no idea what it meant. Hell, I didn't even know he *had* any other friends besides me.

Deciding that to ponder over what Frankie got up to in his spare time would be a criminal waste of my own, I dropped the note and went to make myself something to eat instead.

Now, in the interest of full disclosure, I should probably mention that our refrigerator has never contained much in the way of what one might consider "ordinary" food items. Honestly, it's pretty much just beer. The odd meat-based snack or two. A kid's toy-pistol hovering near the back somewhere, filled with some kind of dark fluid Frankie had put in there years ago, but that we both agreed was now most likely haunted.

Sighing, I pulled out a beer, popped the tab, was just about to take a swig, when —

VRRRRRRMMMMMMM.

My phone.

Goddamnit. Can't a man drink a beer in peace? Just once?

It was Abby.

'Hey!' I said, slamming the phone up to my ear with such force it would leave a mark for a solid fortnight. 'How's everything going?'

'Oh, you know, about as good as you'd expect. I mean, considering everything, and all...'

She sounded tired. And possibly malnourished — though, granted, that might just have been me projecting. I was very hungry.

I should probably also mention it had been established by this point that her father was suffering from a particularly aggressive form of Lymphoma. Supposedly, it was in the latter stages. He didn't have long left.

I know I should have been left devastated by this knowledge, but if I'm being entirely truthful here, the most I could bring myself to feel for the guy was, at best, a kind of *vague* sense of apathy; the kind that comes wrapped in indifference, served with a generous side-helping of *who-gives-a-fuck*.

Because, seriously — this was a guy who'd cared more about the opinions of the townsfolk than the wellbeing of his very own daughter, who had let somebody he was supposed to have loved and protected be tossed out like yesterday's trash.

As far as I was concerned, Lymphoma was the least he deserved.

'Have they said anything else?' I said.

A long sigh from down the line. 'No. It's just a waiting game at this point.'

'Is there anything I can do?'

Forced euthanasia, perhaps? A long walk off a short cliff? Exactly how buoyant is your old man, anyway?

We talked like this for a while before the subject eventually moved on to home.

'So—how's everything on your end? You boys staying out of trouble?' said Abby.

A pause from my side. Too long.

'*Dan?*'

I cleared my throat. 'Oh, you know. *Fine.*'

'*Fine?*'

'Uh-huh. *Fine.* I mean—more or *less...*'

'No weird stuff? Like with that thing the other day, you know with the...'

I'm sure she said more, but I'd stopped listening.

My eyes had just settled on the rock-thing sitting propped on the coffee table.

I suddenly went very still.

Every muscle tensed, like I was getting electrocuted again. I think I even stopped breathing. Hell, I might have just had a stroke.

'*Dan?*'

I barely heard her.

It was the rock-thing. After giving up on trying to get it to do something the other day, we had since repurposed it as a kind of minimalist paperweight. That was the last I'd really paid any attention to it. Looking at the rock-thing now, there was definitely something different about it. Its shape was all wrong, for starters, and there were small bits of it lying scattered around on the carpet like debris from the world's smallest explosion. I could see a hole in one side, about the size of an infant's head, almost as if something had —

I stiffened.

Oh you have got to be kidding me.

'I have to go...' I said.

I could almost see Abby frowning on the other end. 'What? What do you mean you have to — ?'

'Talk to you later!'

I hung up and immediately went into defence mode, snagging a spatula from the wall by the stove and brandishing it above my head like a javelin, or how I thought you were supposed to hold one of those.

I threw myself behind the breakfast bar and ducked low.

I peeked over the top.

Everything was quiet. Or at least, from what I could see from my limited vantage point. As far as I could tell, it was still just the living room, same as I'd left it that morning — save, of course, for the now-broken rock-thing, and the several different parts of it currently collecting dust on my carpet.

I ducked back down and considered my options.

Now, I had seen enough movies in my time to know a discarded alien-egg when I saw one. Which meant that there was now probably a little alien baby in my apartment somewhere — maybe even a whole *litter* of them — just waiting for me to fall asleep so it/they can go ahead and put alien-eggs in my belly. And if that was the case, shouldn't I be getting the fuck out of there?

I thought it over.

Of course, on the *other* hand, if there really were a half a dozen miniature ETs running around my apartment somewhere, I couldn't just leave them to get up to... whatever it was little ETs got up to. What if they got into my dirty laundry and ate all my clothes? Or made a succession of long-distance calls on my phone? Jesus, think of the charges. It would be a nightmare. And besides, they were probably only tiny things. Like babies. I could kill a handful of babies if I had to, couldn't I?

Of course, then there was the whole "world being in danger" thing to consider, too. When you looked at it like that, there was really only one thing to do.

Taking a deep breath, I steeled myself.

Then I called Frankie.

'Mike's Abortion Clinic, you make 'em, we break 'em.'

I let out a breath. *'Frankie! Oh, thank Jesus, there's — the rock-thing, it — and then I —'*

'What? Slow down, Dan. I can't understand you.'

'The rock-thing, Frankie! I think it just... hatched.'

A moment of silence from down the line.

'Hatched? You mean like a Pokémon?'

'Like an egg, you ass! Why — ?' I caught myself. 'Look never mind that, okay? Just *get over here.*'

'Have you seen what came out of it yet?'

There was no mistaking the excitement in his voice.

'Don't you think I'd have mentioned that if I had?!'

But he wasn't listening. The fever had taken him now. 'Ooh, I bet it's something *gross,* Dan. And *scary.*' Another pause, then, 'I wonder if it bleeds acid...'

'YOU'RE NOT HELPING.'

'Relax — it's just been born, right? It's probably only a baby. You can handle a baby, can't you?'

'Frankie!'

He sighed. 'Okay, okay. I'll be over as soon as I can. Just got to finish up here, first.'

'Finish — *what*?!'

'Didn't you get my note?'

I pinched the bridge of my nose and sighed.

Somebody just fucking kill me already.

'It'll be fine,' Frankie continued. 'Just try not to die in the meantime, okay?'

'But — '

He was already gone.

Balls.

I turned back to the living room, gripping the spatula so tight it would have taken a team of surgeons and the fire department both working together to be able to pry it loose.

Okay — you can do this. You're brave. Remember when you ate that Jelly Baby you found under the couch cushion that one time, all because Frankie said you wouldn't, but then you totally did? You got this, man.

On legs suddenly like rubber, I forced myself into the living room.

Immediately I could see that my initial observation about the rock-thing had been correct — in so being that, at the very least, this thing was seriously weird as shit. Also, that it was indeed an egg. Peeking into the hole, I could see what looked like a thin, membranous material coating the inside, almost like a shower curtain. At the bottom of the rock-thing was a collection of oozy fluid-stuff, not unlike sperm, if sperm was green and glowed in the dark. Charlie Sheen's sperm, perhaps. I briefly contemplated reaching in and scooping a little bit of it up with my fingers. Then I remembered that I wasn't an asshole, and so didn't.

I straightened.

Hmm. Empty.

I looked down at the collection of rock bits on the carpet by my feet. It was funny; looking at them from this angle, they almost looked like a —

I stiffened as realisation suddenly hit me like a pie to the face.

It was a trail.

I stood there, fear rooting my feet to the spot.

Again, this was one of those moments where I really should have gotten the fuck out of there. Seriously, there's a reason people in these situations always die in movies — and it's not through using their brains.

But, like the idiot that I was, I didn't get the fuck out of there.

Instead I burglar-walked across the living room, spatula held high, wondering if I was about to become another one of those tragic cases you're always hearing about on the news about so-and-so getting murdered to death in their own homes. Solemn-looking reporters with nice hair and shiny teeth would later relay the fine details of my horrific and untimely demise to an — at best — indifferent public, all whilst in the background men in paper suits and funny shoes struggled with the logistics of ferrying what remained of my mangled corpse towards a waiting (and wholly too-late) ambulance. And the people of America would learn a valuable lesson about the importance of home security. My death would have meaning. I would be like Jesus, in a way.

I followed the rock pieces out of the living room and into the hall, before finally coming to a stop just outside the bathroom door.

I took a deep breath.

Okay. Now, remember — be brave. Besides, it's probably long gone by now.

I pushed open the door and immediately let out a scream like a nineteenth-century damsel. I fell back against the wall and scurried back into the living room, farting the entire way.

So much for being brave.

After what felt like a very long time, I pried myself from behind the breakfast bar and slowly edged my way back towards the bathroom.

I peeked around the frame.

And there it was. The thing from the space-rock. Sitting on my toilet, and taking what for all intents and purposes looked to be its normal, mid-afternoon dump.

What did it look like exactly, you ask? Well, that's hard to say. I guess a little like a monkey, only nothing like a monkey at the same time. Kind of like what a monkey might look like if drawn by a blind, mentally handicapped boy — one who had drawn it badly on purpose.

It was small, about the size of a chimpanzee, with stumpy little arms and legs, and eyes all big and black like a puppy's. Thick, brown fur covered its body in its entirety, speckled here and there with white.

Okay — it was fucking adorable.

The thing-that-was-not-a-monkey and I regarded each other in silence a moment.

I said, 'Uh... hi?'

And that's when shit got, for lack of a better word, "crazy".

Faster than you could say "surprise twist", the thing-that-was-not-a-monkey flung itself at me, its little monkey fingers attaching themselves to my head with manic dwarf-strength.

I screamed and thrashed around, swatting at my face with the spatula and knocking shit over.

For exactly how long this went on, I can't say. Longer than I'd have liked to admit, put it that way. I'll spare you the exact details. Just know that by the time I finally managed to pry it loose, I was covered in sweat, and not a single standing toiletry remained.

Thinking fast, I grabbed the thing-that-was-not-a-monkey and flung it at the shower curtain to my right. It sailed through and hit the tiled wall behind it with a clown-like *honk!* before falling into my tub, out of sight.

An eerie stillness followed.

When I could summon the courage to move again (and against every part of my body urging me otherwise), I slowly forced myself over to the bathtub and, with a quick breath to steady myself, yanked back the curtain.

Gone.

I blinked, surprised.

It had been there three seconds ago, I was sure of it. Was it possible I'd simply imagined the whole thing? Where the hell did the little bastard —

THUMP-THUMP-THUMP.

I spun around, startled.

The front door.

Ah, man, not now. Are you fucking kidding me?!

I wondered if I remained very still and quiet, whoever was knocking would think I wasn't home and go away.

THUMP-THUMP-THUMP-THUMP-THUMP.

'Mr Pratt, this is the police. Open up. I know you're home. I can hear you breathing,' said a woman's voice from behind the door.

Crap.

'And besides, your car is here.'

Not knowing what else to do, I pulled the door shut tight, and, taking a moment to correct myself as best I could, quickly crossed the hall and pulled open the door.

It was the detective from the lake the other day, the one who'd questioned us — Espinosa, I thought her name was.

She was attractive, in a terrifying sort of way. Dark-skinned. Tall. Slim, with jet-black hair tied tightly behind her head in a neat ponytail. Grey pantsuit, with well-polished shoes. She was the very image of professionalism. The personification of all things neat and orderly.

She took one look at the disheveled state of me and frowned.

'Am I interrupting something?'

There was a moment where I couldn't think of a single thing to say. Like my mind had just drawn a total blank.

'Uh... *what?*'

She looked over my shoulder. 'May I come in?'

I began to tell her no, but she waltzed past me and let herself in anyway. She looked around, saw all the empty beer cans and stacks of pizza boxes. 'Nice place you got here.'

I suspected she was being sarcastic.

'Yeah, it's uh... all right.' I cast a glance around the apartment, trying to catch a glimpse of where the little monkey-bastard had got to. I couldn't see him, though.

'So, you're probably wondering why I'm —' She frowned. '*What the hell is that?*'

There was a moment where my heart completely stopped beating. I began to fear the worst.

But then, after following her gaze into the living room — more specifically, to the coffee table — I suddenly realised what it was she was looking at.

The rock-thing! You forgot to hide the rock-thing, dumbass!

'Oh — *that?*' I said, trying to sound as casual as possible — which is harder than you'd think when there's an infant alien-monkey running amuck in your home somewhere. 'That's just, uh...'

82

She stepped over to the coffee table and looked it over. 'You make this?'

'Yes. Yes, I did.'

'What are you—some sort of artist, or something?' She ran a finger over the hole in the rock-thing's side—which, now that I looked at it, reminded me an awful lot of an exit-wound. 'What's it supposed to be, anyway?'

'It's an abstract piece. I like to leave my work open to interpretation.'

She shrugged, like she didn't really care anyway. She wiped her finger on the arm of my couch and turned back to me.

There was something different about her face, now. Before, there had been an air of indifference about her. The air of a woman just doing her job. No longer. Now she was all business, her face carefully neutral, expressionless.

I suddenly felt very afraid.

'I'm going to be honest with you, Mr Pratt,' she said, in a tone that made me instantly believe her.

'Okay.'

'I looked into you. Your past. Seems wherever you go, people always seem to either wind up missing, or dead. That's odd, wouldn't you say?'

'Uh-huh.' I snuck another glance around the living room. I still couldn't see the monkey-thing. It didn't make sense; the apartment really wasn't all that big. Where the hell could it have got to?

If I was a baby alien-monkey from outer space, where would I hide?

'And yet, every time there's an incident—you walk,' Espinosa continued. '*Every time.* You're like an enigma. A *puzzle*. I really don't like puzzles.'

'Puzzles are very hard,' I agreed.

The bedroom? The broom closest? Do we even have *a broom closet?*

Before I knew what she was doing, she crossed the living room and placed herself in front of me. I noticed suddenly how close we were. I wondered if we were about to make out. Was it illegal to refuse a kiss from an officer of the law? Wasn't that an abuse of power, or something?

She thrust a finger in front of my nose. 'I'm on to you, Mr Pratt. The others might not see what you are, but I do.'

'Yeah.'

'I'm going to be watching you. Wherever you go, whatever you do, I'll be there. Watching. *Waiting*. Right up until the day you finally slip up and I arrest your ass — *capiche?*'

I came back to myself. 'I'm sorry — what were you saying?'

She strode past me and crossed the hall in the direction of the front door.

In the doorway, she turned back.

'Be seeing you, Mr Pratt.'

And with that, she spun on her heels and left.

I stood there a moment, not moving. I was very confused. I had the peculiar feeling I had just made things worse for myself, but wasn't entirely sure how that could be.

A moment later, I was running.

'Okay, you little bastard,' I said, various items of cutlery poking out from inside each closed first. 'Prepare to —!'

I stepped into the bathroom and froze.

The bathroom window was open.

I let my hands fall to my sides.

Houston. We have a serious fucking problem.

***

'A monkey,' said Frankie.

It was later that morning. I was sitting on the couch, a blanket wrapped tightly around my shoulders, a cup of lukewarm coffee resting in my lap. I was a nervous wreck. I felt traumatised. I realised this must have been how those Chilean miners felt that time when the mine they were working in collapsed down on top of them, only worse, because at least those guys got a movie deal out of it. It was like I was suffocating to death. Even if Hollywood *was* going to make a movie about me, it couldn't be worth this.

Because it was bullshit. First the Jellies. Then that "other" thing, of which we don't speak. Then the albino dudes—*now this?* It was like some kind of sick cosmic-joke, with me as the punch-line. I mean most people go their entire lives without bumping into even the one type of extra-terrestrial fuck-bag. Four in the space of a year?

It was all so unfair.

'Like an *actual* monkey? Like with a tail, and shit?' Frankie went on. He shook his head and sighed. 'This is bad, Dan. This is really bad.'

I dragged my gaze over towards the window. It had ceased snowing by this point—though, if the news was anything to go by (and it almost never is), the respite would not last for long. Supposedly, there was some real bad weather on the way. A "white-out", I think was the term used.

'We need to get out there and find this thing,' said Frankie.

I almost spat coffee in his face. '*Excuse you?*'

'Come on, *Dan!* There's a newly born space-monkey out there— one that likes to attack men's faces, if I recall. We can't just leave it to do... whatever it is newborn space-monkeys do. I mean, shit, who knows what kinds of nefarious things it might be getting up to right at this very moment?'

'I don't care. I'm done, Frankie. Count me out.'

'But we *stole* it, Dan. We stole it, and we took it home. Like it or not, this thing is our responsibility.'

'Okay, first of all, *you* stole it. And secondly —'

Before I could finish, there was another knock at the door.

Frankie and I shared a glance.

I frowned.

Seriously? Again? Isn't this sort of thing classed as police harassment?

Feeling very much like a man skipping along the tightrope that was his own sanity, I pushed myself up and dragged my feet across the apartment towards the door.

Okay, Detective. You want to play hardball? Fine. Let's —

Now, to describe exactly what happened next, it's probably best I take you through it frame by frame. So here goes.

I opened the door.

Immediately, I became aware of two things. First, that it was not the detective knocking at my door, as I had just automatically assumed. Instead I was greeted by what I can safely say — without a hint of exaggeration, mind you — was the biggest man I had ever seen. Eight feet tall, maybe more. Long, black coat, stretching down to his knees. Another of those stupid, retro businessman-hats on his head.

No eyebrows.

The second thing I noticed was just how slow the human body is in reacting to threats. Because — seriously — I didn't move. Sure, it might have been shock. Or maybe something worse, like some new type of full-body, incurable paralysis, like the type Christopher Reeve was always going on about — I don't know; I'm not a doctor.

All I know is, the giant albino and I stared at each other in silence for a very long time.

Then he was pushing me back into the apartment, his giant body pausing momentarily to duck below the frame before stepping through and following me inside.

I made a sound like a cat giving birth and fell backwards into the hallway.

There was the rustle of shoes on carpet from behind me as Frankie quickly pounced into action.

Not hesitating for a moment, he barrel-rolled over the couch's back — whether as a diversionary tactic, or some kind of new, strange, tactical manoeuvre, I'm not sure — before landing with a heavy thud on the couch's other side. Then, before I could register what it was he was doing, he popped his head up from behind the couch, and, shouting a barrage of curse words, threw his boot at Albino Man.

There was a muted *thump* as the boot ricocheted off of Albino Man's chest.

It hit the floor with a *thud*.

We all stared at it.

Frankie nodded. 'Oh, don't worry — *there's plenty more where that came from!*'

He reached for the other boot.

'Uh, Frankie,' I said. 'I don't think that's —'

He barrel-rolled over the couch again.

'*Would you please stop doing that!*'

But he wasn't listening. He was fully committed, now.

As I watched helpless from the floor, he launched himself over furniture item after furniture item, his body pirouetting through the air like a salmon fighting its way upstream. Again, I'm not sure what he was hoping to achieve by all this. But it was very graceful.

He made to hurdle the TV, slipped, caught his head on the side of the coffee table, and went immediately still on the carpet.

The sound of snoring filled the living room.

I sighed.

I was on my own.

Using the opportunity Frankie's theatrics had provided, I jumped to my feet and immediately sprinted for my bedroom. In hindsight, it was probably the least tactful place I could have chosen. But there was a blanket there, and if I could just get under it—maybe be very quiet, too—perhaps the guy would just go away.

I got about four paces.

Before I could realise what was happening, Albino Man grabbed me by the back of the head and launched me screaming across the apartment. I collided with the breakfast bar, momentum tumbling me over it, and then I was lying on my back in the kitchen, the wind knocked out of me and gasping for breath as I contemplated the secret, hidden world that was the dustball-riddled space beneath my refrigerator.

Hey, look—my G.I Joe! So that's where that went...

I hitched in a breath as hands found my collar, first pulling me to my feet, then off them. I became airborne. It's a strange sensation, being weightless.

'WHERE IS THE NAOGGRATH?!' screamed Albino Man in his odd, quavering voice, even though I could already hear him perfectly fine.

'The... *what?*'

'DO NOT PLAY GAMES. I KNOW YOU HAVE IT. TELL ME.'

I frowned. Things were becoming more mysterious. I had no idea what a "Naoggrath" was. And even if I did, I certainly wouldn't have told this asshole.

I began to tell him this, when—

Fingers clenched around my throat. It suddenly became very hard to breathe.

'TELL ME!'

I tried to say something—anything, but I couldn't. All I could manage when I tried was a kind of strangled cry.

'*Aggg!*'

A darkness was creeping in around my vision now. It occurred to me I was probably about to pass out. Oddly, the realisation was not nearly as alarming as you'd have thought it would be. I felt my consciousness slipping, my limbs relaxing, as my body quickly gave way to unconsciousness—and, presumably, death.

But then, just as I was sure this was it, that it was all over—

There was a loud noise and a cry and all of a sudden I wasn't passing out anymore.

I hit the kitchen's tiled floor, rolled over—

Dustballs!

—before ending up on my back, gasping and choking, clawing at my throat and neck with my hands like a fat kid clawing at the world's very last Twinky.

I glanced up—

I gasped.

Albino Man had shrunk—only that wasn't *quite right*. What I mean is that there was less of him.

It was then I became aware of the thing lying on the kitchen's tiled flooring beside me, still wrapped in the coat sleeve it had first entered the apartment wearing.

I blinked.

Oh, look at that. His arm came off. How about that.

'WHO'S THE BITCH NOW?!' cried a familiar voice from somewhere above me.

I looked up again, spotting Frankie now standing at the entrance to the kitchen, looking what could only be described as irrationally angry. In his hands was a large steel-something, long as a javelin, only thicker, with something like a —

I groaned.

It was a battle-axe.

He pointed it at Albino Man, who I noted was now busy inspecting the stump of what had until very recently been his right arm.

'OH, I'M SORRY — DID THAT HURT? HERE — LET ME GIVE YOU A *HAND!*' He tried to heft the battle-axe again, managed it, but then completely missed his target, smashing the steely instrument of death right into my kitchen cabinet instead.

'Frankie, don't —'

But he wasn't listening.

'YEAH — YOU LIKE THIS BATTLE-AXE, DON'T YOU?' he shouted. 'I KEEP IT UNDER MY BED. YOU KNOW — SO IT'S ALWAYS CLOSE TO *HAND!*'

The toaster exploded.

'Frankie!'

I turned my attention to Albino Man. I saw his expression still hadn't changed — something I thought was especially weird, given he was now missing a part of himself. And shit, if there was ever a time to show emotion, spontaneously losing your arm by battle-axe was definitely that time.

Frankie continued to wrestle the battle-axe.

When he was finished, he lowered it to the floor, panting. 'Okay. Time out. In all seriousness, I think I might actually have concussion.'

He helped me to my feet.

We regarded Albino Man.

'What the hell do we do now?' I said. My voice came out croaky. It was hard to talk — probably because of all the strangling. That dick.

'Just you leave that to me,' said Frankie, patting the battle-axe.

I should have said no, of course. No way me leaving Frankie alone with this guy was going to turn out well — not for any of us. But then, I really was very tired. And I *had* almost just died.

So I left it up to Frankie.

And of course, it was a mistake.

***

Fifteen minutes later and we were sitting in my living room again, Frankie and I on one side, the one-armed giant albino man on the other.

Lacking any rope, we'd been forced to improvise when it came to the task of securing our new, one-armed friend. We tried sellotape — nope. Handcuffs — which actually started off promising, until we remembered the guy only had one hand, and so that was a no-go. Eventually it was decided that wrapping Albino Dude in a bedsheet was the best way with which to restrain the guy. You can probably imagine how that looked, so I won't go into it. Worked surprisingly well, though.

'Okay,' said Frankie, now on his feet and pacing back and forth in front of him. He still had the battle-axe, which he now held cradled in his arms like a newborn. He was growing pretty attached to that thing. 'You want to tell us why it is you and your eyebrow-less compadres keep attacking me and my buddy Dan, here? You some kind of a dick, or something?'

'You do not understand,' said Albino Man. 'The Naoggrath—it has to be *stopped*. It cannot be allowed to feed, do you hear me? If it feeds, this world—*all* the worlds—are doomed.'

I frowned. 'You mean the monkey?' It hadn't struck me as the destroyer of worlds-type. *Weird*, sure—but not *dangerous*.

Not *that* dangerous, anyway…

'To you, perhaps, it is a monkey. Others, an octopus, or a bird. Truthfully, it has no real form. It only appears to you as such because that is the closest your puny human brains can compare it to without being driven completely insane.'

'What is it?' I said. 'I mean, *specifically*.'

He sighed. 'The Naoggrath—or Novamites, as they are also known—were among the first of the Old Ones' creations. Fierce. Relentless. Imbued with incredible power, power to rival that of the very gods themselves. They almost brought the universe to an end. There… was a war. The Old Ones knew they had to do something. So they imprisoned them in capsules—like the one the two of you stole—and scattered them across the universe, where it was hoped nobody could ever find them again. That was the last anyone had ever heard. We had thought they were all extinct.' He paused. 'That was, until a week ago.'

My head almost exploded.

Novamites? Old Ones? Man, just when I was beginning to think things couldn't possibly get any dumber. Touche, universe. Touche.

'And you? What's your part in all this?'

'We are the First Men. The Keepers of Man. Charged by the Old Ones to watch over mankind, ensure they do not destroy themselves, like so many others before them. Since the time when this planet was nothing but rock and ocean, we have been here. Watching from the shadows, constantly saving you from yourselves. When the Cuban

Missile Crisis happened, we were there. When it looked like Hitler was going to bring humanity to a screeching halt, *we were there.*'

Did he just say they killed Hitler? Holy fuck.

'But—*wait*,' said Frankie suddenly from beside me. 'That still doesn't explain you going around exploding everybody. I thought you wanted to protect us. Exactly how is blowing us into a gazillion pieces supposed to achieve that?'

Albino Man looked away. I saw something pass over his face. It was only there for a second, but I thought it looked suspiciously like regret. 'Sometimes saving humanity requires sacrifice. In order to make an omelet, you have to be willing to break a few eggs.'

'These weren't eggs, you *ass*. They were people—*kids*.'

'*What would you have us do?* Let them go tell all their friends about the extra-terrestrial they found? Can you imagine if the world were to find out about the things that scurry about in the darkness? About the things lurking right beneath their very noses—even now, as we speak? It would be chaos. *Anarchy*—believe me, I have seen it.'

I had to admit, he had a point. Not everybody was as well equipped to deal with this sort of thing as Frankie and I were—emotionally speaking, that was.

Albino Man continued. 'Listen to me. Both of you. *You cannot allow the Naoggrath to feed.* If it feeds, it is all over.' He turned his head suddenly to look at me. 'We have heard great stories about you, Dan Pratt. You have done humanity a great service—but your journey has only just begun. There is a war coming. Everyone will be seeking the Naoggrath, now. Those who control the Naoggrath, hold the power. The O'tsaris are a barbaric bunch, but at least they kept the other undesirables at bay. You defeated their leader—their *king*. The balance in the food chain has been disrupted. Now, it will be a free-for-all.'

He looked me hard in the eye, so hard it made me feel almost naked.

'And I am sure I do not need to tell you what would happen if the O'tsaris were to ever gain possession of the Naoggrath...'

He didn't. It would be the end of everything. They'd take over the planet, turn all our bodies into jungle gyms for their bastard offspring to play around in. Tentacles would enter orifices by the thousands — hell, *millions* — and not in that cool, hentai-way. It would be a nightmare.

As I contemplated this, Albino Man suddenly pulled free his remaining hand — with very little effort, I noted — and reached into his coat.

When he pulled it out again, there was another of those truncheon-things in it. Blue flames sparked around the tip like lightning flashes during the world's smallest electrical storm. I could feel the vibration even from as far away as I stood — a kind of *heavy* feeling, deep in the gut, like right before that first big drop on a rollercoaster. The taste of battery acid filled the air, tangy and bitter and awful.

He nodded. 'So long, Dan Pratt. And good luck — you're going to need it.'

He put the truncheon-thing to his neck.

You've probably never seen a man explode before. Ordinarily, it's about as messy as you'd expect. All that blood, that gore. Really, it's not that bad. Surprisingly, Hollywood has prepared us quite well with regards to how to cope in the event one of our fellow citizens decides to up and pop right next to us.

Unfortunately for us, however, this was no ordinary suicide-by-kaboom.

Instead of showering us in his gore, we were instead enveloped in a cloud of what could only be described as "albino dust". If this sounds like a better deal to you than a bucketload of blood and flesh, that's only because you couldn't smell it. Jesus, Cloud Albino Man *stank*. Like egg and shit and sewage and death, all rolled up inside one horrendous dog-fart. And it was *everywhere*. Over our clothes, our faces — in our *mouths*. I'd have a taken a blood showering over that stench any day.

'*What the dick?!*' cried Frankie, once the dust had settled. He waved a hand in front of his face, coughing. '*What the hell just happened?!*'

'I think he exploded himself,' I said.

'Jesus, *another one*? Seriously, I'm starting to think it's us, Dan.'

I didn't answer.

It was happening again. *The retardation*. I could feel it closing in around me, smothering me like an overzealous child's hand around a frightened mouse. Despite my best efforts, the God of Retarded Things had found me, and now his slow ruination of me would resume, and would *keep* resuming, until I was nothing but a bloodied, beaten bundle of man on the sidewalk. Songs would be sung of my tragic, retarded life for centuries to come, and they would all be too loud and off-key, in registers not even dogs would be able to tolerate.

This... this was my destiny.

'Why'd you think he did it?' said Frankie.

'I have no idea.'

He shrugged. 'Well, one thing's for sure, he won't be causing anybody any grief now.' He thought about it. 'I guess you could say he's *harm*less...'

We observed the couch a while.

'So what do we do now?' said Frankie. 'I mean, if this thing really is as dangerous to all humanity as Mr Explodey over here says it is, we need to start looking for it, Dan. Like, *right now*.'

I shook my head. Not because he was wrong, of course, but because if what the late Albino Man had said was true, that would mean this whole thing was way bigger than us. We were in over our heads—which was not exactly an unfamiliar position for us, true, but that still didn't mean I had to be happy about it. But more than that, I just really, really didn't want to get involved anymore than we already were.

Because I wasn't a hero—hell, I wasn't even a *sidekick*. I was the innocent bystander, watching the superheroes duke it out from the sidelines, but who somehow still manages to get fucking decapitated or whatever because of, you know, *"reasons"*. Even at my very best, I was collateral damage. And I was fine with it. Every war has casualties. The most someone in my position can hope for nowadays is a quick death.

I blinked as sudden inspiration struck. 'Wait—let's call Kinsey!'

'*The president?*'

'Sure—*why not*? Isn't this sort of thing his problem now, anyway?'

He thought it over. 'You know what, Dan? You might be onto something there.'

He reached into his pocket and pulled out his cell. A second later, he raised it to his ear.

I frowned. 'You have the president on speed dial?'

'Sure—don't you?'

'Of course...'

I did not.

I paced whilst Frankie did his thing. 'Well?' I said, a couple minutes later. 'What did he say?'

Maybe he'd send the army, or something. Surely the military would be better at finding extra-terrestrials than we were. Didn't they have a division for that, or something?

Frankie shook his head. 'That was his secretary. She, uh... said she'd have me arrested if I didn't stop, and I quote, "being weird".'

Balls.

'Well... *what about Chuck?*'

Chuck Norris. As in *the* Chuck Norris. Like with the president, we'd met during the whole Belmont Grove-thing. We'd actually become pretty close. Yeah, we have cool friends.

Frankie shook his head. 'No good. He's in Bermuda, shooting a movie. Something about mermaids, if I recall.'

I looked down at the floor.

We were on our own.

Frankie shot me a glance. 'We could always call—well, you know...'

I shook my head. 'Uh-uh. No way. Absolutely not.'

'She *is* a lot braver than us, Dan. And smarter.' He thought it over. 'And tougher.'

'We're not calling Abby, Frankie. I've spent too much time getting her away from all that crap, only to pull her back into it again. The answer's no.'

And besides, she's got her own problems to deal with right now.

'So what are you saying? You want to go look for this thing, after all?' He rubbed his chin. 'Well, I'll admit, I had my reservations in the beginning. But you've really talked me around, Dan. When do we start?'

I noted the gleeful look in his eye again.

Balls.

SIX

WE TOOK A MOMENT to go over provisions before heading out in pursuit of the alien monkey-thing. I say "provisions". Really, they were just things Frankie had put aside in the event something terrible and ridiculous happened again — à la now.

Salt. Beer. One of those portable, hand-held vacuum cleaners, for some reason. Eleven dollars in change, wrapped up in a dirty Hello Kitty sock — and that was just the *normal* stuff.

'Check this out,' he'd told me, before dragging me into his bedroom.

They'd been in a little wooden trunk, sitting at the foot of his bed.

Swords. Battle-axes. Maces. What may or may not have been one of those toy lightsabers you can pick up off Amazon for like twenty bucks — you know, with the lights?

Somebody had evidently been preparing themselves for just such an occasion.

Then, just as we were piling out the door, my cell beeped.

I groaned.

Oh, man, not now.

'Who is it?' said Frankie.

'The guy. You know — the blackmailer dude.'

'Chang?'

'Yeah.'

I stared down at the screen in dismay. With all the stuff that had happened recently, I'd completely forgotten about him.

'What's he saying?' said Frankie.

'He wants to meet.'

'Right now?'

I shrugged. 'Apparently so.'

'What are you going to do?'

It was a good question. Acquiring the monkey-thing was clearly the priority here, what with the fate of the world hanging in the balance and all. But if I didn't go meet with Chang, he'd go tell the cops about the whole Mr Stewart thing. Then I'd go to prison. *Forever.* And I was far too androgynous-looking to go to prison. Jesus, I'd be like one of Jennifer Lawrence's nude pics, passed around from man to man, faster than a goddamn STI. They'd rip me to pieces.

Can a man drown from ingesting too much semen? What would you even call *that?*

I shook my head.

Either way, I was still screwed.

I sighed. 'Fuck it. Split up. I'll meet up with you once I've dealt with Chang.'

'You sure?' said Frankie, frowning. 'I mean, not to be a dick about it or anything, but the fate of humanity *is* kind of hanging in the balance, here.'

Spermicide? No, that's already a thing. Rapeicide...?

I shuddered. 'I'm sure. Besides, I'll be quick. I won't be long.'

He sighed. 'Well, all right — but don't come crying to me if I've got this whole thing wrapped up by the time you finish blowing this guy or whatever.'

I sensed overconfidence on Frankie's part.

He thrust out a hand. 'Okay — put her in.'

I stared at his hand like there was a dick and balls hanging from it. 'I'm good.'

'Come on, Dan! Where's your team spirit? Besides, we both might die tonight; we may never have another opportunity.' Before I could object any further, he suddenly grabbed my hand, placed it over his. 'Ready? On three. One, two, three — GOOOOOOOOO DUCKS!'

I squinted at him. 'You worry me — you know that, don't you?'

He grinned. 'Yeah.'

And so we split up, Frankie setting off after the alien monkey-thing, whilst I set off to my long-overdue meeting with the one and only Wesley Chang.

Things only got worse from there.

***

So I drove. Across town. In the snow. In a car that would have struggled on a clear, sunny day, never mind the middle of winter.

It was a treacherous drive. The Accord's wheels slipped and caught constantly on the icy sludge, every once in a while causing the back end to slide out and damn near giving me a heart attack. Wipers worked frantically to clear the snow accumulating on the windshield, like a fisherman desperately tossing water from his quickly sinking boat. It's a miracle there weren't many other cars out on the road tonight, as somebody could have gotten seriously hurt — namely me. Every corner was a near death experience, my life flashing before my eyes so many times I could have walked you through it frame by frame.

As I drove, I took in all the whiteness. Like a white sheet had been thrown over the city. I couldn't remember the last time it had snowed this hard. True, it wasn't quite the white-out the fear-mongering weather broadcasters had promised (at least, not *yet*), but it was still enough to make my butthole quiver—not that *that* took a lot, exactly. But you know what I mean.

I thought about what Albino Man had told us. About this "Naoggrath", or Novamite, or whatever the hell it was called. About the First Men, and these supposed "Old Ones"—whose existence I couldn't even begin to contemplate. And of course, about those "other things" supposedly out there somewhere, who would no doubt be looking for this alien monkey-bastard right at this very moment.

Mostly, though, I thought about Abby, how she was doing. I've never been what you might call an "overly sentimental" guy, but now, with humanity once more hanging in the balance, I couldn't help but miss her—her, *and* her kung fu.

It was a little after 10:00pm when the Accord's headlights finally flashed over Chang's place.

Perhaps unsurprisingly, Chang's residence was a shady-looking trailer park across town, in what could have been considered one of Amerstow's "poorer" neighbourhoods.

It was pretty much exactly what you'd expect. Trailers. Trucks. Mean-looking dogs with saliva conditions, tied up outside the front of people's properties on too-thin ropes. People arguing. Babies crying. Trash fucking everywhere.

Now, I'm not saying for certain this was where all of Amerstow's meth and heroin was manufactured, but I wouldn't have been surprised.

I pulled up outside the number Chang had given me and immediately switched off the engine.

I stared through the windshield at it.

Chang's trailer was like a time machine from the future. All tin, raised up off the ground on what looked like stacked cinder-blocks. Somewhere close-by I could hear what sounded like the thrum of working generators, though I couldn't see any.

Pulling the collar of my jacket tighter around myself, I dragged my feet up the steps and gently rapped on the door.

Chang answered on the fourth knock.

'Mr Pratt! What a surprise! Please, come in! Come in!'

He looked even greasier than last time I'd seen him. Like he'd just taken a bath in the stuff. I noticed he was still wearing the same clothes from our meeting the other day. Same cargo pants. Same stained Ramones T-shirt. True, he could have just washed them and put them on again. I didn't think that was the case, however.

I followed him inside into a trailer covered head-to-toe with a vast collection of what looked to be anti-establishment paraphernalia — and not just your *average* anti-establishment paraphernalia, either. Your fucking *Che Guevara* poster, or whatever. I'm talking *hardcore* paraphernalia here. Posters with declarations like **DEATH TO CAPITALISM!** and **KILL THE PIGS!**, with pictures of various world leaders below, their heads replaced with those of pigs.

Well somebody had a happy childhood...

He led me over to a table positioned at the trailer's front. It wasn't your ordinary dinner table, I noted, but rather a desk, like something you'd have in a study. Loose sheets of paper lay spread all along its length in untidy piles, boasting more anti-government propaganda. I registered the position of the chairs — mine on one side, his on the other.

I almost laughed.

He's turned the place into his very own office.

'Please — won't you have a seat?' he said, gesturing at the chair in front of me.

I should also mention the place was almost unnaturally dirty. Like it was so dirty, it broke some kind of natural law, or something. Empty fast-food boxes, plates with old, rotting food still on them — a whole bunch of empty Diet Coke bottles for some reason, all stacked together in the corner like a kind of poor man's bowling-pin set. It was startling. I didn't know how a person could live in such a place without contracting some kind of fatal disease — not that my apartment was exactly spotless, of course, but at least mine wasn't going to kill you.

I grimaced and — pausing a moment to brush down my seat — slowly lowered myself into my chair.

Chang clasped his hands on the desk and grinned. 'Okay. All right. Here we are. *Finally.* You and me. Ready to confess your sins, Mr Pratt? I imagine you must be practically fit to burst, in that regard.'

'Can we just please get this over with?' I said.

He nodded solemnly, as if that was exactly the reaction he'd been expecting. 'As you wish.' He reached below him to some place I couldn't see and pulled out a little black box, like a remote, but that wasn't a remote.

It was a tape recorder.

He hit the button.

'Whenever you're ready.'

I looked down at the recorder, its steady red light.

I didn't want to tell Chang about Belmont Grove. Despite already not having said a single word on the matter, I'd still had dozens upon dozens of emails from people just like him, who had somehow managed to deduce my involvement. If I went on record with Chang now, whatever the outcome, one thing was for certain — these fuckers would never leave me alone. I'd be hounded. From today until the day I died, from other conspiracy-theorist whackjobs also looking to make a name for themselves by getting that "exclusive scoop". I'd be like this generation's Neil Armstrong — legendary, but for all the wrong reasons.

Of course, if I didn't give Chang what he wanted, I'd go to prison. I'd go to prison, and become entertainment for the other inmates, who would no doubt nickname me something awful, like "Swallows Whole" — for reasons that should not need explaining. And if I could say only one thing for my aspirations in life, it's that I never wanted to know what another man's balls tasted like.

And so I told him. About everything. About Mr Stewart and Baxter & Klein. About Carter's group and the whole fiasco up in Massachusetts. And, of course, about the Phonies. I spared no detail, however small or seemingly irrelevant. And the more I told him, the better, strangely, I felt. It was like confession. I was unburdening myself, purging myself of all the ridiculous crap that had been weighing so heavily on my soul this past year.

Did it feel good, you ask? No. Not even close. I *was* still speaking under duress, after all.

But it felt all right.

When I was finished, I glanced up. He didn't have a clock anywhere I could see, but I sensed some time had passed. Maybe an hour, or so. I wondered how Frankie was getting on, if I'd have been able to sense if he'd died yet, like how it works in *Star Wars*.

'So,' I said, with a sigh. 'That's it. Now you know.'

I was like a new man. *Changed*, like a Transformer, only not really — though that admittedly would have been freaking awesome.

Chang stared at me across the table for what felt like a very long time.

When he was finished, he said, *'Do you think this is a joke?'*

I blinked.

I hadn't been sure of exactly what reaction I'd been expecting, but certainly "anger" wasn't it. *Of course* I didn't think it was a joke—how could I? I'd almost died—a *dozen* times, if I remembered correctly. If it was a joke, I wasn't the one making it. And I certainly wasn't laughing.

'Um...'

'Do you really expect me to believe that "aliens" were responsible for killing all those people?' He looked furious, his greasy cheeks now glowing and vibrant with anger. That, or sunburn. But at this time of year? What wattage were those lights, anyway? 'What—do you think I'm an idiot?'

I wasn't sure how to answer that without making him even madder.

I raised my hands like I was being held at gunpoint instead. 'But... it's the *truth*, I swear—besides, isn't this what you wanted?'

'Don't lie to me, Pratt!'

He was on his feet now, leaning over the table and jabbing at the air in front of my face with his bloated, sausage fingers. Frothy spittle flew from his mouth in a fine spray, showering me like those times back when you were a kid when you'd look up into the rain, even though that's probably really dangerous.

Holy fuck—he's got rabies! Don't let him bite you, Dan!

'I know it was the government, Pratt!' Chang went on. *'What was it—some kind of experiment? The government testing out chemical warfare on its own citizens again?'*

I almost choked on my own spit. 'What? No! Why would they—?' I paused. *'Wait—they* do *that?'*

106

Man, this day just kept on getting worse and worse.

'*Tell me!*'

Spit continued to fly. He was like a goddamn spitting-machine. If he didn't settle down soon, I'd need an umbrella.

'But I—'

'*You're working for them, aren't you?*' he continued, face now the colour of an overripe tomato. His eyes were bugging out of his head, like one of those insects that do that for some reason. It occurred to me the guy looked fucking insane. 'WHO ARE YOU WORKING FOR?!'

Plump hands found my collar, tried to pull me onto my feet. For the second time in less than twenty-four hours, I was manhandled— only not in that good, consensual way people are always writing songs about.

'TELL—!'

Suddenly, there was a cry and a *whoosh*ing sound.

Before I knew what was happening, I was released from Chang's grip, falling backwards into my chair and almost toppling the fucking thing over.

When I was certain I wasn't about to go spilling backwards, I looked back across the desk.

Chang was gone.

I blinked. 'Uh... Chang?'

Maybe he went for a lie down, or something...

I peeked over the table. 'Wesley, *hey*. Are you—?'

It all happened in the space of a few seconds.

Just as I was leaning over to check on him, Chang suddenly sprung up from behind the desk.

I recoiled like a startled cat, arms pinwheeling, shit flying out of my asshole at such terrible velocity it could have punched right through a bunker door.

'*Mother of fuck!*'

There was something on Chang's face. Some kind of *furry* something, small, like a —

I stiffened.

LIKE A MONKEY.

'*Get it off me!*' cried Chang, as the Novamite clamped around his head promptly began its attack, pummeling and clawing, scratching and pulling at his hair. And hissing. The fucking thing was hissing at him. What was more, it looked... *different,* now. Bigger. Not a lot — it was still only tiny. But definitely not as tiny as it had been before.

Well, that can't be good.

'*Pratt!*'

Oh yeah.

'Okay! Hold on! Stand still —'

The Novamite bit down.

To this very day, I have never seen blood shoot out of a person the way it did Chang that night. Like one of those volcanoes they were always trying to force you to make back in science class — only this one worked. The word "geyser" came to mind. You seriously wouldn't have thought blood was capable of moving at that speed. It was amazing.

I threw up my hands as hot, coppery redness began to rain down on me like I was the main attraction in the Devil's bukkake.

Even in my horror, I took a moment to acknowledge the fact it was the second time in only twenty-four hours I had been engulfed in another living being's bodily matter. I wondered if it was a sign of the times, what that might mean for my inevitable prison-stretch.

Oh, Jesus God, no...

Thinking fast, I grabbed a Taco Bell box from a unit next to me and flung it.

Exactly what I was hoping to achieve by this, I'm still not sure. But it was the adrenaline, man—I had to do *something*.

Whatever the reason, it sailed through the air, and—through some miracle or another—struck the monkey-thing directly on the back of the head.

I'd like to tell you this is the point where the little monkey-thing collapsed down dead—a limp bundle of semi-chimpanzee, unmoving on the trailer's floor in a jumbled heap of its own crumpled limbs.

Instead, the monkey-thing shot me a look, as if to say—*Seriously, dude? A Taco Bell box?*

Then before I knew what it was doing, it unclamped itself from Chang's head and shot off somewhere back down towards the other end of the trailer.

There was a *crash* and a *bang*. A waft of something uncannily like wet dog.

Then—

Silence.

The monkey-thing was gone.

I stood there on the trailer's worn, filthy carpeting, not moving, listening to what I thought was the quickly fading sound of the monkey-thing's departure from the scene.

When I looked back at Chang, I almost puked right in my mouth.

I've seen some things in my time. Terrible, awful things. I've seen people explode. Watched celebrities getting pulled to pieces like stale bread. You could say I was not unaccustomed to the odd bit of blood and gore.

But looking at Chang then, all that stark red and hanging lengths of what I supposed was his neck-flesh, I couldn't deny the retching feeling bubbling in my guts.

Christ, look at it. It's like spaghetti.

'*I... I think I'm dying,*' he said.

'Yeah.' He was.

'*You... have to... help me...*'

I'd like to tell you that the idea of simply bugging out of there and leaving Chang to his fate never crossed my mind. Truth was, Chang dying right then was probably the best thing that could have happened — for me, I mean. Not for him. I had no real reason to want to keep Chang alive — but plenty of reasons to want him dead, not least of which because he was technically the indirect keeper of my anal virginity. And besides, this was a fully grown man who lived in a trailer and spent the majority of his time on YouTube watching videos about the freaking *Illuminati*, or whatever. Really, letting him die would have been the responsible thing to do.

He reached for me, eyes wide and pleading.

'*Please...*'

Goddamnit.

I got an arm under his shoulder and shakily pulled him to his feet. I made for the door, thought about it, then quickly back-pedaled and snatched up the tape from Chang's recorder — because, seriously, I had enough problems right then as it was.

Then, before I could give myself any time to reconsider, I kicked open the door to the trailer and shambled out into the frigid cold.

Hey — I never said I was a smart guy.

***

So I guess this is the part where I'm supposed to tell you how I raced Chang to the hospital, how I broke every driving law known to man and risked my own life as I desperately fought to get him help, taking corners like a man possessed and shouting the occasional word or two of encouragement, things like *"Hang in there!"* and *"Don't you die on me, damnit!"*

Truth was, I drove at a very reasonable thirty miles per hour, both hands constantly on the wheel, making sure to use my blinkers whenever making turns, and stopping at each and every light — and I didn't say a single word. Seriously, there's a reason we have speed limits, folks. And besides, it had been snowing, hadn't it? What was I, an asshole?

We reached Amerstow General twenty minutes later, pulling to — what *I* thought — was a very reasonable stop outside the main doors.

I looked Chang over.

He was not looking good. He was very pale, for one thing. There were dark bags under his eyes and his lips had turned a faint blue. What was more, his skin had taken on a somewhat *waxy* quality. He really needed help. *Fast.*

'Okay,' I said, with a sigh. 'We're here.' I paused, waited for him to open his door — or at the very least say *thank you*.

When he didn't, I said, '*Chang?*'

I wondered if he was waiting for something, like a prompt, or a pep talk or whatever.

'Um... good luck?'

Nothing.

I groaned. '*Chang?* Chang, we're here. Come on, big fella. Upsy-daisy. Time to go.' I pushed his shoulder, but he didn't move. Christ, he was fucking deadweight. 'Come on, wake up. Wake up, you asshole.'

I punched his shoulder.

After several minutes of this, he finally opened his eyes. They settled on me sitting in the driver's seat beside him and he frowned. 'Oh — Pratt. It's you...'

'Yeah, it's me. *Dick*. Now get out of my car. You're bleeding all over my upholstery.'

He took a deep, rattly breath. I noticed he still wasn't moving. 'You were right... about the aliens... about everything—God, I'm such an asshole!'

'Yeah.' He was. 'But seriously, Chang, my upholstery—'

'Will you forgive me?'

I sighed. 'If I say yes, will you get the fuck out?'

Before I could object, he suddenly took my hand and squeezed.

'Thank you. That means... a lot...'

Oh goddamnit.

After a lot of effort, I eventually managed to get Chang into the emergency room, where I'm pleased to say he was quickly taken out of my hands. Then I had some questions to answer. Questions about who I was, what had happened, exactly how I knew the patient etc. Seriously, you'd be amazed the kinds of lies a person can come up with when they really have no other choice.

And so, several minutes later, "Sven Larsson" emerged from Amerstow General, covered more than a little in his "best friend's" blood.

Once outside the main doors, I hesitated a moment before making my way over to my car—not least because it was a goddamn bloodbath in there.

I ran my fingers through my hair.

I didn't think I'd ever been more emotionally drained. I wondered what the time was. It felt very late, though probably wasn't. I really needed to get some sleep.

I watched the snow settling on the parking lot a while, feeling like I could use a cigarette, even though I didn't smoke.

At some point, I became aware of eyes on me, and I turned.

There were people staring at me. A couple of nurses hovering by the main doors. Old guy in a robe, who had apparently stepped outside for a smoke, the chill night wind occasionally blowing said robe up around his head like Marilyn Monroe that one time and affording me a much better glimpse of his bare, withered ass than I would have liked.

But there were other people, too. People in normal clothing, whose presence there I couldn't determine. True, they could have just been visitors — family members, or whatnot, coming to check on their sick relatives.

But the way they all *stared* — all blank-faced and expressionless, the way they refused to look away, even when I held their gazes... it was unsettling. Okay, *yes*, I was covered in blood, so that could have been why they were all staring — *whatever*.

Something told me that wasn't why, though.

Suppressing a shiver, I pulled my jacket tighter around me.

Then I got the fuck out of there.

SEVEN

THE FOLLOWING FEW HOURS passed in a frenzy of bleach and shampoo.

I showered—fast and hard, like the kind of sex guys think all girls want, even though realistically that's probably a statistical impossibility. And I wept. For longer than I would have liked to admit, in a manner I would have denied if confronted with. I think it was a purging-thing.

I thought about penguins. It's not often said, but penguins are very much like nature's joke. They're weird-looking—that's the first thing. They have wings, but can't fly. They mate for life, and the female always chooses, so if you're fat or an especially weird-looking penguin, you're fucking doomed. Then there are all those sharks trying to take a bite out of them all the time. Face it, nobody wants to be a penguin.

And yet that's exactly what I was—a lone penguin, trundling lost along the shores of his insignificant, yet strangely eventful life, unaware of the myriad monsters waiting just out of sight for me to turn my back before pouncing on me and tearing me to pieces like a fucking man-shaped piñata. I was nature's joke. I had to be; it was the only thing that made sense.

When I was done crying and showering, I went to clean the blood from the Accord's seats and footwell, realising the second I started what a poor order I'd chosen to do said task in.

After cleaning the Accord and showering for what felt like the fifteenth time, I tried to get some sleep — even managed it a little, too, until I had a dream about being a separated Siamese-twin, and awoke, sweating in the dark, wondering exactly where the hell the other part of me had gone. I've never been able to explain my dreams.

At around 5:00am, just as the sun was peeking its head over the horizon, I went to meet Frankie.

I met him at a diner across town, just off the main highway. A glass-all-the-way-around joint, called — I kid you not — the Chili Fiddler.

Giant, flaming chili above the entrance. Two fake-as-shit palm trees flanking the main doors, for reasons I'm still not able to fully explain.

I found Frankie at a booth near the middle and slumped into the seat opposite.

He looked awful. His hair was all tousled, and there were dark stains like mud and something else I didn't even want to think about all over his clothes. Something like oil over his hands and face, like how mechanics sometimes look after a hard day's work. The not-so-faint odor of fresh garbage came off him in waves, so strong it made me nauseous.

I shook my head.

So many questions.

Whilst I waited for my coffee to arrive, I listened as Frankie filled me in on his progress thus far.

He'd looked everywhere he could think of that a newborn alien-monkey might go, never mind the fact he couldn't possibly have known such a thing. Firstly, the mall (his logic here being that was where everybody went—which I guessed wasn't totally inaccurate, when you think about it). The dump (because, you know, "reasons"). The flood drains, where the city's homeless all like to hang out and be homeless and stuff—easy meal.

And still—nothing.

I told him about Chang, the monkey-thing's arrival, how much bigger it had looked.

'*Bigger?*' said Frankie. '*You mean like it evolved?*'

'Well, I guess you could say—'

'*Like a Pokémon?*'

I groaned. 'For the last time, Frankie, *it is not a Pokémon.*'

He held up his hands. 'Hey, I'm just looking at the facts, here.'

My coffee arrived and I sipped it in silence, watching through the glass front as early morning commuters bound for work flooded slowly past, wet sludge spraying up from their back tyres like explosive diarrhoea. It was still snowing, though no harder than it had been last night. I wondered what would happen when this "blizzard" finally hit, if they'd be forced to shut the roads. Seriously, it's amazing just how ill-equipped we still are to deal with the elements. We can put a man on the moon, but functioning when there's snow on the ground? Uh-uh—that shit's complicated.

Frankie glanced up. 'Wait—what if we've been going about this all wrong?'

I considered the expression on his face. Only two things got Frankie that excited — girl-on-girl wrestling, and the prospect of impending death.

I thought girl-on-girl wrestling was too optimistic, however.

'What do you mean?'

'This thing's a baby, right?'

'Sure.'

'And who was the first person it saw after punching its way out of that fucking Poké Ball, or whatever?'

I stared at him as realisation dawned. 'Wait — *are you saying this thing thinks I'm his mom?*'

Holy crap, what a week.

He shrugged. 'Yes — *no*. I mean, what if it like, I dunno... *imprinted* on you, or something? Because think about it — why would it attack Chang? And while we're on the subject, why *didn't* it attack you?'

'Well —'

He leaned forward. 'Because Chang was *threatening* you, Dan — *it was defending you.*'

I thought it over a moment.

Could it be? Had it really just been rising to my defence, concerned for the wellbeing of its only parent?

'But it *did* attack me...' I reminded him. 'Back at the apartment. Here — *look.*' I pointed to the scratches on my cheek and forehead. Not exactly life-threatening, true, but a wound is a wound. And besides, it really stung. '*See?*'

'It was taking a *crap*, Dan. You interrupted it. Shit, I would have tried to scratch your eyes out, too.'

'And let me guess — that's when it imprinted on me and I became its mother, right?' I shook my head. 'Goddamn it, Frankie.'

'I don't think you're like its mother. More like you're just *linked* with it, or something—you know, like E.T? Like maybe it sensed your fear at Chang's place, and that's why it attacked him.'

I let out a long breath. 'This is so retarded.'

Frankie grinned. 'Yeah.' He plucked a fry from the table and pointed it at me. 'So, going by that logic—*where's the one place you'd go if you were hungry and frightened and desperate, Dan?*'

I began to tell him how stupid that was, then paused as I realised suddenly I *did* know.

I held his gaze steadily across the table. 'This is so retarded...'

Frankie pushed his plate of fries away and stood, sending a fresh waft of garbage my way. 'Grab your shit—it's go-time.'

***

Back in the parking lot, we were surprised to find we had a visitor waiting for us.

She was sitting propped against the side of my Accord, arms folded, shoulders bunched against the biting cold. She looked very angry—but then, to be fair, that might have just been her normal face. We really didn't know each other that well.

'Mr Pratt,' she said as we approached.

I groaned.

Espinosa.

I nodded. 'Detective.' I looked past her at my car, simultaneously acknowledging just how screwed I'd currently be if I hadn't decided to clean the car last night. 'What a pleasant surprise.'

I was feeling sassy.

She turned her gaze toward Frankie. 'And you are?'

Frankie frowned. 'Me?' He rubbed his chin thoughtfully. 'Well, on a biological level, I guess you could say I'm mostly carbon—though it's been noted I am unusually attracted to inanimate objects.'

A moment of confused silence from Espinosa. 'You—?'

'By which I mean I'm magnetic...'

She looked questioningly over at me.

I nodded. 'It's true.'

It wasn't.

She looked us over again, an expression on her face like she was wondering if that was enough with which to arrest us. After a moment, however, she shook her head. 'Right. Well, you're probably wondering why I'm here—'

Nope.

'—so I'll just cut right to it. A man was taken into the emergency room last night suffering from deep lacerations to his face and neck; *a Wesley Chang?'*

That pain in my stomach again. Like a battalion of angry elves attempting to hack their way out using the world's dullest pickaxes.

'Never heard of him,' I said.

'Oh, no? Funny, because we visited his trailer. Guy kept a diary. Want to take a wild guess as to who was set to meet with him yesterday?'

Balls.

'We also have witnesses claiming a man of your description was seen dropping him off,' she went on. 'A skinny, nervous-looking fellow. Bit of a coincidence, wouldn't you say?''

Frankie leaned towards me and covered his mouth with his hand. 'Got to admit, that *does* sound like you, Dan.'

I swallowed dryly. 'How, uh... is he doing? This guy I've never met.'

'He's in a coma. He's lost a lot of blood. It's touch and go.'

'Oh.'

I looked around, wondering what the stance of an innocent man looked like, if that was a thing you could fake. 'So... am I under arrest?'

'No—not *yet*. But I *will* be asking you to come down to the station with me to answer some questions.'

I nodded like I thought that was a very reasonable course of action. 'What, like, next week, or—?'

'*Now*, Mr Pratt.'

I hesitated. To our left, cars continued to amble by on the highway, their passage through the icy sludge making a sound like someone slowly pulling out a length of tape. 'Like *now*-now?'

She took a step towards me, eyes narrowed to slits. '*Get in your goddamn car.* You're going to follow behind me—unless you'd both like to ride in mine, that is?'

I looked over to where she was gesturing. A coffee-coloured, boxy-looking something—what I thought might have been a sedan. Wire-mesh grill in the back, separating the front from the rear. I knew without having to check those doors only opened from one side—and not the side the two of us would be sitting.

'We're good.'

'Okay. Now, listen—*do not deviate*. Deviate, and I swear to every god out there I will jam my foot so far up your asses you'll both be tasting dog-shit for the rest of your pathetic little lives—understand?'

Frankie and I looked at each other.

Brutal...

She nodded. 'Good. Now let's go. I'm freezing my tits off out here.'

She climbed into her car and we reluctantly climbed into mine.

She pulled away, and we followed.

'What are we going to do, Dan?' said Frankie from the passenger seat. 'We can't go give a statement *now*. That little monkey-bastard's still out there. If we don't find it, someone is going to get hurt.'

I followed the what-might-have-been-a-sedan onto the slip road, feeling the Accord's tyres fighting for traction on the incline.

'I know.'

But what did he want me to say? She was a cop. A really scary cop, for that matter. Citizens did what the cops told them. That was how society worked, the reason we weren't all out on the streets throwing faeces at each other or whatever. Obeying the law was how we all avoided ending up covered in shit.

'We have to ditch her, Dan,' said Frankie.

I was silent a moment as I considered this.

'You *do* understand how that would look, right?' I said. 'I mean, we already look guilty. Now you want to flee her custody?'

He let his hands drop into his lap. 'Doesn't seem to me like we have much of a choice.'

I hate it when Frankie's right.

Before I could have a moment to come to my senses and realise what a fucking terrible idea what we were about to do was, I gripped the Accord's wheel tight and, crossing three lanes in an instant (and whilst causing a procession of angry yet completely understandable horn-blares), pointed us towards the turn-off.

I looked back across the highway, catching a fleeting glimpse of Espinosa's face just before she fell out of view.

YOU MOUTHERFUCKERS, she mouthed.

We were fucking screwed.

***

Fifteen minutes later, and we were pulling to a stop inside Speedy's lot, our arrival there marked by a bluster of snow-packed wind.

More a theme park than a restaurant, Speedy's had everything any small child could ever ask for. Play-pits. Arcades. Ice cream parlours and animatronics—though these ones weren't haunted, so far as I knew. It was opened in the fifties by a man named Hans as a simple pizzeria—that was, before success had seen it go supernova. Now it was the apex in child entertainment. A place where parents could go drop off their kids and leave them for hours on end so they could go pretend they weren't parents for a little while. The parents got time away from their kids, and the kids got to have fun without the constant nagging from their overbearing parents.

It was the place my Grandma Helen had taken me a lot in those early months following my parents' sudden abandoning of me. We would sit in the same booth, eat the same food (Speedy Burger Special), and have more or less the same conversation:

Gee, my parents are assholes, huh?

Yeah.

I'm not sure what it was about Speedy's that appealed to me so much. It certainly wasn't the food. But whatever the case, one thing I could always count on with Speedy, was that the guy would never, ever leave me—he couldn't, he was fixed down.

There had always been something comforting about that.

The place was unusually empty for this time on a weekday. Ordinarily there'd be posses of small children dashing all over the place, their frazzled parents—those without the good sense to run the second the kids were inside—following quickly behind them, arms outstretched and faces pained, looking like they were about to have a major fucking aneurysm. Now it was mostly just teenagers, spread around in booths, sipping milkshakes and laughing in that totally annoying way teenagers do, unaware of the sheer misery that awaited them. The occasional adult or two, having no doubt pulled over to grab a quick bite to eat before continuing on to wherever it was they were headed. No sign of the space-monkey.

I stared up at the giant, porcelain Speedy Bear guarding the restaurant's front, face now partially obscured with snow.

I nodded.

Hello, old friend. It's been a while.

'Okay, so how are we going to do this?' I said to Frankie sitting beside me.

Whilst I hadn't really thought about it during our desperate dash over here, it occurred to me now I had no idea how to approach what it was we were about to do — that was, providing Frankie's reasoning was correct, and that the Novamite was actually even *here*. Which I think we can all agree probably wasn't. One thing was for sure, we'd have to be discreet. The last thing we wanted was a panic on our hands.

Frankie turned to me, face unusually serious. 'Leave it to me,' he said.

I suddenly got a very bad feeling.

Wind gusting all around us, we stormed through the entrance doors.

Without so much as a pause to consider just how stupid what he was about to do was, Frankie jumped up onto a table, raised his hands above his head, and — in a volume you could have heard from space — shouted, 'EVERYBODY! MAY I HAVE YOUR ATTENTION, PLEASE? I'M LOOKING FOR MY MONKEY. I REPEAT. HAS ANYBODY SEEN MY MONKEY?'

A bout of confused laughter from around the restaurant.

He jumped down. 'No good. Doesn't look like anybody's seen him. We should try out back.' He thought it over a moment. 'I'll, uh... I'll go check the ball pit.'

'Maybe we should stick together, hmm?' I said.

He sighed. 'You're right, Dan. Besides, he's probably playing the grabby-thing, anyway.'

And so, long story short, we searched around Speedy's, looking in, what I thought, were all the wrong places. We checked the diner, the ice cream parlour. Behind the counter where they stuffed the bears the kids all got to take home with them as part of the company's draw. Nobody tried to stop us, or ask what we were doing there—which was a good thing, really, as I wouldn't have been able to answer if they had. But I wasn't that surprised; it's hard to give a shit about anything when you're on minimum wage and your primary responsibility is clearing up over-excited child vomit.

Once we were sure we had checked everywhere, we stepped into the centre of the restaurant and paused.

The Novamite wasn't here—which meant this had all been a giant waste of time. What was more, in choosing to come to Speedy's instead of the police station as instructed, I had also brought upon myself the angry wrath of an officer of the law—one who already had a bug up her ass for me, as it happened.

I shook my head.

Things just kept getting worse and worse.

'Okay—now what?' I said, glancing around.

Frankie put his hands on his hips and sighed. '*Ball pit?*'

'*Think*; where else could this thing—?'

Before I could finish, there was a cry.

To be clear, it is not unusual to hear the occasional scream or two whilst at Speedy's. From the kids, mostly, whenever their elation grew too strong for them to hold in—but also from the parents. Because parenting is really, really hard.

But this was no cry of elation or parental distress.

Startled, we threw a glance over towards a door by the back, where it had sounded as though the scream had come from; a little nondescript metal-plated door, with one of those round windows on it like they always have on boats—portholes, I thought they were called.

A moment later, we were running.

The kitchen was a lot smaller than you'd have expected for a restaurant of this size. Sinks. Freezers. Fryers and stoves. Long silver counter down the centre, above which multiple different cooking utensils hung like the heads of defeated enemies. Black-and-white tiled flooring.

This wasn't what caught our attention, though.

What caught our attention was the man we spotted the instant we entered the room—a cook, if his get-up was to be believed. Some Asian guy, short, with balding hair and a too-fine moustache. He was standing on a counter, a spatula in his hand (which I could appreciate), face pointed to a spot in the corner we couldn't yet see from our position just inside the door.

We stepped into the strong smell of fried food and halted.

'*What is it?*' said Frankie. '*What's wrong?*'

Asian Guy pointed with the spatula. '*Th-th-there!*'

We stepped further into the kitchen.

And there he was. The Novamite—my *baby*—squatting before an open refrigerator, his face buried in what looked to be an entire frozen chicken.

What followed next was a great example of biology taking over.

Instinct kicked in.

It was that kind of primal, *raw* urge, like what our ancestors no doubt felt whenever they found themselves faced with a potential life-or-death situation or a freaking T-Rex or whatever. The sudden realisation that this time there would be no backing away, no retreating. That, for better or worse, it was time to finally plant my feet and be a man.

I pushed Frankie towards it.

'*Get it, Frankie! Show it your kung fu!*' I jumped onto the counter next to Asian Guy. I nodded and he nodded back, understanding passing between us. I just hoped he had another spatula. '*Quick!*'

But Frankie did not show it his kung fu.

Instead he walked over to where the Novamite squatted, hands limp by his sides, with not even the one kitchen utensil between them.

As I've mentioned already, Frankie has never been good at making informed decisions.

'Hey, little guy!' he said, kneeling down next to it. '*What'choo got there?*'

The Novamite turned, saw him. I expected it to gouge his eyes out, or bite off his head or something—which, really, would have been exactly what he deserved.

Instead, it let out a *coo*—exactly like a baby might—before quickly turning back to its food.

Frankie turned back to me, the biggest, dumbest grin on his face. 'You didn't tell me it was this cute, Dan!' He reached out and petted it—never mind the fact that doing so was the literal scientific equivalent of petting a nuclear bomb. 'Oh, you're a handsome fella, ain'tcha? Hmm? Who's a handsome fella?'

The Novamite continued to coo and gurgle and—I swear—giggle.

After a moment's hesitation, Asian Guy and I climbed down from the counter and tentatively stepped over to join them.

We leaned over Frankie's shoulder.

Okay, so it was cute—I mean, when you considered what it was, and all. The big eyes, fluffy body and whatnot. But that didn't change the fact this thing was dangerous as *shit*. Appearances are deceiving. Throw a dress and some lingerie on a lion, it's still a *lion*. However much you might want to spoon with it, it's still gonna eat your face off.

Asian Guy leaned further forward and gestured at the Novamite with his head. I noticed he didn't look that frightened anymore—didn't look frightened at *all*, actually. 'Does it have a name?' he said.

From in front of me, Frankie held up a finger. 'Okay, I'm just gonna throw this out there—*Gizmo*.'

'Will you please get serious?' I said. 'What the hell are we going to do about this?'

Wood-chipper? Volcano? Where exactly does the government dispose of nukes, anyway?

He thought it over a moment, face pointed toward the ceiling. I sensed something stupid coming.

'*Take him home?*'

Ah.

'Are you fucking kidding me?' I said. 'A minute ago you were looking to kill this...this... *thing*—'

'*Gizmo.*'

'Okay—*Gizmo. Whatever.* Now you want to, what—keep him as a pet?'

'Well we can't very well leave him here, Dan. I mean, look at him. It's a miracle he's managed to survive this long.'

I lowered my voice. 'We could always, well—you know.'

Frankie gasped. 'Uh-uh. No way. We're not killing him, Dan. Absolutely not.' He put a protective arm around the Novamite, who I noted had placed itself directly in Frankie's lap.

I blinked. '*What?* No, I meant phone Kinsey, you ass. See if he'll take him off our hands for us.'

Because that worked so well last time, didn't it, Dan? God, you're an asshole.

'Are you *crazy*? Have you any idea what will happen to Gizmo if the government gets hold of him? *Don't you watch movies, Dan?'*

'But what if it—'

I paused as I suddenly became aware of a sound approaching. A kind of *whirring* noise, growing louder by the second.

I frowned. 'What the hell is that?'

Funny. It almost sounds like a —

Before I could complete the thought, there was a world-shattering *crash* from behind us. A sound like the very Earth itself cracking in two.

The three of us fell backwards, crying out as the wall separating the kitchen from the dining area suddenly exploded in a spray of plaster and fine wood-chips.

Ears ringing. Dust everywhere, so thick I could hardly see.

When I finally managed to collect myself, I looked back at the wall, surprised to find there was now what looked to be a garbage truck parked there.

It was your typical-looking garbage truck. Big, hateful grey, with one of those compactor-things on the back that no matter how old you get still reminds you of that one scene in *A New Hope*. Unlike the rest of the city's garbage trucks (which I remembered now were more of an *olive* colour), this one had no city-affiliated markings on it anywhere that I could see.

I stared at it.

Man, that has got to be either the best or the worst parking job ever.

There was the *clunk-clunk* of doors being opened.

Two figures stepped out of the dust cloud.

They were tall men. Probably six foot. Wearing heavy-looking work-boots and dressed in your typical midnight-blue overalls. Interestingly, I saw they also had no faces — only that wasn't quite right, as, technically speaking, whilst they might not have had any eyes or mouths or noses to speak of, looking at them now, it appeared as though someone had drawn a set of features on their faces in the places they would normally have been. I'd like to also point out that whoever did so did a pretty shocking job, as not only were their noses in the complete wrong places, but neither eye was the same size as the other, either, giving them both a *squinty* look.

If you'd have asked me earlier, I'd have said that things couldn't possibly have gotten any more retarded than they already were. That we had reached the threshold of what was the allowable amount of retardation before the universe simply noped-out and imploded in on itself.

I'd have been wrong.

I shot a glance around for Frankie, saw he was still recovering on the kitchen floor behind me, face and body plastered with so much dust he now looked like a Geisha girl, only one nobody would ever want to have sex with.

Moving in eerie unison, the faceless garbage men stepped towards me.

'DAN PRATT,' they said — despite the fact they didn't even have mouths (don't ask). 'HAND OVER THE NAOGGRATH AT ONCE.'

I frowned.

Now who the fuck are these guys?

'We, uh... don't have it,' I said.

'YOU LIE. HAND IT OVER, OR —'

They suddenly fell deathly silent and turned to each other. I sensed something passing between them. If they had eyes — *real* eyes, I mean, not drawn-on ones — I had the feeling they'd be pretty fucking wide right now. 'SHE HAS COME. WE MUST RETREAT.'

And with that, they bunched up their "faces", before disappearing in a *poof* of smoke, leaving behind nothing but a bundle of overalls and boots.

I sighed.

Seriously? Again? Hasn't anybody ever heard of a front door?

Before I could ponder any more over this question, a voice called to us from somewhere over bullhorn:

'MR PRATT? MR PRATT, ARE YOU THERE? HELLOOOOOOOO? PAGING MR PRATT?'

It was a girl's voice — one I didn't recognise, either. A cheery, sing-song quality to it, surprisingly in-key.

Ah, man, now what?

Ears still ringing from the crash, I reached back and slowly helped Frankie to his feet, noting the monkey-thing now clasped tightly against his chest. Together, we scooped up Asian Guy.

'Who the hell is that?' said Frankie, gesturing towards the voice.

'I have no fucking idea,' I said.

He grunted. 'Better go take a look.'

Frankie still cradling the Naoggrath tightly in his arms, and with the three (or was that four?) of us now covered head-to-toe in dust, we shambled out through the new hole in the kitchen's side and immediately halted.

A small army of people now stood waiting for us just inside the entrance. About fifty, possibly more. All in various items of clothing, like they'd just been called away from whichever job they'd been performing to tend to this specific matter in hand.

I didn't need to see the glow of their eyes to know who these guys were.

Phonies.

I sighed.

And that, ladies and gentlemen, is what's called the icing on the cake.

My eyes settled on one of them standing in the middle of the group. Young girl, maybe fourteen, fifteen, with mud-coloured hair down to her shoulders — what I thought looked purposely tousled and messy (*kids*) — dressed in an oversized Korn hoodie and jeans so baggy they could have been socks.

She saw me frowning and grinned.

'*We meet at last, Kingslayer!*' she said, letting the bullhorn fall to the restaurant's floor with an angry clatter.

Frankie and I shared a glance.

Kingslayer?

It was then I noticed all of Speedy's other patrons were now gone, hopefully having gotten the fuck out of there the second the garbage truck made its surprise appearance — though granted that was probably being a little too optimistic.

'I have to admit, though, I'm disappointed,' she went on. 'You aren't what I was expecting at all.'

'I'm sorry — *who are you?*'

She blinked. 'Oh, of course! Where are my manners?' She stepped forward and, to my complete surprise, curtseyed. 'My name is Boot, and I am the new King of this region.'

There was a moment where my brain completely stopped working. Like the gears, now clogged with an influx of new ridiculous material to sift through, had simply given up and gone on strike, ashamed and embarrassed for us all.

Luckily, Frankie's hadn't.

'Your name is *Boot*?' he said. He laughed. 'As in *shoe*?'

Boot gestured towards the creature cradled tightly in Frankie's arms. 'Hand over the Naoggrath, Mr Pratt. If you cooperate, I promise I'll—'

'*You'll let us go?*' I said.

Holy crap, maybe things would turn out okay after all. We could even be back for dinner.

She laughed. 'Oh, no—I *am* going to kill you. What I was going to say was I'll make it quick. Seriously, a day or two *tops*. You'll barely feel a thing. Sound fair?'

'*Three days!*' cried Frankie.

Frankie never really understood haggling.

'Hand it over, Kingslayer—this is your last chance,' continued Boot.

I suddenly became aware of movement in my periphery, and turned to see several of the group had now begun to circle around us.

We were being flanked.

So that couldn't be good.

'If you want Gizmo, you're going to have to pry him from our cold, dead fingers!' said Frankie. He lunged into what was possibly a fighting pose, though probably wasn't.

From behind us, Asian Guy cleared his throat. 'Uh, actually, I should probably just—'

'*Stay out of this, Shrimp Eyes!*' cried Frankie.

The people circling us began to close in.

We backed up. I don't know where exactly we thought we were going. Nothing but brick wall that way.

One of them—a woman in a blouse with librarian glasses and angrily back-combed hair—suddenly reached for us.

Before she could grab us, however, there was another loud *whirring* sound.

We all spun to face where it was coming from, turning just in time to witness a shape growing on the other side of Speedy's glass front. Some *white* shape, moving in fast.

Huh. Kind of looks like a —

I gasped.

Uh-oh.

Boot cried, '*MOVE! MOVE!*' moments before the restaurant's window-front exploded in a spray of glass.

The three of us dived to the side as the white, paneled FedEx truck blasted its way through Speedy's entrance and smashed directly into the rear of the faceless dudes' garbage truck.

BANG!

A moment of dazed silence from inside the restaurant.

Everyone stared at the FedEx truck, its crumpled hood, the smoke rising from it in little wispy tendrils, giving off a sound like a giant pleading for silence.

But that wasn't what had caught everybody's attention.

No, what had caught everybody's attention was the message that had been painted on the FedEx truck's side—a message written in what looked to be oil.

HO-HO-HO! NOW I HAVE A MACHINE GUN!

I stared at it, dumbfounded.

Okay, now this is just getting ridiculous.

From across the entrance, Boot shouted, '*Don't just stand there — go check it out!*'

Bodies closed in around the truck, moving cautiously. I noted the pistols now in their hands—black, sleek-looking things. Because even body-snatching jelly-slugs from outer space can appreciate the practical advantages of firearms, apparently.

They reached the FedEx's front and paused. A "man" — this one in full construction worker's get-up — grabbed the driver's door and yanked it open.

Empty.

He started to turn around, no doubt in an attempt to relay this information —

There was a sudden cry of surprise from behind us.

We all turned back towards the front again, me wondering exactly what the fuck was going to happen next, if it could possibly be any more ridiculous than what had already happened, if that was even *possible*.

It was.

As I watched in dumbfounded silence, Burrito Stalker launched himself through the hole in Speedy's entrance, barrel-rolling over the stuffing counter like it was the hood of a police car back in the '70s.

He raised a hand — a hand I saw held the little fake, imitation pistol from the other day — and began shooting people with it.

Now, I say "shooting" — really he was just pointing it at the people he wanted to die and shouting "*Pew! Pew! Pew-pew!*"

The Phonies fell to the ground like dominoes, wailing and grabbing at their bodies — bodies that looked totally fine, by the way. At least, to me.

I stared at them, the sheer stupidity of it all.

OH COME ON.

Burrito Stalker threw himself back behind the stuffing counter as the Phonies quickly returned fire, little wood splinters kicking up from the counter in sprays.

Burrito Stalker and I locked gazes.

His lips moved.

GO!

I didn't need telling twice.

Gunshots echoing around the restaurant like thunder, we ducked low, began to creep our way towards the exit, shit shooting out of every single one of my bodily orifices – at a velocity that would have surprised you. I would have been fucking terrible at war.

Burrito Stalker returned fire, drawing attention on himself, allowing us the distraction we needed to get away.

Pew! Pew! Pew-pew-pew!

About halfway there I heard a cry from behind us and turned.

It was Asian Guy. He was lying on the floor, fingers clawing at his leg, face now contorted in a rictus of pain.

'What's wrong?' I cried, as a chorus of gunfire played out over our heads. It was then I noticed the red patch blooming on his pants. 'Holy shit – *are you hit?'*

'What's is it?' cried Frankie.

'Asian Guy – he's hit.'

We turned back to Asian Guy. We saw his lips move. It looked like he was trying to say something, but because of all the gunfire going on around us, it was hard to hear exactly what it was he was saying.

I frowned. *'What?'*

Asian Guy stared dumbfounded at us, at his leg, back to us again. 'GODDAMNIT HELP ME YOU ASSHOLES.'

I turned to Frankie. 'You hear what he's saying?'

'I think he wants us to go on without him.'

'Yeah.' That was probably it.

Asian Guy's eyes widened. 'WHAT? NO, I DIDN'T SAY –'

Frankie raised his hands to the sides of his mouth. 'OKAY – THANKS!'

Asian Guy stared expressionlessly at us. He began frantically gesticulating with his hands — urging us on, no doubt.

I shook my head at the sheer guts of the man.

Your sacrifice will not be forgotten, brave soul.

After a huge effort, we finally reached the entrance.

Not hesitating for a moment, we immediately made for the doors, feet skidding on broken glass, thunder rolling over our heads —

'*Dan!*' cried Frankie.

I turned back.

Boot had Frankie pinned on the ground, was trying to pry the Novamite — sorry, *Gizmo* — from his hands.

Eyes glowing. Tentacles uncoiling from inside her open mouth like wet noodles.

I didn't think.

I ran back and kicked her directly in the crotch.

She rolled over, gripping her lady parts, her eyes wide with a combination of pain and rage. 'OH NO YOU DIDN'T.'

But I did. (And before you go accusing me of being a misogynist here or whatever, I'd like to point out that men get hit in the crotch a heck of a lot more than women do. When you look at it that way, really it would have been sexist *not* to kick her in the crotch.)

Ignoring Boot's feminist cries, I grabbed Frankie under one arm and quickly hauled him to his feet.

We turned to run —

He grabbed my arm. '*Gizmo!*'

I looked back over my shoulder, turning just in time to witness another of the Phonies, this one in what looked like a power-company jumpsuit and hardhat, throw a net over the little guy, scoop him up like the fucking catch of the day.

Through the holes in the netting, Gizmo's eyes shone with fear.

Frankie made to go after him, but I grabbed him. 'No time! We have to go!'

'But—'

I looked back round at Boot, who I saw was now starting to get up. Jesus, she looked pissed—no doubt because of the blistering punt I had just unleashed upon her Bat Cave. *'Now!'*

Gunfire booming all around us, we booked it through the hole and didn't look back.

EIGHT

CHESTS HEAVING. EARS BURNING. Fear-sweat stinging our eyes. I could feel bile trying to force its way up my throat in that way it always seems to do whenever you happen to be running for your life — something I was growing uncomfortably used to.

Boots crunching over fresh snow, we took shelter in some dingy-looking alley a good handful of blocks away, behind a dumpster bleeding trash bags.

We crouched low.

'Okay,' I said. 'Okay, don't panic. We need to think. To make a plan.'

Clearly, going home wasn't an option. Which meant we'd have to come up with some other place to live if we wanted to continue on with our lives unhindered by the constant possibility of a sudden, grizzly end. Mexico, probably — although I'll admit I wasn't big on tacos. Maybe I could call myself Juan and start a mariachi band or something. Was learning mariachi hard?

Maybe I could join a gang...

'*Yeah*,' said Frankie, who I saw was now pacing the alleyway, hands balled into fists, looking especially angry — for Frankie, at least.

'I'll make a call to Josh and Kenny. See if they can meet us at the border.'

Have to remember to ask them to bring some sombreros, too — camouflage.

Frankie quit pacing and turned to me, eyes wide. '*Piss on that! They stole our Gizmo!*'

'Frankie —'

'We *can't* leave, Dan! Have you forgotten what Albino Dude said? DESTROYER OF WORLDS. You really want to leave something like that in the hands of those fuckers?'

'But —'

I winced a moment as a battalion of cop cars zoomed suddenly past, their lights flashing and sirens blaring, scaring the living piss out of me.

I had a pretty good idea where they were headed.

I waited until they'd passed, then turned back to him. 'Look, I get what you're saying, but think — what the hell are the two of us going to do about it? *We're nobodies.* I log people's information, and you —' I thought of the best way to say it without being an ass. 'You're *you*, Frankie.'

He shrugged. 'So?'

'*So?* So we're not exactly the best people to be running off into battle with these guys, don't you think?'

He crossed his arms. 'That didn't seem to stop you last time.'

'*Last time* — ?'

I caught myself.

Breathe, Dan. Just breathe…

I took a deep breath. 'Look, I'm just saying, *what are we supposed to do?*'

Before he could answer, we were interrupted by the sudden sound of brakes squealing.

We spun back towards the mouth of the alley, where we were surprised to find what looked like an old Chevy Impala now sitting there, idling.

Jet-black. Obscene orange and red flames down the sides like it had just burst straight out of a burning building, or Hell perhaps. From the rearview hung a set of black, fuzzy dice, swinging low like a pair of old man's droopy testicles. It was like bad taste given form. I could barely look at it.

For a second this confused me.

Then I saw whose face it was staring back at us from behind the windshield.

I groaned.

It was Burrito Stalker.

He leaned over and pushed open the passenger door. *'Get in!'*

Frankie and I shared a glance.

Did I think about it? Sure. A strange man offering me a ride in his flash car? That was some stranger-danger shit right there. I mean what was I, an asshole?

Of course, on the other hand, the guy *had* just saved our lives — even if, granted, in the most ridiculous fashion possible. Really, it would have been rude to refuse. And hey, on the bright side, he might even have some candy.

Just remember, if he tries to put anything in your butthole, just say no.

Clenching our butt-cheeks tight, we crossed the alley and hesitantly climbed in.

The Impala took off at once.

Burrito Stalker turned to me. He was sweating and his face looked waxy, though I didn't think too much of it — not *then*, at least.

'Are you hurt?' he said.

He began to pat me down —

Stranger-danger!

—but I swatted his hands away. 'No, I'm—*would you stop that*? I said I'm fine.'

He stopped pawing at me and turned his attention back to the road. 'Good. That's good.'

From the backseat, Frankie said, 'Yeah, I'm, uh... fine, too.'

I turned back to Burrito Stalker. 'You want to tell us what the hell just happened back there? Who were those guys? And whilst you're at it, who the hell are *you*? Why do you keep stalking me?' Not that I was complaining, of course, but it was still pretty creepy.

'I told you already. It's complicated.'

'So *un*complicate it. What's your deal?' I blinked as realisation slowly dawned. 'Wait—you knew this was going to happen, didn't you? That's why you warned me, isn't it? The other day?'

Silence for a moment. Just the revving of the Impala's engine and the gentle beating of snow on the windshield before us.

Finally, he sighed. 'It wasn't supposed to happen like this. *The Council*—' He shook his head, as if he'd already said too much. 'Let's just get to A'doy—he'll know what to do.'

I began to ask him exactly what the fuck that meant, when—

'There's just one problem, though.' He turned to me. 'You'll have to drive.'

I blinked. 'Why will I have to—?'

He pulled his hand away from his trench coat, affording me a glimpse of the ragged hole that had suddenly appeared in it, singed around the edge like a cigarette burn.

The dots connected.

'Wait—*are you shot?!*'

As if in answer, Burrito Stalker suddenly slumped forward over the steering wheel, hands by his sides and limp as a partially deflated sex doll.

HOOOOOOOOONK!

'Jesus!'

I fought for the wheel as the Impala suddenly weaved from left to right, wheels spraying snow-sludge, the Chevy ricocheting off of parked car after parked car like a goddamn pinball, each impact sending my heart shooting into my mouth and yet more diarrhea out of every available orifice.

Frankie and I working together, we finally managed to pry Burrito Stalker from the wheel.

I guided us to a shaky stop and simply sat there a moment, trembling and breathing hard, listening to the snow beating down on the Impala's hood, more shit in my pants than a senior at an old-people's home on curry night.

Yep. Almost died again. Fucking Fridays, man.

After a while, Frankie said, 'Well. That was unexpected.'

'Help me!' I said.

We grabbed an arm each and hoisted Burrito Stalker around to the backseat.

As we were laying him down, his eyelids fluttered. Christ, he looked awful. *'Must... get... to A'doy...'*

Before I could ask exactly what an "A'doy" was, he suddenly grabbed my hand. For a moment I thought we were about to shake, which would have been inappropriate, given our current predicament—that, and I still hadn't learned how to from last time. It would have been a whole thing.

When he released my hand, I was surprised to find there was now a piece of paper in it.

I frowned. 'What's this?'

But he was gone. Well... not *gone*-gone. He wasn't dead or anything. I mean asleep or passed out or whatever.

I looked at the scrap of paper in my hand.

It was a map—though not like any map I had ever seen before. There were weird markings and what I thought were supposed to be numbers on it. Some of the roads I recognised, most I didn't. Like a road atlas where the manufacturers, having not heard of Google, couldn't be bothered to check out every single road, so simply decided to make them up instead.

At the top of the map was a name, a glaring red ring drawn around it.

TWO CRESTS.

Frankie hovered over my shoulder. 'Now, I'm not much of a betting man, Dan, but if I had to take a guess, I'd say that's where this "A'doy" character is.' Before I could reply, he suddenly launched himself at the front seat. '*Shotgun!*'

I stared down at the tattered scrap of paper in my hand.

Here we go again...

NINE

WE DROVE THE IMPALA west out of the city, following the directions said Burrito Stalker had given us as the Impala's wipers worked frantically to cope with the sudden influx of snow. It was really coming down. Whilst admittedly still not the blizzard we'd been promised, if things continued on the way they were, I knew it wouldn't be long. And I thought a snow-induced standstill on the highway would be the last thing we needed.

Every half hour or so Frankie would lean round and check on Burrito Stalker (if that was even his real name) — by which I mean he would simply lean into the back and poke repeatedly at the guy's face until he begged him to please stop doing that.

It wasn't until a good three hours or so had passed that we finally reached the turnoff for Two Crests.

Acting on a whim, I pulled over onto the hard shoulder and switched off the ignition.

I stared through the windshield at it.

Just a sign, like any other you've probably seen a million times before, now speckled with a combination of sleet and snow.

Now, I was not a well-traveled person by any definition of the term, but I *had* journeyed many times past this particular stretch of the I-64 — on holidays, visiting relatives as a kid and whatever — and not once did I recall ever seeing a turnoff for a "Two Crests". Not that *that* meant anything, of course; I could have just missed it. I'm just saying, it was weird, is all.

'Hey, pass me that other map, will you?' I said, nodding at the glovebox. 'The, uh... normal one.'

Frankie reached into the glove box and handed it to me.

I placed them side-by-side. 'Look,' I said, pointing at the maps in my lap. 'This town — according to this map, it shouldn't be here.'

Frankie gasped. '*A ghost town...*' He thought it over. 'Or, you know, it's just not been incorporated yet. I mean people build new towns all the time, right? Maybe the map's just outdated or whatever.'

A fair point. Still, there was something about all this that just didn't *feel* right. I mean, sure, the fact we were on our way to a place we had never been before, to meet with a man of whose intentions we had not the faintest idea, could have had something to do with it. Then there was the fact we had a trench-coat-wearing burrito man bleeding to death on the backseat, too.

But for whatever reason — call it ESP or woman's intuition or whatever — I didn't think that was it.

And yet, bad feeling aside, we had no choice. Boot and her gang now had the Novamite, and if what Albino Man had said was true, that meant we had very little time before the world and everybody in it went the way of the dinosaurs — and by that I don't mean they got their own theme park.

I nodded at the rear-view. 'How's our new friend doing?'

Frankie looked round, did the whole pokey-thing again.

A low *groan* from the backseat.

He turned back. 'No good, Dan. I'm afraid he's gone.' He reached back and gently patted his leg. 'Good night, sweet prince. Do not go gently into that good night.'

Another irritated groan, louder this time.

Groaning myself, I climbed out of the Impala and quickly trudged my way round towards the back, gusts of snow-laden wind whipping my hair back from my face like I'd just jumped out of an airplane.

I should probably mention at this point I have no experience whatsoever tending to a gunshot wound. Like most people, the extent of my first aid abilities is resigned to band-aids, back rubbing, and the occasional soothing word or two of encouragement.

Still, there were certain things I expected going in, having watched many movies in my short, insignificant life — the least of which was blood; though, oddly, as I pulled back the material of Burrito Stalker's trench coat, I couldn't see any. Like, not at all. Not a single drop.

Looking back now, this is probably the part where I should have begun to suspect something fishy was afoot — and surely would have, had I been a smarter man.

But, like I said — I wasn't a doctor. And I *had* been driving for a long time. I'm telling you, my brain was frazzled.

So instead of jumping up and running a thousand miles in the opposite direction, as I rightly ought to have done, I simply said, '*Huh*,' and continued pulling back clothing.

I pulled back his shirt, noting another charred ring like the one on his jacket, no doubt from where the bullet had passed through, still not overly concerned —

I paused.

There was no blood.

I could see the entry wound the bullet had made as it had passed through his abdomen — a little mark of punctured flesh, like a finger-hole punched into a ball of dough.

But no blood.

Again, this is the part where I really should have sensed something peculiar going on, but I didn't.

I know, I know — I'm an *asshole*. I'm a *dick*; but I *was* very tired. And I had been through a lot in the past forty-eight hours, hadn't I? Look, you weren't there, okay?

I stared at the wound, a frown creasing my brow, confused into a state of near paralysis like a YouTube video refusing to buffer. I don't think I even breathed, just continued to stare down at the little dough-hole like a robot whose primary CPU had just gone and blown a major fuse.

It wasn't until, turning finally to look into the back seat, my eyes had instinctively settled on Burrito Stalker's, and the obvious had suddenly become apparent.

It was like being electrocuted again.

I threw myself backwards out the door, yelping in surprise and flailing out with my arms.

I landed with a thump on the snow, my head bumping against the central reservation — though I hardly felt it, wouldn't have cared even if I had.

I stared back through the open rear door, my mouth hanging so far ajar you could have parked a fucking plane in there.

Burrito Stalker's eyes.

They were *glowing*.

I pounced to my feet like the ground was made of larva. '*JESUS CHRIST!*'

'*What? What's wrong?*' said Frankie, climbing out the passenger side after me. He shot a look back into the Impala at Burrito Stalker and gasped. 'Wait—you're a *Phony*?!' He shook his head. 'Oh, man, what a twist. I did not see that coming. You see that coming, Dan? That's some Shyamalan-shit right there. I'm so surprised. Seriously, I am numb with shock right now.'

'*Frankie!*'

'Oh—right!' He sprung into a fighting pose, or whatever the equivalent was when you had cabbage for brains.

He turned to Burrito Stalker. 'Okay, asshole—*prepare for a dick-pounding!*' He kicked his legs like he had stepped in something nasty and began punching wildly at the air. I became aware of cars passing us on the highway, slower than usual, and not, I knew, because of the snow. 'I'm gonna go to town on that dick!'

'Uh, Frankie...'

'I'm gonna be all over that thing!' he continued. 'Seriously, when I'm done with that dick, you're not gonna be able to walk for a week!'

Burrito Stalker stepped awkwardly out onto the snow, one hand pressed against his side, the other outstretched and pleading. He didn't look overly like an evil, body-snatching jelly-slug. But then, they never did, did they?

'*I... can explain...*'

'EXPLAIN THIS—!' said Frankie, who then attempted to kick Burrito Stalker, but slipped on the snow and hit his head on the ground instead.

The sound of snoring immediately filled the air.

I groaned.

OH GODDAMNIT.

I turned my attention back to Burrito Stalker, who I saw was now about as pale as the snow he walked on. Like a mannequin come to life, only one I would not ever want to have sex with, like in that one movie that one time. Whatever that was called.

'*Please,*' he said. '*I can explain everything, just... get me to A'doy —*'

Before he could say anymore, he suddenly hit the deck.

Sighing, I walked over to Frankie and kicked him. 'Hey. Wake up. Wake up, you asshole.'

Frankie's eyes fluttered, then slowly opened.

'Did... *did we win?*' He turned his head, spotted Burrito Stalker lying facedown in the snow.

A moment later, he was on his feet. '*Ye-ah! You see what you get? Huh? Didn't I tell you not to mess with me? Like a Jedi master, son!*' He reached down and snatched up a clump of snow, momentarily balling it up in his hands before reaching back his arm and launching it at Burrito Stalker's back, who took it without protest — mostly because he was still unconscious.

When the fever had passed, I said, 'So — what the hell are we going to do with this guy? Got any ideas?'

Frankie slowly tilted his gaze back down towards the ground —

'That's *not* pelting him with snow,' I said.

He shrugged. 'Leave him here? I mean, shit, he *is* a Phony, after all.'

This was true. Whatever else may have been going on here, the guy was definitely a Phony.

I shook my head. 'Still, he *did* save us. And besides, if he wanted to kill us, don't you think he'd have done so already? He's had plenty of chances. And yet — here we are.'

'So that's a *no* on leaving him? Just so we're clear.'

I stared down at Burrito Stalker's unmoving body, the snow-angel he had unwittingly made — that was actually not too shabby, now that I looked at it.

I didn't think I'd ever been more confused. I didn't know what this guy being a Phony meant, or how that figured into our plans. Probably nothing good, if our luck so far was any indication. But we had driven a long way, and despite myself, I had to admit, I was kind of intrigued. And besides, it wasn't like we had any better ideas.

'Let's just throw him in the trunk,' I said.

Frankie nodded. 'Good plan.'

And so we threw him in the trunk and carried on towards our destination, unaware that by the time we came to leave, the world and everything we knew about it would never again be the same.

***

If there's one thing that cannot be argued with, it's that the world is full of rabbit holes – both literally, and metaphorically. Like little Alice herself will no doubt tell you, the world is rarely what it seems. You think you know the world, your place in it, until one day you suddenly find yourself the guest of honour at a tea party hosted by a borderline-psychopath, being riddled at by a narcoleptic mouse. And like little Alice will no doubt also tell you, once you've cracked the shell on that egg, there's no putting this Humpty Dumpty back together again.

We continued on down the barren stretch of country lane, our odd carriage leaving twin grooves in the snow behind us.

I had begun to get a bad feeling. Sure, part of it was no doubt due to the unusual nature of our visit to this particular part of the good ol' US of A, or whatever the fuck was waiting for us up ahead.

But it was other things, too.

Firstly, the radio died – which was not that peculiar in and of itself, given the state of the weather and all, and that it was my radio;

however, it had worked fine thus far, and I saw no reason why it should have suddenly stopped working now.

The second thing I noticed was that it had stopped snowing. And I don't mean like it had slowed down; I mean it had *literally stopped*. And considering the storm that was supposedly due to hit us any minute, this struck me as particularly odd.

Weirdest of all, however, was the town itself — which looked to have been transported here from somewhere over in Canada or something.

Mostly just one road. A straight-shot through town, unoriginally called Main Street. A procession of bland, flat-faced buildings flanking it on either side, with the occasional road or two to break up the monotony. A snow-capped mountain stood just behind it, seeming to loom right over the town itself — something I thought was especially odd, seeing as we didn't really have any mountains out this way. Didn't have any at all, in fact.

Then, of course, there were the people themselves.

Now, specifically what it was that was so odd about them, I wasn't sure. I mean, they all *looked* normal enough — at least, for the most part. They didn't have two heads or anything. I would have mentioned that by now. Still, there was something about the way they all smiled that seemed a little, well... *off*. Like they were all just faking it, or something. Too-wide eyes above plastered-on smiles. It was creepy as hell.

And, for whatever reason, I got the feeling it was all for our benefit.

'Are you seeing these guys?' said Frankie, having turned to look out the window. 'I'm getting a real Stepford Wives-vibe here, Dan.'

We rolled to a stop outside a generic-looking diner called Wallie's and quickly switched off the ignition.

We stared through the windshield.

'So — what now?' said Frankie.

I thought it over. I had no idea who this A'doy was, or where he might be — or shit, what he even looked like. And seeing as we hadn't been given a specific address or means with which to contact the guy, it wasn't like we could simply roll up to his front door or whatever — which, really, was enough incentive to just turn the Impala around and blow right out of this creepy, pretend town as fast as the Impala's engine could manage — treacherous roads or no.

But then, if we did that, all hope would be lost. Boot and her gang would do... whatever it was they planned to do with the Novamite — something I had the sneaking suspicion wasn't good. Then the world would end, all because the two of us got spooked by a town that wasn't what it appeared to be.

I sighed.

'Let's just go inside and see who's there. Maybe they know where this A'doy guy lives.'

'Should we, uh... go get Burrito Dude?'

I shrugged. 'Nah. Besides, he could probably use the rest.'

The inside of the diner was pretty much exactly what you'd expect. Just your typical American diner, populated with an array of different men and women, all of whom really should have been at work, now that I think about it. Blue, shiny upholstery. Checkered floor. A jukebox that looked approximately a billion years old in the corner, blaring some old Elvis song or other I didn't remember the name of. The rich smell of frying grease in the air.

Frankie and I made our way over to a booth, trying not to notice all the slanted glances pointing our way as we walked. It was like that scene in *An American Werewolf in London*, where the guys walk into that pub, only to have all the regulars stop and stare at them. Christ, I hoped there weren't werewolves, too.

After what felt like an inappropriately long time, a waitress appeared, dressed in a mint-green waitress' uniform and white apron (an apron I noted didn't have a single stain on it, just by the way).

She was a young girl—maybe late teens, early twenties—with dirty blonde hair tied loosely behind her head in a half-assed ponytail, fine strands bleeding out every which way like a star exploding. I'd never owned a ponytail, but I'd been late to work practically every day of my adult life, and so knew just-got-out-of-bed-hair when I saw it.

'Welcome to Wallie's!' she said. *'C-can I get you b-boys anything?'*

I noted the forced smile, the way her hands shook and jerked the pencil in her hand as she spoke.

Jesus, look at her. She's fucking terrified.

'Some c-coffee, perhaps?'

I cleared my throat. 'Actually, we were just after some information. We're looking for someone—*name of A'doy*? Maybe you know him?'

What happened next surprised me.

The pencil in her hand fell to the floor.

Her eyes widened, and her face went alarmingly slack, like she'd just had a major stroke or aneurism or something.

I thought—with no exaggeration whatsoever—I might have just killed this girl.

'Are... you okay?' I asked.

I noticed the conversation inside the diner had stopped, could feel the eyes on me, like an actual, physical weight.

She tried to speak, but her voice cracked. She mumbled a handful of poor excuses, bent and scooped up the pencil, before hurriedly disappearing off somewhere out back in a whoosh of skirt and perfume.

Frankie and I shared a glance.

'That was weird, right?' I said.

Frankie leaned forward and put a hand to the side of his mouth. 'You know what I think? I think some people are actually robots. I mean we already know aliens exist. Think about it — *robot people*, Dan. It would actually explain a lot.'

'How exactly would that explain a lot?' I asked.

'Well, for starters —'

'*And what about the people who are aliens?*' I said. '*Are they robots, too?*'

Frankie shot me a look. 'Don't be ridiculous, Dan. They made the robots, of course.'

Of course.

We sat there a while longer, listening to Elvis song after Elvis song, me wondering where the waitress had gone, if she was now dead.

After several minutes of this, we got up and stepped back out into the cold.

Frankie put his hands on his hips.

'So. That went well.' He thought about it. 'Although I never *did* get that coffee...'

'So what do we do now?'

He shrugged. 'We could always go ask that guy.'

He gestured over my shoulder to where a navy-blue panel van sat parked along the roadside behind us. A sign on the side for some local business or whatever — something to do with plumbing, if the little caricature plumber staring gleefully back at me was anything to go by. Even from where we stood, I could see the front cab was empty — that, or the person driving it was invisible. Maybe he was even a ghost. At this point, nothing would have surprised me.

I began to ask what the hell he was talking about, when I noticed what it was he was pointing at—a pair of boots, shuffling back and forth on the panel van's other side, just visible under the chassis.

'He's been following us since the moment we arrived,' Frankie went on. He thought it over. 'Not very discreetly, either, I might add.'

'And you're only just telling me this now?'

He shrugged.

Goddamnit.

'What do we do?' I said.

Frankie nodded. 'Follow me.'

I followed him half a block down to a little side-alley next to what looked like an old video store.

And then, before I knew I was doing it, for the second time in only twenty-four hours, I ducked low behind a dumpster and waited to see if I was about to get murdered to death or not.

'Okay, so now what?' I said. 'What's the plan here, exactly?' It occurred to me suddenly if things went badly, we had effectively just trapped ourselves—which technically I guess you could say was our own fault, though if I'm honest I like to believe that was all Frankie's bad.

Frankie nodded. 'We wait until he comes, then jump him. I'll hold him down, you punch him in the dick until he tells us why he's following us. Got it?'

'I'm not punching anyone in the dick, Frankie. Besides, he's probably just some—'

So this is the part where I'd like to tell you how I explained to Frankie all the logical reasons why it was highly unlikely the man in the heavy-duty snowshoes was following us. That we waited for a couple minutes, then when the guy didn't show, we simply said *screw it* and went to go play video games or something.

156

But, in the typical backwards-logic that is my life, that's not what happened.

The man in the heavy-duty snowshoes rounded the corner into the alleyway behind us. Some tall dude, black, dressed in a bulky winter-onesie, despite the fact that — here, at least — there wasn't a single flake of snow on the ground.

There was that moment where the three of us just kind of froze and stared at each other, like a trio of strangers might upon entering an elevator to find they were all wearing the exact same outfit.

Then before I knew what was happening, Frankie was lunging out from behind the dumpster, salt dripping from each closed fist like sand.

'EAT THIS, DICK-BAG!'

The man bucked in surprise as a handful of my kitchen's finest struck him directly in the face.

Then there was some sneezing. And crying. A lot of crying, if I'm honest — more than you'd have thought for an evil, body-snatching space alien, anyway.

After about a minute of this, the man said, 'YOU THREW SALT IN MY EYES?!'

Frankie and I looked at each other.

Umm... what?

I frowned. 'Wait — *you're not a Phony?*'

'*No,*' he said — somewhat pissily, too, I thought. Maybe it was all that salt in his eyes. 'I'm not a "*Phony*".'

Frankie gasped. 'I knew it. He's a robot. See, Dan, what did I tell you?'

'He is not a robot, Frankie.'

At least, I hope he isn't.

The man finished wiping at his face and stared at us. 'Look, I'm not a "Phony" —and I'm not a *robot*, either.'

'Are you sure?' said Frankie. 'I mean, if you were a robot, how would you know?'

'I AM NOT A PHONY OR A ROBOT.'

'Please excuse us a second,' said Frankie, pulling me over to the dumpster for a group huddle. He put his hands on his hips and sighed. 'Okay, so I'm pretty sure this guy is a robot, Dan. They must have programmed his brain not to remember or something. Poor guy. Question now is, is he a good robot, or a bad robot? Because I've seen *Terminator*, Dan.'

'Have you considered the possibility the guy might be human?' I said.

Frankie rubbed his chin thoughtfully and frowned. 'You know something, Dan? That's so crazy it might just be true. Hold up —' He turned back to the man in question. 'Hey, are you human?'

Angry glare from Snowshoes.

Frankie frowned. 'Hmm. Guess he isn't sure. I don't like this, Dan. I don't like this one bit.'

Slowly, we stepped back over to him.

'Okay, pal,' said Frankie, thrusting a finger at him, 'you've got exactly three seconds to explain why the hell it is you're following us before my buddy Dan here goes ahead and makes your balls his own personal Disneyland. Capiche?'

The man just stared at us. Man, his eyes were red.

'You're looking for A'doy, right?' he said.

A pause.

Frankie and I shared another glance.

'Who wants to know?' said Frankie.

'Follow me —I can take you to him.'

Now, again, I'd like to reiterate that I am not usually the sort of person to readily accept help from strangers. Call me antisocial or a little diva-bitch or whatever, but I've seen enough movies to know that well-intentioned strangers — *truly* well-intentioned strangers — are few and far between, that in most cases the supposed Good Samaritan is just your typical Buffalo Bill-type looking to hatefully rape-murder you through the asshole before up and making a suit out of your skin. And I didn't want to be somebody's prom dress.

But then, it wasn't like we really had many other options, was it?

And so, ignoring my instincts, Frankie and I followed the man in the winter-onesie out of the alley.

Things only got weirder from there.

TEN

DRIVING AGAIN. BACK IN the Impala. Following the panel van as it led us swiftly out of town, the buildings flanking us being quickly replaced by pine tree after pine tree, interspersed by the occasional telephone pole.

Up, up. Steeper than you'd have thought—steeper than I was comfortable with, really. It was like those early moments during rollercoaster rides, where it begins to dawn on you you've just made a terrible mistake.

Huh. Would you look at that? We're going up the mountain. Holy shit, I hope there aren't bears.

After what felt like a very long time, the panel van finally pulled to a stop in a crunch of loose stone.

I looked through the windshield.

It was a cabin. Small. Quaint. Rickety-looking porch for a front. Several cords of old-looking wood, all stacked up off to one side like a mass grave. It was the kind of place you'd only live when your primary goal in life is to remain as far away from other people as possible. Of course, I say "people" — but you know what I mean.

Not hesitating a moment, we climbed out of the Impala and onto the gravel, our footfalls crunching loudly as we slowly made our way over to the panel van. I turned my attention once more to the cabin. Up this close, it actually looked more like some kind of frontier-era trapper's shack — although I'll admit I wasn't really sure I knew exactly what one of those looked like. But still.

I was expecting Snowshoes to get out and give us a pep talk, or whatever, maybe explain to us what exactly we were getting into — or at least elaborate on the whole bear situation. But he didn't.

Instead, the panel van suddenly banked round, brake lights flaring. Then it was pulling away, loose stones kicking up in a fine spray from its wheels as it quickly took off back down the path we had just come.

Frankie and I shared a glance.

Now where the fuck does he think he's going?

I let out a long breath. 'I'm starting to get a bad feeling about all this, Frankie.'

And I was. I mean, shit, first the town, now *this*? As if things weren't bad enough already. Jesus, this was turning into the worst day ever — and I still wasn't any wiser as to our current bear situation.

Frankie shrugged. 'Well — might as well get this over with.'

He stepped over onto the porch, the old wood creaking loudly under his feet as if in protest at the sudden, unexpected weight.

Now, in the interest of complete honesty, I should probably tell you I was pretty much shitting in my pants by this point. And I don't just mean because of bears. It was the cabin. I had seen my share of horror movies, and so knew that this was how they always started; the unwitting heroes, walking around in circles with their thumbs up their asses, charmingly oblivious, right up until the point some monster or another suddenly ups and bites their genitalia off or whatever. Really, it was unfair of us to put our genitalia on the line like that. A person has a responsibility towards his or her genitalia, after all.

I swallowed, hands now clasped tightly over my balls. 'Hey, you know, maybe we should just forget—'

Frankie rapped on the door.

He waited.

He waited some more.

Nothing.

I let out a long sigh. 'Well. Looks like nobody's home.' I cast a quick glance around—you know, for bears. 'Guess this was all just a waste of time. Come on—I'll buy you a milkshake.'

Canada—that's where we'll go. Let the Phonies have the Novamite and take over the world. That's fine. We'll just stay up in Canada. Nobody wants to go to Canada.

I started to make my way back to the Impala, then paused as I heard a stiff *creak*.

I looked round—

The door was open.

Oh, come on...

The inside of the cabin was not what I had been expecting at all. For one thing, it was a hell of a lot bigger. There were tables all along the walls, filled with a selection of what looked like old ceramic pots and utensils. A collection of fur pelts on the walls—none belonging to bears, I noted, which was a good thing really, because I didn't think I would have been able to handle that. A squat little metal-thing sat in the corner—what I thought might have been an old wood burner, though I couldn't be certain.

We became aware of a soft light emanating from somewhere further in back.

'Uh... hello?' said Frankie.

Nothing.

He stepped a little further forward, bent low in anticipation of an attack. I gripped my balls tight and tried to imagine I was somewhere else. For the first time ever, I found myself wishing Frankie still had his battle-axe on him, then scolded myself, because even if we were about to get our junks bitten off, that was just ridiculous.

We stepped past a gnarled, wooden beam, and —

We froze.

There was a man sitting there. At least, I *thought* it was a man. He was sitting slumped in a chair, his body turned away from us, pointed towards the fire that was raging in the fireplace before him. Soft light flickered off the walls, casting shadows that seemed to move of their own volition, like shadowy limbs reaching out to grab people too slow or stupid to run away.

Luckily for me, I was neither slow nor stupid.

On legs suddenly alive with adrenaline, and whilst still gripping my balls tightly, I turned for the door —

Frankie grabbed my arm.

'Wait. Something's not right.'

'*No shit!*' I hissed. I tried to pull my arm free, but he was insistent. Maybe if I bit him, or something...

'No, I mean — *look*. He's not moving. See?'

I looked back round to where the guy was sitting. True, we could only see the top of his head, but it was enough to see that the guy hadn't moved so much as an inch since we'd got here. Which meant he was either a ridiculously heavy sleeper, or...

Releasing my arm, Frankie suddenly stepped over to the chair.

He frowned.

I held my breath. '*What? What is it?*'

When he made no move to answer, I followed him round to the front of the chair and looked down.

I frowned.

It was a doll—a mannequin, to be exact. And a girl one, too, I noticed—not least of which because someone had apparently gone to a lot of effort to apply makeup to her.

Lipstick. Eyeliner. Fucking *rouge*. It was all there. She was dressed in a leopard-print nightie, exposing a plunging neckline. A pair of fluffy pink slippers hung from the end of her rigid doll's feet.

I blinked.

I was just so confused.

From beside me, Frankie said, 'Uh... *A'doy?*'

'It's a doll, Frankie.'

If he heard me, he gave no sign. 'Do you think it can see us?' He leaned forward and waved a hand in front of its face. 'Helloooooo? A'doy? Your friend sent us. We've come to ask you some questions.'

'Frankie, for the last time, it's not—'

I felt my balls shoot suddenly up into my throat as, from behind us, a voice cried, 'FREEZE, MOTHERFUCKERS!'

I let out a yelp, hands flying above my head—

'NOW TURN AROUND—*SLOWLY*. KEEP YOUR HANDS WHERE I CAN SEE 'EM!'

Slowly, we turned around—

And then, just like that, my mind broke. With the finality of a high-speed car crash, we suddenly reached the pinnacle of what was the allowable amount of retardation before the universe and all its bullshit imploded in on itself. The God of Retarded Things had played his final trump card, and boy, was it a doozy.

It was a bunny rabbit.

Now before you say anything, I know, I know — it's dumb. Believe me — I know. When you spend as much time around ridiculous crap as I do, you get to know it when you see it.

But it was what it was.

The silver-grey talking bunny rabbit gestured with the revolver in his paws — oh, yeah, he had a revolver, too. Did I mention that? Yeah; seriously, fuck my life.

'NOW STEP TOWARDS ME — AND DON'T TRY ANYTHING FUNNY. TRY ANYTHING, AND I SWEAR I'LL BLOW YOUR FUCKING BALLS OFF.'

I stared.

How the fuck is he even holding that thing? Do bunny rabbits even have *opposable thumbs?*

'NOW!'

We stepped forward, hands still raised high, my stomach cramping against the crippling retardation now coursing through it like wildfire.

The heavily armed talking bunny rabbit looked over our shoulders at the chair. *'Charlize? Did they hurt you, baby?'*

Nothing from the doll. Just the stiff crackle-pop of the fire.

He turned back to us. 'I swear, if you've hurt her —'

Frankie held out his hands. 'Wait — *no.* You've got it all wrong. We're not your enemy. Your friend sent us. You're A'doy, right?'

The bunny rabbit frowned — which is a hell of a thing to see a bunny rabbit do, by the way.

'How do you know that name?' he said.

'Your friend — *the burrito guy*? He sent us.'

A look of confusion from Mr Rabbit.

I said, 'Uh... trench coat? Looks kind of like a young MacGyver, only not really?'

He blinked. '*Mr G?*'

Mr G?

'Sure.'

'*Where is he?*'

'Oh, he's fine. He's in the trunk.' I heard how it sounded. 'I mean, sure, he *did* get shot, but —'

The talking bunny rabbit stared back and forth between us. 'Who are you?'

Before I could stop him, Frankie said, 'Well, on a biological level, I guess you could say we're mostly just carbon, though I should probably mention —'

I cut him off. 'Look, my name's Dan. This is Frankie. We're not actually as big a pair of dumbasses as you're probably thinking right now.'

Oh, that's right, Dan. Lie to the guy. Way to start a relationship.

Rabbit Dude's face changed. The revolver he'd been pointing steadily at our crotch regions fell suddenly to the floor with a heavy clunk.

'*You're* Dan Pratt?' he said.

There was no mistaking the awe in his voice.

'Um...'

He raised a paw to the air. 'It's okay, everyone — you can come out now.'

Before I could ask exactly who it was he was talking to, bodies began to emerge from out of the shadows around us. Big bodies, little bodies. Fat and thin bodies. Bodies wearing clothes, others, unfortunately, not so much. I'd like to tell you they were all human, but really that would have been a lie.

I gawped at one standing by the wood burner, a trunk-like appendage hanging from his chin like a length of taffy.

Jesus, is that a tentacle, or – ?

I stiffened.

OH GOD.

A'doy gestured with his furry little rabbit's paw. '*Come.* We have much to talk about, and very little time.' He jumped up onto the shoulder of a guy with a nut-sack-looking appendage for a nose. 'Come.'

They walked towards the front door, the rag-tag gaggle of non-humans following quickly behind them.

Frankie and I looked at each other.

Oh god. The retardation. I can hardly move. Is this really happening?

We followed.

*****

Forty minutes later, and I was sitting back on the Impala's front seat, thinking about lemmings.

Remember that old myth about how lemmings will occasionally get together to perform mass suicide by one-by-one leaping to their deaths?

Well, turns out that's only half true. Rather than an urgent desire to off themselves, recent studies have determined it's actually part of some deep-seated migratory behaviour. Supposedly they have these "strong biological urges", urges that are apparently so strong that not even the prospect of a nasty death-by-kersplat is enough to stop them.

And that was how I felt then, sitting in the driver's seat of a car that was not my own — like a small animal led by forces it does not understand, into a situation that simply cannot end well for it.

The universe is a cruel, cruel place.

We stepped out of the Impala and onto the sidewalk, a fierce wind kicking up around us and making our clothes dance.

We had followed A'doy and his band of not-so-merry men back into town, to a large building I had missed during my initial reconnaissance of the town that I would have sworn was a church, had it not looked so desperately unlike any church I had ever seen before. It was all brick, for one thing, white and flat and glaring like bleached bone, and there wasn't a sliver of stained glass anywhere I could immediately see – mainly because it had no windows. Also, not that many doors – which *had* to be a fire hazard, when you really think about it.

We followed A'doy and his gang up the concrete steps towards the building, Frankie and I sharing more than the occasional nervous glance between us.

Inside was more like a museum than a church.

There was shit everywhere. *Weird* shit – what you might call artefacts, only, again, not like any artefacts you'd have ever probably seen before. Also, *actual shit*; a great, coiled mound of it, thankfully fossilised (or at least, I *hoped* it was). Suits of strange-looking armour and machines and trinkets and little round objects – what I could have sworn were actually just Magic 8 balls – filled the space, spread out generously from one side to the other.

Frankie and I stared around the cavernous room, our mouths open.

'*Jesus, would you look at all this stuff, Dan?*' said Frankie. He gave a low whistle. 'I mean, shit, there's got to be a bazillion things in here.'

I thought that was an exaggeration, but whatever.

'Look at that thing!' he said, pointing to an object hanging on the wall across the room from us – what may or may not have been some kind of extra-terrestrial battle-axe. 'I bet you could do some serious damage with that thing, am I right?'

Oh Jesus.

'*And are those Pokémon cards?*'

I looked to where it was he was pointing.

Huh. Look at that. They even have a Charizard.

Frankie shook his head, his eyes wide and glistening like a kid's on Christmas morning, only sadder, because this was an adult. '*What is this magical place, Dan?*'

We followed the posse of weird-looking alien dudes across the vast space, footsteps echoing loudly, taking in more bizarre and obviously alien objects as we walked. Eventually we reached the back of the room, and we stopped.

I looked around.

We were in a small alcove, a plinth just inside it, around which a half a dozen or so wooden benches sat. Upon the plinth sat a little black book, not unlike a Bible, but that I had the sneaking suspicion was not.

A'doy gestured for us to take a seat, and, after a moment's pause, we did.

'What is this place?' I asked, unable to hold back my curiosity any longer.

'This —' said A'doy, hopping down from Nut-sack Face's shoulder and settling himself into what — I swear — was a La-Z-Boy, ' — is the Library of Knowledge. The place where we, The Council, seek to remember and honour those who've passed.'

I looked around at the cluster of fucked-up-looking dudes standing around us.

They didn't *look* much like librarians...

'And this place?' I said, gesturing around. *'Two Crests? Is everybody here all...'* I tried to think of a polite way to say it, *'...not from around here?'*

He chuckled. 'In a manner of speaking, yes — although not in the way you're probably thinking. Two Crests is in a lot of ways a refuge — a *sanctuary*, if you will, for any Outerling seeking escape.' He held his paws to the side and smiled. 'Despite what you might think, you humans are not the only ones the O'tsaris wish to eliminate.'

'So Two Crests is a, what... *a safe house*?' said Frankie.

A'doy nodded. 'Indeed. In fact, many of the men and women you see standing around you now came here for just that very purpose — take Craig, for example.' He gestured at a pretty ordinary-looking dude hovering near the back of the group. Well, I say "ordinary". He was pretty fat. 'Step forward, my son. Don't be shy.'

The walking wall of man known as "Craig" slowly waddled forward, head lowered, multiple chins jiggling.

'The O'tsaris came for you, didn't they, Craig? Tell our guests,' said A'doy.

Craig nodded and rubbed a hand over his neck. 'We were asleep at the time. Larnie and I — my wife. We had a farm back in those days. Ninety acres. Just cows and sheep, mostly. They must have found out we were there, surrounded us one night. I barely managed to get away.' He hesitated. 'Larnie, she, uh...'

He trailed off a moment as he relived his tragic backstory.

'How did you get away?' I heard myself ask. I mean, not to be a dick or anything, but I just couldn't see this guy evading anybody. And not just because of how overly conspicuous he was.

What he said next surprised me.

'Oh — that was easy. I shot fire out my ass and used the distraction to get away.' He must have seen the look on my face, because he frowned. 'It's a defence mechanism? You know, like how when an octopus...'

I'm sure he said more, but I'd stopped listening.

I looked around at Frankie, who I noted now had the biggest, smuggest smile on his face.

Suppressing a groan, I turned back to A'doy. In all my procrastinating over the Phonies and their evil ways, it had never once occurred to me there might be other people out there somewhere, also casualties of their agenda—not that that made things any easier to swallow, of course, or that these were people. But it was very surprising. I wondered what more I didn't know, if I would ever get a chance to find out, considering the world was now about to end or whatever.

I began to ask A'doy this, when—

There was the sound of doors crashing open from behind us.

More of A'doy's group. They were carrying something between them. Some *beige* shape, one that looked vaguely familiar...

I blinked.

Oh, hey, look! It's Burrito Guy! Burrito Guy's joined the party!

They carried him quickly past us, feet dragging on lush carpeting, through a small red door I hadn't even noticed yet.

When they were gone, I turned back to A'doy. 'What will you do with him? Mr G?'

A'doy shook his head, looking suddenly troubled. 'We are a community of peace, Dan Pratt. We survive because we remain hidden. Our job is not to intervene in the affairs of Man, but merely to *observe.*' He shook his little rabbit head again. 'Mr G broke the cardinal rule. We will heal him—he *is* one of our own, after all. But then I'm afraid he will be... excommunicated.'

I stared. 'Wait—*you're banishing him?*'

That just seemed overly harsh.

'The matter is out of my hands. He knew what the consequences of his actions would be. He was only supposed to observe and report. The rules must be enforced, Dan Pratt, lest everything collapse into chaos — *this* is how we have survived through the ages. Not through renegade acts of violence.'

I stared at the door through which Mr G had vanished. Even if the guy *was* a Phony, I had to admit, I felt kind of bad for him. I mean, don't get me wrong, I wasn't about to break down and cry or anything. But it was still a tough break.

'But *why*?' I said. 'Why do you care what happens to us? What's it to you?'

A'doy nodded over our shoulders at the men and women standing behind us. Almost immediately, they began to disperse, disappearing off to do whatever it was they all did here — fucking probe each other, or whatever.

When they were all gone, the large wood door booming shut behind them, he said, 'Walk with me.'

We followed him over to the plinth, where he quickly scaled it, little paws scrambling up it like a squirrel up a tree.

He flipped open the cover.

'Many years ago, there was a man. Rao' Tarth, his name was,' he said, beginning now to flip through pages. 'He was a great warrior — but also very wise. Some say he could even see the future, though this has never been fully substantiated.' He shrugged, as if to say — *what you gonna do?* 'Either way, it was he who prophesied that the reign of the O'tsaris would one day be ended, not by an Outerling — but by a Human. A *Man*. That this man would first kill the King of the O'tsaris, before going on to eventually free the rest of the galaxy from their evil clutches.'

He flipped another page and placed his paw on it.

I looked down.

It was the picture of a man, positioned in your typical hero's pose, shirt ripped, heavily muscled torso just visible between the tears. Like the cover for an '80s action flick—one nobody would ever want to watch, by the looks of it.

A'doy turned to look up at me, little black eyes gleaming.

I had a feeling I knew what was coming next.

With the dramatic delivery of a seasoned theatre actor (albeit a very short one), he said, 'We believe that man is *you*, Dan Pratt.'

I burst out laughing.

I know, I know, I shouldn't have. We were guests, after all. And they *had* technically saved our lives—whether directly or indirectly. But still—come on.

That shit was just too funny.

I laughed for a very long time—much longer than it was funny, anyway. I wondered if I'd finally lost my mind. That would be all I fucking needed.

'*Me?*' I said, when the fever had abated.

'You defeated Amonamanon, did you not?'

Actually, that was more of a group effort...

'But... I'm just a data key entry operator for an insurance firm. What makes you think I'm qualified to—'

He placed a little paw on my shoulder, stopping me. '*Listen to me.* Over the centuries, do you know how many people have ever stood up to the O'tsaris and survived?' He waited for me to answer, like I had it fucking written down somewhere or something. He shook his head. '*None*, Dan Pratt. The answer is *none*. Not a single one. And yet, not only did you stand up to them—you *beat* them.' He held my gaze, little black eyes unblinking. 'I'd say you're uniquely qualified.'

I gave a reluctant nod.

I *was* very brave...

But that didn't change the fact I simply didn't want to get any more involved than I already was. Some people, they spend their entire lives waiting for that dare-to-be-great situation to swing by and imbue their lives with sudden meaning. Me? I could care less about being a hero. Because seriously, do you have any idea of the kind of life expectancy of somebody like that? Sure, they might seem all badass now, with all their utility belts and gadgets and fucking skin-tight leotards or whatever, but let's be real, not one of them is ever going to make it into old age — and those are the ones who are actually *good* at the whole superhero-thing. Hell, even Superman died in the end. And now, what — I was supposed to be everyone's saviour? Are you fucking kidding me?

I shook my head.

Fuck this. This wasn't my destiny. No way.

If this was my destiny, I wanted a refund.

'But even if I *wanted* to stop them,' I went on, hearing the whining quality to my voice, but unable to stop it. '*How could I?* Boot and her cronies already have the Novamite. Even if we did know what they were planning to do with it — *which we don't* — we have no idea where to find them.'

What he said next caught me off guard.

'We already know what it is Boot and her companions are planning,' he said. 'It's the same thing they're always planning, of course.' He waited for me to fill in the blanks again. When I didn't, he frowned. '*Open a doorway into the Neverwas? To bring Her through?*' He caught the look on my face. 'You really don't know anything, do you?'

That's what I've been saying! Why doesn't anybody ever listen to me?!

He hopped down.

'She goes by many names. *Nidreth. Khavhu. Yithyla.* An evil so vast, so very... *evil*, not even the Old Ones were willing to stand up to Her. So instead they banished Her to the Neverwas — what you might know as the Deep Dark — where it was hoped all memory of Her would fade from existence.' He shook his little rabbit head. 'Only, as would turn out, evil of that calibre does not simply "vanish". Evil bleeds through. Whenever a mother drowns her infant child in the bath, that is *Her* will. Whenever a man kills another man out of passion, that is *Her*. Her influence seeping through. Black blood spreading through a clear body of water, darkening every inch it claims.'

I blinked as the obvious finally dawned. ' "*Her*"? Wait — *are you talking about the Queen?*'

In case I haven't mentioned it already, the Phonies have a hierarchy similar to that of bees. See, you have your drones — which are pretty much your normal, everyday Phonies. On top of that, each region also has a "King", whose job it is — from what I understand — to coordinate the Phonies' efforts in the Queen's stead. Then of course, there's the Queen herself, who is harder to find than a fart in a hurricane. I was pretty sure she was just a myth at this point.

From beside me, Frankie said, 'So, wait — you're saying the Phonies *aren't* alien, after all?' He shook his head. 'Oh, man, what a twist. And after all this time, too. I'm just so surprised, Dan. Seriously, I am numb with shock right now.'

Well, at least that explains why nobody's ever been able to find Her — She's in another goddamn dimension.

'So the Phonies that are here now, already, they're like, what — the advance party?' I said. 'Making the necessary preparations in order for them to bring their queen through?'

He nodded. 'That is their MO, yes. Infiltrate the population, acquire the leading positions of authority. Only then would they ever risk bringing Her through.'

'And what happens then?'

'Let's just say there is a reason She is known as "The Eater of Worlds".'

Oh.

He quit pacing and turned to me. 'Boot and her companions must be stopped. If a doorway to the Neverwas were ever to be opened, it would mean not only the end of this universe, but *all* universes. Do you understand? We're talking the end of all existence. Like a brisk hand, sweeping all the chess pieces off the board in a single swipe.'

Frankie gasped. '*A touchdown...*'

I decided not to comment.

We reached the huge front doors and stepped out once again into the blistering cold where the rest of A'doy's gang now stood waiting — though there were others standing with them now too, I noticed. People from the diner, their human disguises now all shed, exposing how they all really looked — which, to be honest, wasn't that great. Among them I spotted the waitress who had attempted to serve us earlier before disappearing off to go cry in a backroom or whatever, saw she had cat's eyes and what looked like an extra arm protruding out from her belly button. Not gonna lie, it was pretty gross.

What was more, I saw they'd also fetched the Impala for us — even given it a clean, too, by the looks of it. So that was nice of them.

A'doy turned to me, wind rippling his fur. 'A man does not choose his fate, Dan Pratt,' he said. 'But he *can* choose how he reacts to it.' He put his paw on my pants leg again. I'd never get used to that, I decided. '*Embrace* your destiny, my son. For like it or not, *you* are the chosen one.'

He knelt down, paws outstretched on the blacktop — or, you know, as much as they could. He was still a bunny rabbit, after all.

'HAIL, KINGSLAYER!' he cried.

A cacophony of elated cheers from the group.

I frowned down at him, his stupid little rabbit's body. 'Stop that. Stop that, you asshole.'

But he would not.

On and on they cheered, their alien fists (those that *had* fists) pumping in the air, whooping like animals caught in the middle of a particularly violent sex-frenzy. I looked round and saw Frankie was cheering too, clapping and pumping his fists over his head, having what looked like the time of his life. That bastard.

I continued to watch from in front of them, wind cutting at my face, cold and miserable, my hands in my pockets, wondering how they'd all react if I suddenly up and punted their little rabbit-leader right through a fucking shop window —

A stiff *pop* cut through the sound of people cheering, silencing them in an instant.

With a gasp, I jerked around to where it had sounded as though the pop had come from —

Oh crap.

'ALL RIGHT!' shouted Espinosa, her voice deafening in the new silence. She had her gun pointed towards the sky, smoke rising from the barrel, the wind taking it and quickly whisking it away. 'NOBODY MOVE! EVERYBODY STAY WHERE YOU ARE. YOU ARE ALL UNDER ARREST!'

I blinked.

Wait — did she follow us all the way from Amerstow? Holy crap, what is she, the fucking Terminator?

She walked briskly towards us, the gun still pointed up into the air. 'DO NOT—'

Her eyes settled on the group of rag-tag-looking extra-terrestrials standing around the Impala and they widened. *'What in the name of...?'*

I took a tentative step towards her. 'Look, Detective. I can explain—'

She whirled the gun on me, eyes wide and blazing. *'Stay where you are! I... don't...'*

Her eyes darted from person to person. It occurred to me she looked fucking terrified. But then, it wasn't every day you discover the world you've been led to believe is a complete and utter fucking lie. *'What is this? Some kind of cult?'*

I blinked. *'What?* No—look, it's complicated. If you'll just let me explain, I can—'

'I said stay where you are!'

Gun in my face. Hands trembling. The barrel wib-wobbling in the air in front of my eyes like it was made of jelly.

If she doesn't calm down soon, somebody's going to get hurt.

It was at about that moment that A'doy squeezed himself through the crowd.

He hopped to a stop at Espinosa's feet and looked up. 'Young lady, I can appreciate your alarm, but you really have nothing to be afraid of.' He held up his paw. 'Now, if you'll just go ahead and hand me the gun, we can get this all straightened out.'

It's an odd thing, watching somebody's mind implode. Like watching a car crash in slow motion. But then, not everyone's brains were as resistant to this kind of ridiculous crap as mine and Frankie's were.

Espinosa opened her mouth to say something else, perhaps to try and make sense of what she was seeing—who knows.

Then, with a feminine sigh, she collapsed to the blacktop, unconscious before she hit the ground.

From beside me, Frankie sighed. 'Man. Some people, am I right?'

'Yeah.'

We walked back over to the Impala and climbed in. I saw they'd also given the inside a clean too — which was also very nice of them.

I flicked on the ignition, the Impala growling to life beneath us.

A'doy appeared in the window.

'Good luck, Dan Pratt,' he said, having once more hitched a ride on Nut-sack Face's shoulder. 'And God-speed. Remember — we're all counting on you.'

I looked through the windshield at his followers. 'You know, we'd stand a lot better chance if you came with us. A hundred men are better than two.'

He shook his head. 'As I've told you already, Kingslayer. We are merely —'

I held up a hand. 'Observers, yeah — I got you.'

Thanks for the help. Asshole.

'What about her?' I said, nodding to Espinosa still lying spread-eagled on the ground. A couple of the not-men had gathered around her now, were poking at her leg with what looked like a hockey stick.

A'doy followed my gaze. 'Her? Oh, she'll be all right. I'll have the men take care of her. When she wakes up, she'll think this was all nothing but a bad dream.'

I had my doubts about that, but whatever.

We shook.

Then, with A'doy and his men waving us off, we drove out of Two Crests, back into the cold, the snow once more picking up the further out of town we got.

By the time we got back to the highway, it was a goddamn blizzard.

'Jesus, would you look at that?' said Frankie, leaning forward in the passenger seat. 'Looks like the end of the world.'

'Uh-huh.'

'Hey, Dan.'

I turned to look at him.

'*Winter is coming...*'

'I hate you so hard right now.'

I looked into the rear-view, unsurprised to find the road we had just travelled down now entirely vanished, as if it had never been there in the first place. Just a line of pines now, barely visible through the raging snow.

I had the feeling that was normal, however.

I turned back to Frankie. 'So how do you want to do this? I mean, we still have no idea exactly where Boot and her asshole friends are planning on creating this "doorway". How are we supposed to find them?'

Frankie thought it over. 'Maybe it's time we, well—you know.'

I gasped. 'You don't mean...'

He nodded. 'Uh-huh. And hell, if there was ever a time to use it, it's now.'

I groaned.

I hate it when Frankie's right.

And so, blinkers flashing, and with visibility now at about a foot, I pulled us back onto the highway, wind and snow raging around us and causing the Impala to shake and shudder with the force of it.

Frankie turned to me. 'Oh, hey, you know something—I just realised what A'doy's name backwards is...'

I pointed my face at the windshield and didn't look back.

ELEVEN

NOW BEFORE I BEGIN, I would like to stress that I am not unaware what you are about to read is beyond ridiculous. It is. I know — believe me, I do. But I would like to also remind you that, apart from the whole "creature" part, what is to follow is actually not as unlikely as it might initially seem. For instance, did you know that it's possible for a rat to squeeze itself up through your wastewater system? That's right. Like right up there. Turns out their ribs are hinged at the spine or whatever, allowing them to squeeze through even the tightest of spaces.

Of course, this was no rat, and if it had a spine, I had no freaking idea where it was. Probably because of all those eyes. Did I mention it was a severed hand? Yeah. Probably should have mentioned that first.

'Okay — ready?' said Frankie, turning to look at me from his place in the passenger seat.

It was several hours later. We were back inside Amerstow, idling in a clearing, in a patch of sparse woodland located just outside the city limits. The plot of land in question belonged to Frankie's Uncle

Ger, a Vietnam vet who, after a particularly hairy experience overseas back in the '70s, had returned home convinced it was only a matter of time before the, and I quote, "slanty-eyed little monkey-fuckers" made their way over and started "shoving bamboo into everything".

So being the case, Ol' Uncle Ger went out and did what any other responsible red-white-and-blue-blooded American would—he stockpiled.

Guns. Ammunition. Porn. SO MUCH PORN—though, to be fair, I think this last may have been unrelated.

From what Frankie had told me, it was but one of several plots he owned all across town—his "emergency cache", as he put it.

I stared through the windshield at it, squinting against the driving snow.

It was one of those sheds like the ones you can pick up from Kmart for like a couple hundred bucks. Mint-green. Seven feet tall, by about maybe ten feet wide. All corrugated metal, with a set of big sliding doors on the front, its arched roof covered in what looked to be several inches of accumulated snow. A set of big, heavy-duty padlocks on the doors.

I grunted. 'Let's just get this over with.'

We climbed out of the Impala and trudged our way over towards the shed, heads lowered, jaws clenched against the cold. I'd never been in a blizzard before, but I had seen plenty of movies, and so you'd have thought I'd have had some idea of what to expect. But I didn't. It was louder, for one thing, the wind howling all around us like a mother wolf mourning the death of her cub, only right in our ears. Snow stung at our faces, our necks, the velocity alone enough to make you want to nope the fuck out and scramble back to your car, crying hysterically, peeing the whole way.

Once at the doors, Frankie removed his keys and began sifting through them whilst I kept watch, not really expecting to see any bears, but not exactly wanting to take the chance, either.

After a moment of cursing and fumbling, the doors slid back with a shriek and a clatter, causing an avalanche of snow to rain down on us.

We looked into the shed.

It was like staring into a black hole. Just total darkness, or what Kim Kardashian's soul must look like.

Frankie bent down and fished through pockets. '*Here, Jonesy! Come here, boy! Look what Daddy's got for you!*'

I shot him a look. 'You named it?'

'Uh-huh.' He pulled out his hand, which I was surprised to see now held a packet of Pop Rocks. He poured a small pyramid out onto his palm and shook it back and forth. '*Here, boy!*'

It was then that I realised—all of Frankie's disappearing acts. The notes he'd been leaving for me recently.

He's been coming here and feeding this thing. That sneaky motherfucker.

He leaned in and threw the Pop Rocks just inside the doorway, scattering them across the small, rectangular patch of light spilling in over the shed's floor.

As we waited for the "thing of which we do not speak" to show itself, I thought back to the day we had first seen it.

It had been one night a few weeks back, whilst on my way to the bathroom. I had been up all night, having been suffering from a bad case of drinking too much coffee before bed, and had thus far put off going to the bathroom because of my natural—and completely understandable—fear of walking through a dark space in the dead of night. Even if that space is yours, and you have the lights on. Also, ghosts—though I had no real evidence to suggest my apartment was haunted. But as I'm sure you'll agree, you can never be too careful with those sorts of things.

So I'm standing there, preparing to unload, when all of a sudden I look down and—*bam*—there it is; sitting on the edge of my toilet and staring—that's right, fucking *staring*—up at me with its half a dozen people's eyes.

By this point you're probably thinking things can't possibly get any dumber, am I right? I mean, come on—*a severed hand covered in eyes? Oh man, what next?*

A penis.

It had a goddamn penis.

Was it a big penis, you ask? Well, that's hard to say. I was still half-asleep, and it wasn't like I was staring at it or anything. Technically, I guess you could say it was "average sized", though when compared to the rest of its "body", it was actually frighteningly large.

I let out a scream like I was being stabbed to death and threw myself up against my bathroom wall.

The hand and I regarded each other.

It was like something out of a nightmare. Stumpy, gore-slicked wrist. All those awful, unblinking eyes. Where had it come from? What did it want? What is the correct penis-to-body ratio for something that size, anyway?

These are questions I still ponder over to this very day.

Then, suddenly, the hand-thing lunged at me.

I tried to throw up my arms, but even with the adrenaline now racing through me I was still way too slow. I stumbled backwards instead, gasping in surprise. Then before I knew it I had a penis in my face, and really that's the last thing you want when it's three o'clock in the morning and you're not Ricky Martin.

The multi-eyed penis monster dug its fingers into my hair as it sought to do... whatever it was it was about to do. I closed my lips tighter than I ever had in my life and pawed at it, trying desperately to block out the realisation that this... *thing*, whatever it was, had just crawled right out of my goddamn toilet, and was thus probably covered in poop particles. Nobody ever thinks about poop particles as much as they should. You know whenever you smell something nasty? That's little bits of said particles going straight up your nose. That's right — think about that the next time you walk into the bathroom after someone.

Thinking fast (and whilst taking special care not to make any form of contact with its, uh, "dangly" bits), I threw it back into the toilet from whence it came and slammed the lid.

I jumped on it.

What the sweet baby Jesus fuck?!

'Dan?'

I threw a startled glance round at the doorway.

Frankie!

He rubbed at his eyes, yawning. 'Everything okay? You're making a lot of noise.'

I blinked. 'Frankie — *Jesus*! There's a... a *thing*! In the toilet!'

He squinted. '*A what?*'

'A HAND! With... I think eyes, and — IT HAS A FUCKING PENIS, FRANKIE.'

He was quiet a moment as he considered this. 'How big?'

'FRANKIE!'

'Specifically how big are we talking here, Dan? Because you know, there's a very specific penis-to-body ratio —'

He was interrupted as the thing in question suddenly threw itself at the underside of my toilet lid.

THUMP.

Frankie and I stared at each other.

'HELP ME,' I moaned.

'Okay, don't panic. I know exactly what to do.'

Before I could say or do anything, he reached past me and, to my utter surprise and disgust, hit the flusher.

I glared at him. 'ARE YOU KIDDING ME? THAT'S NOT GOING TO—'

There was a terrible suctioning sound.

Slowly, I lifted the lid.

'Oh no, wait, it's worked. Huh. How about that.'

We stared down into the empty bowl a while.

'So. What do you want to do now?' said Frankie. 'Want to go watch cartoons?'

And so we watched cartoons for a while—I sure as shit wasn't going back to bed.

We didn't see the multi-eyed penis monster for a while after that. Well, not *immediately*, anyway—but, really, that's a whole other story. I was hoping we'd seen the last of it.

'Hmm,' said Frankie, frowning. He rubbed his chin thoughtfully. 'He's not usually this shy.'

I rolled my eyes.

"He." Like it's a person...

I sighed. 'Let's forget this. Besides, we don't really have the time to be—'

Before I could finish, the multi-eyed penis monster—AKA Jonesy—leapt suddenly out from the shadows, snatching up a handful of Pop Rocks, before quickly skittering away again into darkness.

I let out a cry and fell backwards onto the snow, catching the door with my arm and causing yet more snow to rain down on top of me.

Looking all of a sudden like a crap snowman, I glanced up.

"Jonesy" tentatively crept out into the light.

It was even more disgusting than I remembered. All those eyes, those fingers — *ugh*. What was worse, since our last meeting he had somehow gone and procured himself his very own little Christmas sweater; basically just a fingerless glove, with a little Santa face sewn into it, the quality of which told me all I needed to know about its creator, who was obviously Frankie.

'*There* you are,' said Frankie. He knelt down to greet it, patting the floor by his feet and ushering the little guy over. '*Did you miss me?*'

It skittered over on its little finger-legs, penis dragging on the floor behind it, causing it to make a sound like a man rubbing a hand over his stubble.

Frankie poured another pile out onto his hand and held it out for "Jonesy", who quickly dug-in, fingers raking up the Pop Rocks, curling them back into somewhere inside its palm where I assumed the equivalent of its mouth must be.

He patted it. 'There's a good boy. You like Pop Rocks, don't you? *Hmm?*'

The multi-eyed penis monster shuddered with delight.

I almost threw up all over myself.

When he was finished, Frankie knelt down. 'Now listen, Jonesy. This is important. *We need your help.* Will you help us?'

Confused squint from Jonesy.

Oh, great. It's retarded, too…

Frankie pointed back through the snow towards the Impala. 'See that car over there? Well, there's a very bad man in that car, with very bad friends. Friends who want to *hurt* Daddy. We need to know where they are, so that we can stop them. Understand?'

Jonesy recoiled back on his fingers, squinting furiously.

Hurt Daddy, you say?!

Frankie nodded. 'That's right. We need your help to stop them.' He lifted it up in his hands, held it in front of his face like a princess about to kiss a frog. 'Will you help us?'

Instead of answering, Jonesy suddenly shot up Frankie's arm, perching itself on his shoulder like a parrot. Only it was worse than that, because this parrot was a severed hand, one whose disproportionately large penis hung down over Frankie's shoulder like a sports towel flung there after a good workout.

Christ, look at it. It's like a goddamn fireman's hose. How does it even walk with that thing?

We waddled back over to the car.

I lifted the trunk.

So here's probably the perfect time to tell you we had taken a little detour before making our way over to Uncle Ger's Emergency Cache. And by "detour", I mean we had driven to a building I thought I would never visit again, for reasons that would be obvious to you if you knew the sorts of things I did about the people who worked there.

In the end, it had taken surprisingly little effort to get him to come outside. A single text, in fact.

Then, the second he'd stepped out through the doors, we'd thrown a bag over his head and bundled him protesting into the trunk, whereupon I had swiftly set about smacking him with a snow-shovel—not that doing so was exactly necessary, per se, but I like to keep all my bases covered. And besides, it had felt pretty good.

I stared down at him.

'Hello, Brett. Been a while.'

Brett regarded me from the trunk's floor with glowing eyes.

Once upon a time, we had been colleagues, he and I, back when I had still worked for Baxter & Klein, and all this ridiculous bullshit had yet to begin. He would come over to my cubicle, irritate me for a little while, before disappearing off again to go photocopy his balls or whatever. I don't mean to make it sound like we were friends, or anything like that—we weren't. Far from it. In fact, I liked him a whole lot more as a Phony than I ever did as Human Brett.

He'd evidently somehow managed to remove the bag from his head, despite the fact his hands were bound. Did I mention he was a Phony yet? Yeah.

'*MMMMFFFF!*' said Brett.

I blinked. 'What? I can't understand you.'

'*MMMMMMMFFFFFFF!*'

Really trying, now. Body thrashing like a shark's washed up on the shore, desperate to get back into the water.

Frankie and I shared a glance.

'Looks like he's trying to say something, Dan.'

I nodded. 'I wonder what he's trying to say.'

'I think he wants us to hit him with the shovel again.'

Brett suddenly stopped thrashing, eyes wide and staring.

I grunted. 'That's better. Now, I'm going to remove this tape. If I see so much as a single tentacle, you're getting a salt facial—understand?'

Slow nod from Brett.

'Well, good. Now hold still.'

I reached into the trunk and, with a brisk jerk of my arm, ripped the tape from his mouth.

'*Thundering vag-belch!*' he cried. '*Did you have to be so rough?*'

I blinked. 'Oh—sorry.'

Frankie elbowed me.

'I mean—*eat a dick, Brett!*'

'Seriously. *I think my lips are bleeding...*'

191

'Oh, shut up. You know you can't bleed. Quit being so dramatic — or would you like us to put it back on?'

Frantic head-shake from Brett.

'Okay. Now, we have some questions for you. Cooperate, and we'll let you go. However, should you choose to be a dick and not cooperate, we'll be forced to use Jonesy here to extract the information. And believe us when we tell you that is a process you do *not* want any part of.'

Yeah, as it turned out, apart from holding the record for the most impressive penis-to-body ratio *ever*, Jonesy could also read minds — something Frankie and I had discovered one late night, the details of which I am still very much reluctant to talk about. Let's just say there are some things in life you just can't un-experience, and leave it at that.

Brett was silent a moment as he considered this.

'What kind of questions? Like *math*?'

'We want to know where Boot and the others plan to breach a hole into the Neverwas,' I said. I leaned forward. 'And you're going to tell us.'

He looked suddenly terrified — I mean, as much as a trans-dimensional body-snatcher *could*. 'But... you don't understand. I don't do that kind of work anymore. I'm out. Seriously — how would I know where she's going?'

Frankie and I exchanged glances.

'You know, Dan, I think he's telling the truth,' said Frankie. 'Guess we don't need him, after all.'

'Yeah.'

He put his hand on the trunk-lid. 'So long, Brett. Been nice catching up.'

He made as if to slam it, but Brett suddenly jerked bolt-upright.

'*Wait!*'

We waited.

He sighed. 'Look, I *do* know where she is, okay? *But I can't tell you.* If I tell you, I'm a fucking dead man. Seriously, that girl may look harmless, but she's a fucking psychopath. She'll kill the *shit* out of me.'

'And I'm supposed to care?'

'Please, Dan! Just let me go—for old times' sake, huh? What do you say?'

I stared down into the trunk at him, hands balled into fists.

Old times' sake? What, you mean the time you put bleach in my coffee? Or the time you found out I liked Lindsay Bacherman, and then went and told her I had genital warts, and that it was terminal? How about the time you put industrial-strength glue on my chair? You mean those times, Brett? Hmm?

I grabbed him.

I don't know what I was thinking. Probably, I wasn't. All I know is one moment he was in the trunk, squinting up at me with his stupid little jelly-eyes. The next he was falling out onto the snow, landing with a thump, a crumpled bundle of bound limbs.

Now, I know what you're thinking, and *no* I didn't go to town on him or anything like that. I mean, Jesus, I'm not Bruce Willis. Even if I didn't have the physical strength of a nine-year-old girl, I drew the line at beating up on people who were simply unable to fight back—which was a lie, of course, but felt reassuring all the same. Mostly, I was afraid that, even with his wrists and ankles cable-tied, he'd still somehow manage to get the drop on me. I didn't want to take that chance.

I kicked snow at him instead.

'OLD TIMES?!' I cried, spit flying from my mouth like a crazy person. I punted a mound by his head, showering him in snow. 'FUCKING OLD TIMES?!'

Brett recoiled as snow rained down on him. *'Hey! Stop that!'*

But I would not stop.

The red haze of fury stole in over my vision, clouding everything in sight.

This was it—my mental breakdown. The one that had been brewing ever since the night we had first broken into Mr Stewart's house and drawn penises on his paintings and furniture and whatever. The scale had finally tipped into the crazy zone—as it was always going to anyway.

This—this was my Björk moment.

Watch out, world. Here comes Dan, the snow-kicker!

'ARE YOU FUCKING KIDDING ME?!'

I felt a hand on my arm suddenly and turned.

Frankie.

He looked concerned—and rightfully so. I was a crazy person now.

'Dan – stop! He's had enough!'

I reached down and turned Brett over.

I put our faces together.

'TELL US WHERE SHE IS!'

Brett's chest hitched. Like he was crying, only not really, because he was smiling, too. And laughing.

So that was weird.

He tilted his face towards the sky. *'You stupid fools! You're already too late – don't you see?* We have the Naoggrath. *Soon, our fearless King, Boot, will punch a hole into the Neverwas, and then – oohhhhh then, my friends –* then *you will know true horror. The sky will turn red. Men and women and children will be pulled apart on the streets like meaty piñatas, their innards quickly gobbled up like candy. The creatures of darkness will spill over onto this plane and ravage it in the blink of an eye – all whilst* She *watches and laughs.*

He threw his head back and cackled.

Frankie and I shared a glance.

I nodded.

He turned and looked at Jonesy perched on his shoulder, whose penis I noted was still way larger than it realistically ought to have been. I mean, goddamn. 'Okay. Now — just like we talked about. Go on.'

Some stuff happened then. Stuff I don't want to overly go into, if I'm honest, for reasons I also don't wish to elaborate on. What I *will* say, however, is that Jonesy climbed down from Frankie's shoulder and quickly made its way over to a still-laughing Brett.

Then things got... weird.

Like, *really* weird. Again, I don't want to get into specifics.

There was some crying. Some screaming. Some — for lack of a better word — "docking", as Jonesy quickly latched itself onto Brett's petrified face and got to work.

It didn't take long for us to get what we wanted.

'Okay, boy, that's enough,' said Frankie, less than a minute later. He ushered Jonesy back over, who came at once, giddily skittering across the snow before once more settling itself on his shoulder.

I turned my attention back to Brett.

He was lying in the foetal position, eyes fixed on some point in the distance as snow rained down on him like God's frozen tears, now a broken shell of a man. *'All right,'* he said. *'I-I'll talk...'*

Okay, so maybe I exaggerated a little on the whole "reading-minds" part — *whatever*. Still, results are results.

'Where?' I said.

'The Devil's Spire... In Merlot.'

I blinked, surprised.

The Devil's Spire; an outcropping of rock the size of a small mountain, located the next town over — often lovingly referred to by local folk as "God's Nipple", because that was exactly what it looked like. Flat, sheared top, like the stump of a tree. A really *big* tree. Supposedly, it was millions of years old. The closest thing to a national monument this state has.

I stepped back over to Frankie.

'Well. Now we know where they're planning on doing this thing,' he said. He nuzzled Jonesy sat on his shoulder and my stomach twinged.

I shook my head. 'But we're still no better off. I mean, shit, they'll have a whole army of those fuckers over there. Just us two? We wouldn't stand a chance.'

We stood and watched the snow slowly covering the man formerly known as Brett as he lay quietly weeping on the ground.

'So what do you want to do?' said Frankie.

I sighed.

That was the question, wasn't it? So we knew where Boot and her gang were — *so what*? Aside from the fact we were just a pair of hapless assholes, they outnumbered us a hundred to one. No way we'd be able to stop them by ourselves.

'We need help,' said Frankie.

I whirled on him. '*Help? From who?* Chuck's on location. Josh and Kenny are in Mexico. The president's not interested and/or a dick. And even if we *could* somehow get a message to him, it's unlikely he'd be able to get anybody here in time — not in these conditions, anyway.'

Then, of course, there was Abby — though even with the direness of our current situation, there was still no way I was going to call her. Which on the surface might sound like a terrible decision, considering she was both smarter *and* braver than us — and it was. But still, if you love someone, and you're about to take a spiraling nose-dive into

Satan's gaping, fiery butthole, you don't pull that person along with you, do you?

I shook my head.

No. Better just the one of us go. And let's be honest, she had a whole lot more to offer society than I did. Really, it was the only responsible thing to do.

'So what do we do, then?' repeated Frankie.

I shrugged. 'Looks like we're on our own.'

We were both silent a moment as we considered the gravity of this statement.

Ordinarily, this is the part where I'd tell you how I suddenly nutted-up, how I simply said — *fuck it all* — and rode off into battle, all stoic and brave and knightly, undeterred by the overwhelming odds stacked against us. How I gallantly marched my horse right up to the enemy's defences, sword raised high, shouting things about honour and freedom as I fought desperately to keep the tears of utter terror from smearing my face-paint.

Sure, it's a nice image. The selfless hero, nobly giving his life so that others may live. And hell, everybody likes a sacrifice — especially when it's for the greater good, and you're not the one doing the sacrificing.

Thing is, they've got it all wrong. There's nothing brave or glorious about killing yourself — no matter how you dress it up, or whose name you do it in. In reality, the only people sacrificing themselves for the greater good these days are over-confident assholes and people too stupid to fear death. *It's unnatural.* And besides, I didn't even have a horse.

I thought it over.

Of course, if I *didn't* go, everybody I'd ever known or loved would be brutally murdered to death by monsters.

So there was that to consider, too.

I shook my head.

I just didn't know what to do.

Frankie sighed. 'Well, I guess we could always —'

He was interrupted by the sudden sound of a vehicle approaching.

We both tensed and turned our faces back to the road, waiting to see if we were about to get brutally murdered to death or whatever.

The vehicle rounded the corner.

It was a panel van. Navy-blue. Chrome rims.

It pulled over in the snow a half a dozen yards or so away. A moment later, the door opened, and —

I stared.

'Mr G?!'

He trudged over to us, handsome face pinched against the snow, beige trench coat flapping all over the damn place, reminding me once more of a cape.

He nodded. 'Hello, Dan.'

I frowned.

Wait — how did he even know where to find us? What, does he have us on fucking tag, or something?

He nodded a greeting to Frankie, who nodded back. He didn't seem overly concerned by the fact there was a multi-eyed penis monster currently dragging-dick all over Frankie's shoulder — which, really, if there was ever something to be concerned about, this was it. I mean, *goddamn.* To be fair, though, walking the circles he did, he probably saw shit like this all the time. But still.

He looked back and forth between us, the light reflecting back at me from his perfectly shaped cheekbones and blinding my eyes. He wasn't dying anymore either, I noticed — which, ordinarily, would have given me pause for thought, though with everything I'd seen over the past few days now barely made me raise an eyebrow. 'I hear you boys are in need of some help.'

Frankie and I shared a glance.

Frankie said, 'Uh... yeah, how did you —?'

Mr G raised his fingers to his lips and whistled.

Immediately the van's backdoors flew open and a small gaggle of men jumped out. Again, I say "men". Guy in short-shorts and a Yankees cap, his body covered in blister-pink scales. Another guy in a parka, who at a glance looked mostly normal — that was, until you caught a glimpse of him in your peripheral vision, and saw him for what he really was; a hair-covered, spidery-looking thing, with thick, snapping mandibles for a mouth. Long, snake-like appendage for a tongue. But you get my point.

Oh look. The cavalry has arrived. Hurrah.

I peered around them at the van. 'Uh, not to be a dick about it or anything, but I don't suppose you got any more back there?' I mean, sure, it didn't *look* like it could've held any more people, but you never know.

Before he could answer, there was the sound of another car approaching.

We all turned to watch as the coffee-coloured, boxy-looking sedan jerked to a stop beside the panel van, headlights punching dual lines through the snow.

I blinked.

Oh you have got to be kidding me.

Detective Espinosa climbed out of the sedan and paused a moment to pull her jacket tighter around her before quickly joining us on the snow.

'Mr Pratt,' she said, offering me a nod. She looked round at the half a dozen – for lack of a better word – "monsters", standing next to the panel van and, to my complete surprise, nodded.

She let out a breath. 'So – looks like I was wrong about you, after all,' she said, having to shout a little over the wind. 'Guess I owe you an apology.'

'Yeah.' She did.

Instead, she said, 'Your friend here tells me the world's about to end, that you're the only one who can stop it. That true?'

I snuck a glance at Mr G, who gave me a thumbs-up.

Bastard.

I cleared my throat. 'Well, actually –'

'Then you're going to need all the help you can get.' She reached behind her and pulled out her service pistol, cocked it, being – what I thought – overly dramatic.

I stared around at them all, all those stupid, hopeful faces.

It wasn't that I didn't appreciate the gesture – I did. But that didn't make it any less redundant. We were still pants-wettingly outnumbered, with – by my count – only the one gun between us. I mean, sure, there were the several dozen or so in Uncle Ger's Shed of Wonders, but really with all that porn in there too, there was no way of knowing what kinds of cross-contamination might have occurred. Was it-gun-to-porn, or-porn-to-gun? Because that's a lot of hands in a lot of different places, folks. Even if the fate of the universe *was* in jeopardy, that's no excuse for not using proper precaution.

'*Guys,*' I said, not wanting to be a party-pooper, but unable to help myself. 'Listen. We're outnumbered. I mean, hell, the only way we'd stand a chance is if we had a –'

I paused as an idea struck me like a rogue lightning bolt.

It was so simple. So *obvious*. I couldn't believe I hadn't thought of it before.

I turned to Espinosa, frowning furiously. 'How well do you know your boss?'

She looked at me sideways for a moment, unsure if I was being serious. 'We're... pretty tight, I guess. *Why?*'

Frankie turned to look at me, eyes wide with sudden understanding. 'Wait — are you thinking what I'm thinking?'

'Probably not,' I said. I turned back to Espinosa. 'Okay — I'm going to need you to make some phone calls.'

TWELVE

IT WAS LATE EVENING by the time the first of the helicopters arrived.

Not the heavily armoured helicopters I was expecting, mind you — you know, with the missiles, and stuff? It was a little compact-looking thing, black as coal, like something you'd expect some rich tycoon to use to get around in. Smooth, sleek glass for a front, giving the whole thing a *domed* look, with a couple of steel rods for legs. Really, it was a surprise they'd even allowed one up at all, given the state of the weather and all. But then, when you considered the stakes, losing a couple guys by helicopter crash was probably the least of the military's worries.

It touched down in the spot right where we were standing, rotor wash kicking up snow and sleet and sending clumps of the stuff flying in our direction — as if we weren't covered enough already.

The second the helicopter's feet were safely on the snow, the sliding door slid back and a man emerged.

It was the same man who had interviewed us after the whole thing back over at Lake Fairburn — Havisham, if I recalled.

He extended his hand. 'Mr Pratt.'

So I guess here's the perfect time to tell you some phone calls had been made.

First, Espinosa had called her boss, who — after demanding to know every detail of the situation — had eventually agreed to put us through to somebody "higher-up", who may or may not have worked for the CIA.

Now, I know what you're thinking, and *no* we didn't tell him there were "aliens" trying to instigate the end of the world. I mean, *come on*. Truthfully, I'm not sure what Espinosa had told the guy to get him to take us seriously. All I know is that, whatever it was, it worked.

After that, we were put through to somebody over at the NSA, who, after dilly-dallying for a good half an hour, had eventually put us through to somebody at the Pentagon, where, after yet *more* dilly-dallying, we were eventually put through to somebody at the White House. Or at least, I *think* it was the White House. To be honest, it was a very long and confusing process, and it wasn't like I was really paying that much attention anyway.

Again, I'm not sure what was said, or how exactly Espinosa managed to get them to listen to her — though I *did* hear both mine and Frankie's names dropped a couple times, so maybe that had something to do with it, I'm not sure. We're a pretty big deal.

After a very long and awkward handshake, Havisham finally released my hand. He squinted up at the snow and sighed. Like Espinosa, he didn't seem all that bothered by the fact there were a good baker's dozen of extra-terrestrials currently standing around him being all extra-terrestrial and stuff. I wondered exactly how much he knew, if the whole "aliens living amongst us" thing was common knowledge now.

'Hell of a day for a war,' he said, eyes still pointed at the falling snow.

'Uh-huh.'

We talked for a while, as we began to go over what he called our "plan of attack". Emphasis on "our". Yeah—seriously, don't even.

He told me about his team. The "Dead Revenants", they called themselves, which, apart from sounding like a rejected thrash-metal band from the '80s, didn't even make sense. After the whole Belmont Grove incident, the government had supposedly decided to set up a new task force in an attempt to try to cope with the emerging Phony threat. Thus, the "Dead Revenants" had been born—or at least, I *think* that was how it went. Again, I wasn't really listening.

When he was done, I filled him in on Boot and her plan, about Gizmo and this supposed "Neverwas".

To his credit, he listened in complete silence, not even raising his eyebrows when I told him the part about the multi-eyed penis monster—which, speaking of penis monsters, we had since locked back up in Uncle Ger's Emergency Shed, lest he get confused for a baddie and accidentally shot to death or whatever.

When I had finished, he reached into his pocket and pulled out a little silver case. Inside was a row of expensive-looking cigars.

He offered one to me.

I shook my head. 'No, thanks. I'm, uh... trying to quit.'

He looked at me strange a moment, then popped one between his lips. More of the army guys had arrived by this point—all, I assumed, from the Pennyfield Air Force Base, what with it being the closest military installation and all. Hummers. Jeeps. Several of those big, six-wheel personnel carriers, green plastic sides flapping furiously in the wind. No tanks, though, which I thought was a bit of an oversight. If you weren't going to bring out the big guns when the fate of the world was at stake, when *were* you?

As we prepared to move out, I went to go find my "crew".

They were huddled by the panel van's open rear doors, using them as shelter from the raging wind and snow. None were talking. Whereas before they had been all gung-ho and eager, now they just looked anxious. Like a gaggle of skydivers might upon just having been informed that only one of the parachutes they're wearing between them works. Well, all except for Mr G, that was, who I noticed was looking especially calm and composed for somebody who had only hours before been on death's door. Frankie also seemed pretty nonchalant, what considering the fact that, should we fail, the world was *literally* going to end—though that might just have been because of the brain damage he so clearly suffered from. I also had a sneaking suspicion he might have been playing Candy Crush, though I couldn't be sure. And I just didn't care enough to ask.

I found a spot next to Mr G and settled in, welcoming the shelter the van's doors provided.

I followed his gaze out into the snow.

'So,' I said.

He nodded. 'So.'

'Listen, I'm, uh... sorry about the whole "banishing" thing. That's got to suck. But I've got to ask—*why'd you help us*? I mean, you must have known what the outcome would be. Why'd you stick your neck out for us?'

There was a moment where he didn't say a single word, just continued to stare out at the falling snow.

Finally, he said, 'Are you familiar with Spider-man?'

'*The superhero?*' This took me aback. He just didn't look like a comic book kind-of-guy.

'There's this saying Peter Parker uses,' he continued. ' "With great power, comes great responsibility". Basically, it means that those with the power to help others, have an obligation to do so.'

I blinked.

'Are you... telling me you're Spider-man?'

Holy shit. I knew it.

He shot a glance at me. '*What?* No. I'm just saying — it's an apt quote, is all. And unlike our mutual furry-friend, who is apparently happy to sit in his little cabin whilst the walls burn down around him, I, however, am not.'

There was a moment of uncomfortable silence between us.

Finally, I said, 'So just to be absolutely clear — you're *not* Spider-man?'

He squinted at me. 'You sure you're the chosen one?'

I shrugged.

He stared blankly at me a moment, perhaps wondering if he should comment on this, before turning his attention back to the snow.

I followed his gaze, my mind turning — as it always did during the quiet moments between monster-attacks — towards Abby. It felt like months since I had last seen her, even though, really, it was less than a week. I didn't think I had ever wanted to see another human face so bad in my entire life. True, the fact there was a good chance I might never see her again could have had something to do with it. But whatever the case, in that moment, I missed her terribly.

'Here — take this,' said Mr G, pulling me back into the moment. He reached into his trench coat, pulled out the little wooden, imitation pistol from before. It looked even more ridiculous up close — not least of which because, from this distance, I could see it even had the word **GUN** written on it in what looked like faded Sharpie.

'That's okay,' I said.

'*Please,*' he insisted, holding the gun out to me. '*Take it.* Consider it a thank you—for saving my life.'

Well, if you call shoving your unconscious, bullet-riddled body into the trunk of your own car and completely forgetting about you "saving", then, uh... yeah – you're welcome.

I looked at his stupid, handsome face.

I sighed.

'I mean, I *guess* I could—'

He shoved it into my hand.

'There you go. It's all yours—but be careful with that thing. It's not a toy.'

Goddamnit.

Suddenly, a soldier dressed all in black, with a contraption on his head I thought might have been a set of night-vision goggles, appeared. He searched the group, hesitating a moment as his eyes fell on the clearly not human folk amongst us, before eventually turning his gaze upon me.

'Sir,' he said, with a nod. 'Time to head out.'

'Uh... okay?'

He disappeared back off to wherever he'd come from, boots crunching on snow.

I turned back to the van, surprised to see everyone now up on their feet, eyes all bright and wide.

Look at them. They think you're their leader.

I swallowed dryly.

I didn't want to be a leader. Despite what A'doy and his gang might believe, I was not leading-man material. Hell, I was a data key entry operator for an insurance firm — and not even a very good one, if we're being totally honest here. At best, I was the guy killed in the first act by a tragic twist of fate, offering a heart-felt speech to the others before finally succumbing to his injuries, but whose death would provide ample motivation for the *actual* heroes with which to continue on their journey. I was filler. I was fucking *collateral damage*. Really, that was the best I could hope for.

And yet the way they all looked at me, the way their eyes held my own, it was clear that, for whatever reason, these men trusted me. Trusted me enough to lead them to victory, or at the very least not get them killed — which just goes to prove one very important point, one I've been making for years.

People are fucking stupid.

'Okay,' I said, not knowing what to say, but feeling as though I had to say something anyway. 'Who's ready to go kick some ass?'

What happened next surprised me.

They all raised their hands, fists held high, and began to cheer and whoop and laugh. Backs were clapped and palms were slapped; it was like we'd already won — which, if you asked me, was kind of tempting fate. But whatever.

'THE KINGSLAYER!' one of them cried — a guy in a navy snowsuit with bright red suckers on his hands and face, whose name I didn't know, but that I decided I would from then on refer to as "Douche".

The others quickly followed suit, fists pumping the air, undeterred by the sheer ridiculousness of it all.

I slowly nodded to myself.

Yep. We were all going to die.

PART 3
A MELEE OF MONSTERS

Excerpt from *Merlot Daily*, dated October 10th, 2015, from the article 'Devil's Spire sparks concern for locals due to ongoing construction work':

...still unknown exactly what the cause for the ongoing work is, as an official announcement has yet to be issued; however officials for the site have stated that the work being carried out is strictly of a "maintenance" nature, and that no building or expansion work will be taking place.

Furthermore, when asked exactly when members of the public could expect to see the site reopened, council representative Rickard Blakely stated that "Whilst we do not have an exact date at present, we will of course notify the public as soon as one is determined."

End of excerpt.

INTERLUDE—PART 3

LAKE STARED AT ME from across the (possibly) oak desk, his face pinched tight in concentration.

It had been a very long time since he'd last spoken. A good couple hours, in fact. What was more, there was something different about his face now. I don't mean like *aesthetically* different, like he'd suffered a catastrophic stroke or whatever. Regardless, there was a look in his eye now that I couldn't place, and for that reason and that reason alone, I didn't like it.

I glanced over towards the window, noticing for the first time that the light had diminished considerably since first beginning my story. I wondered what the time was, if Lake had any other patients sitting outside in the corridor somewhere, patting their knees with their hands, wondering when the hell they were going to get their brains shrunk already.

Just as I was thinking this, the light on the phone on Lake's desk began to blink.

When he made no move to grab it, I said, 'Uh, do you need to get that...?'

He blinked, seemed to come back to himself.

'*Hmm?* Oh, yes. Yes —' He picked up the receiver, told somebody called "Karen" to cancel his appointments for the rest of the day, before dropping it back into its cradle with a clatter.

I blinked.

Okay...

He settled back in his seat. 'Please — *continue.*'

I noted the eagerness in his voice, the visible change in his posture. Like a kid at story time, only worse, because this was an adult. But there was something else to it, too. Something I couldn't quite place. I didn't know what was going on here, or what the sudden change in his manner meant.

But it was very concerning.

I looked at my imaginary watch. 'Actually, it's getting pretty late. I should probably —'

Lake suddenly leaned forward. 'No — *don't leave.* We're making a breakthrough here. Ending the story now could prove significantly detrimental to your recovery.'

It could?

I didn't want to damage my brain any more than it already was.

I let out a slow breath. 'Well — *okay,* doc. I mean, if you're *sure —*'

'*Oh, I am.*'

That look in his eyes again. That *wild* look. And was he sweating, too?

But what was that old saying — *in for a penny, in for a pound*?

THIRTEEN

WE REACHED THE NEIGHBOURING town of Merlot a little over forty minutes later, pulling up at the entrance to the national park in a not-so-angry squeal of brakes.

It had taken a lot longer getting to Merlot than expected, even when taking into consideration the treacherous conditions inflicted by the unrelenting sleet and snow. With the storm now at full-hurricane levels, we had been forced to abandon the choppers, endeavouring instead to travel to our destination by road.

And it had been hell.

Every road we took seemed to have a crash on it somewhere, forcing us to take detour after detour. It was surprising; you'd think the military would have some kind of contingency put in place for just these kinds of situations. But no. Possibly, it was due to the rushed nature of our mission, or the urgency with which we traveled. Really, I like to think they were simply as ill-prepared as the rest of us, because that would have been just my fucking luck.

For obvious reasons, the ranger station/visitor centre at the entrance was completely deserted, the squat, shack-like little building barely visible through the storm, its lights all off, and not a single other vehicle visible in the small area of snow-blanketed blacktop that made up its lot.

For whatever reason, I thought we would disembark here, travel the rest of the way on foot. But of course, this was the United States military, and so instead we just ploughed our way through, undeterred by all the landscaping work our doing so probably ruined in the process — not that *that* should be our top priority or anything. I'm just saying, it was a shame.

After what felt like a million years, we finally pulled up at the base of Devil's Spire.

Almost immediately, soldiers began filing out onto the snow — a good amount of them, though, granted, not nearly as many as I would have liked. They say safety comes in numbers, but really that's twice as true if those numbers have guns — as these ones did.

Voices shouted orders as men in body armour and funny-looking helmets rushed into formation.

I stared up at the mountain. Even with the wind and snow flying everywhere, I could see that the place was a lot bigger than I remembered. Just sheer, jagged rock, as far as the eye could see, the tip currently concealed by the raging snow. Whilst it had never occurred to me before, sat here now looking up at it, I realised the place looked almost exactly like that mountain from *Close Encounters of the Third Kind* — which, when you really think about it, was actually kind of fitting. I wondered if Richard Dreyfuss was up there too somewhere, if he was any good with automatic weapons, and if — should all else fail — he'd be accommodating to the idea of allowing himself to be used as a human shield. Hey — you never know.

We climbed out of the panel van and approached the soldier dudes, wind whipping all around us.

Frankie stepped forward from the group.

It was then I noticed the item in his hands—what I was unsurprised to find was a battle-axe, only not the same battle-axe as the one from back at the apartment. It was the one from Two Crests. The one that had been hanging on the wall, in the same room as the Pokémon cards and the weird, exotic armour and whatnot, back in the church/museum that little furry asshole had taken us to before sending us off on this suicide mission.

Looking at it now, I had to say it looked more futuristic than extra-terrestrial—a distinction you really had to be there to fully appreciate. Sleek. Smooth. Covered in a myriad of buttons and lights, with fancy patterning down the side that looked more than a little like some company or other's poor attempt at branding.

Now, I know what you're thinking, and *no* I have no idea when he stole it, or how. Or how he managed to keep its presence a secret this whole time without anybody noticing. Seriously, I have no fucking clue.

But trust me when I tell you that, when you've known Frankie for as long as I have, sometimes it's better just to not ask questions and move on.

'*All right, you cowards!*' he shouted, marching in front of the soldiers and, judging by their body language, simultaneously pissing off every single one of them. '*You want to live forever?!*'

Before anybody could answer, he launched himself at the rise, battle-axe raised high above his head like a shitty Viking as he began to zigzag between trees, screaming profanities.

Ignoring all the incredulous looks now pointed my way, I turned back to the others.

'Okay. Let's, uh... go save the world, or whatever.'

They cheered and set off after Frankie — all except for Espinosa and Mr G, that was, who simply fell in line next to me — which, if I'm honest, I was fine with. Because, you know — "human shields". Like Pokémon, you can never have too many.

Heads lowered and weapons bared, we chased them up the rise towards the top.

And our destinies.

***

So we ran. Up the ever steepening rise, chests heaving, thighs burning. Snow whipped constantly around us, bending the trees fleeting past as we ran, making an already hellish journey even worse.

I thought about escalators. Nobody ever appreciates escalators when they're in abundance. They're just those shiny things they have down at the mall that you're still ninety per cent sure won't kill you when the time comes to get off them, but that you get on anyway because the only thing that outweighs your fear of death-by-escalator-treads is your sheer, unashamed laziness. Even if there was a ten per cent chance I'd be sucked down into its gears like a fucking hotdog down a garbage disposal, saving the world shouldn't be this exhausting.

We pressed on, hearts pounding, lungs burning in our chests, until, after a mammoth effort, we finally reached the top.

I spotted Frankie kneeling behind an outcropping of jagged rock and quickly joined him.

'Anything?' I said, having to shout to be heard over the wind.

He nodded over the rock. 'See for yourself.'

I peeked over the top.

It was some small clearing, about the size of a football field, set inside a natural depression in the "mountain's" peak. Large outcroppings of sharp-looking rock and stone stood on all sides, providing at least meagre protection from the storm, giving it an *enclosed* feel. Several of what looked like industrial-scale digging and construction equipment lay scattered around and abandoned, snow accumulating on them like rust. A small army of floodlights, positioned in a rough half-circle near the back, shaking wildly in the wind.

I'll admit, it was a lot less sinister a gathering than I was expecting. No occult symbols or sacrificial plinths. No men in robes uttering murmured chants to each other. I didn't know what opening a door into another dimension was supposed to look like, but I had the feeling this wasn't it.

Banners. Balloons. People in suits and gowns — presumably Phonies — holding glasses of some unknown substance that I'd like to have said was blood, but that was really probably just wine. A large, round structure stood positioned at the space's far end, made of thick stone and covered in more of those hieroglyphs like the rock-thing had had — what may or may not have been a Stargate, but for legal reasons we'll just say wasn't. Sure looked like one, though. Among the cluster I spotted more of those weird-looking garbage men who had jumped us back over at Speedy's, standing around and doing nothing, faces still, unfortunately, like that of a badly drawn child's painting.

I scoffed.

Guess if you can't beat 'em, join 'em...

Laughing. Cheering. Fucking *high-fives*.

And not a single guard in sight.

'This is not what I was expecting,' I said.

And it wasn't. This was the Phonies' end game; what they had been planning — presumably — from the very get-go. Whilst I knew from experience that the O'tsaris were an arrogant bunch, I found it hard to believe they would be so nonchalant as to attempt to perform a dimension-bridging ceremony without so much as a single guard present. I mean, even for multi-dimensional brain-parasites, that was just tempting fate, wasn't it?

Frankie shook his head. 'Yeah. I don't like this, Dan. Something's not right.'

We waddled back down the rocks towards the others.

I turned to Havisham, stood waiting beside a handful of his men whilst the others ventured forth to go get into position or whatever.

'No good. Something's wrong.'

I explained to him about the whole "no guards" situation.

Before I could finish, he suddenly raised his hand to his ear.

'*Do you have eyes on the target, over?*' A moment of silence, then. 'Roger. That's a go. Let's hit these fuckers hard and fast before they know what hit them.'

I blinked. 'Wait — didn't you hear what I just said? *Something's not right*. We have to rethink this thing.'

Whether he heard me or not, I'm not sure.

Whichever the case, he strode past me in that dick-way people in authority always do, chest pushed out and one hand raised in the air, no doubt giving a signal to the others.

From beside me, Espinosa shook her head. She looked very cold, and mad, but mostly just cold. '*Idiot*. He's going to get them all killed.'

I leaned towards Frankie, hand cupped around one side of my mouth. 'Should we, like, stop him or whatever?'

He shrugged. 'Hell if I know — besides, I'm way too drunk to be making decisions right now.'

We followed them back up to the lip of the depression, where we waited for the black-clad soldiers to manoeuvre themselves into position.

I looked back towards the party.

I still couldn't see any guards. Just more party-goers, laughing and talking excitedly with one another.

The soldiers started to make their way down.

It was then, watching from the relative safety of our impromptu hiding place, that I first saw it – movement, from the tops of the jagged rocks circling the enclosure.

I must have been making a face, because Frankie suddenly turned to me, frowning. *'What? What's wrong?'*

I squinted and leaned forward, unsure of what I'd just seen – if, that was, I'd even seen anything at all. It was snowing pretty hard, after all. And it wasn't like I had the greatest –

The shape suddenly moved again.

Then before I knew it, I was on my feet, leaping over the rock and sprinting towards the hundred or so men currently making their way down, arms held high over my head and waving back and forth like a man attempting to flag down a taxi.

Somewhere far away I heard voices shouting my name, pleading at me to stop, to come back.

I barely heard them.

'WAIT! STOP! DON'T GO! IT'S A TRAP! DON'T –!'

The shapes creeping along the rocks began to move.

To the soldiers' credit, they were quick to react – even if, granted, it was still already too late.

The soldiers descended on the party, guns drawn, voices shouting a barrage of orders; a black swarm, like a small army of large, heavily armed ants.

The party-goers all turned to look at them, but didn't move. Just stared at them, the faintest of smiles lighting up the corners of their mouths like they were nothing more than amused by the sudden gate-crashing of their happy little shindig.

One of the soldiers stepped forward, gun rammed tight against one buff shoulder —

And that was when they struck.

They came in a frenzied wave, swooping down from the enclosure's rocky sides before quickly swarming the soldiers like piranhas at a bleeding piglet; dozens of malformed, winged creatures, each about the size of a large dog, with huge, reptilian eyes and little black, furry bodies, hidden mostly — and for reasons I am still unable to explain — beneath what looked to be studded, leather gimp-suits.

Yeah — I know. Tell me about it.

The sound of panicked gunfire filled the air as the soldiers desperately attempted to defend themselves, punctuated every few moments by screams of pain and surprise as the little winged creatures quickly went to town on them, biting, clawing, scratching, picking some of the soldiers up before letting them fall back to Earth with a meaty *splat* I could feel in my very soul.

It was all over in the blink of an eye.

The remaining soldiers, acknowledging their situation, quickly threw down their weapons and raised their hands over their heads in what was the universal gesture of surrender.

The winged Gimp-beasts promptly encircled them, snapping their little jaws as fresh blood dripped from the fabric of their nipple tassels.

I stood there, watching from across the clearing, unable to move — hell, or even *breathe* — shit pooling once more in my pants, until —

Something cold and hard pressed into the back of my neck.

I gasped and went instantly rigid, my own hands suddenly in the air, as a woman's voice hissed, '*Kingslayer...*' directly into my ear canal.

I risked a look back over my shoulder.

It was indeed a woman. Dark-haired. Tall. A mole on one cheek I thought was called a beauty-spot, though probably wasn't. Eyes as white as the snow currently beating down all around us.

I swallowed.

Oh, great job, Dan. Seriously, great stealth work there.

She led me over at gunpoint towards where the remaining soldiers all stood cowering, the two of us having to tiptoe our way over a carpet of mutilated bodies and what looked to be a river of quickly accumulating blood, steam rising off it like a mirage.

I fell in line and tried to keep my eyes off all the viscera at my feet.

It's okay. Don't panic. They might have captured you. But Frankie and the others are still out there. We can still —

'Hi, Dan!'

I looked back over my shoulder as Frankie and the others suddenly appeared behind me, surrounded by yet more glowing-eyed, heavily armed party-goers.

I groaned.

Well. Guess that's us fucked. At least nobody can say we didn't try.

Frankie came and stood next to me, looking his usual unperturbed self.

He looked the Gimp-beasts over, his eyes eventually settling on their nipple tassels. 'Are those — ?'

'Yes,' I said. 'Yes, they are.'

There was a murmuring from somewhere on the crowd's other side.

A familiar woman's voice shouted, '*Step aside!*'

I let out a groan.

Boot.

'Well, hello again, Kingslayer!' she cried, emerging suddenly through the crowd like a game-show host through a curtain. 'Fancy seeing you here!'

She looked different from the last time we had met. She was still wearing the same Korn hoodie, true, and her hair was still that stupid, tousled style it had been the last time our paths had crossed. Same baggy jeans, too. But there was something... *different* about her.

For no reason I could pinpoint, I thought she looked even more insane.

I sighed. 'Hello, Boot.'

'Have you come to witness Mother's grand arrival? Because if so, you're just in time.'

I looked over her shoulder at the Not-Stargate. 'Where's Gizmo — I mean, the Novamite? What have you done with him?'

'See for yourself — *boys!*'

The crowd suddenly parted.

It was then that I saw it.

They came out from behind a stack of large, copper tubing; more Faceless Men, dressed in high-vis construction overalls and pushing what looked to be some kind of large, steel coffin between them, like the ones hospitals use for patients with breathing difficulties — iron lungs, I thought they were called. Thick, coiled cabling trailed off it like tentacles, leading off to some place further back I couldn't see. In the side of the steel coffin was a large, round window, like a porthole.

Frankie gasped.

'*Gizmo!*'

He was strapped down to the inside of the coffin, a combination of different wires and cables poking out of him from a myriad of different and unthinkable places. Plugs in his mouth, his belly-button.

Other places. Thick and exotic-looking cables ran down from his ears and into some kind of conduit in the coffin's side.

Jesus, look at him. They've turned him into a goddamn pincushion.

At the sound of his name, Gizmo slowly turned his head. His eyes were half-lidded, his little monkey face ashen and pale. He looked awful. I was amazed he was still alive.

He placed a small paw on the glass.

Even though we had never gotten along, I couldn't deny I felt bad for the little guy. Even if he *was* the "destroyer of worlds" the others claimed him to be, he didn't deserve this. Hell, nobody did.

They wheeled him over towards the Not-Stargate, where they immediately began hooking him up to what looked like your normal, everyday portable generator.

Almost immediately, the hieroglyphs on the Not-Stargate began to flicker.

And then, just like that, I understood.

They're sucking the life out of him. Like a battery. Using his life-energy to power up whatever the fuck that *thing is.*

Boot paced in front of the Not-Stargate, her eyes alight — and not in the usual, alien way.

'This is it,' she said, staring enrapt at it. 'The moment we have waited countless millennia for.' I noticed she looked even more insane.

She turned back to me. *'Watch, Kingslayer. Watch the beginning of your planet's destruction!'*

Before I could say or do anything, she turned back to the steel coffin and nodded.

The man at the generator hit a switch.

What happened next is still fuzzy in my memory, for reasons that will become apparent shortly.

There was a blinding flash of light. A deafening *crack* of electricity — so loud it felt like my entire head was splitting in two.

In the millisecond interim before the doorway opened I had time to think of those old test-clips they're always showing on documentaries of those early nuclear bomb-tests, the way the trees would bend backwards with the force of the blast before them and everything else unlucky enough to be caught in its vicinity got levelled to ash — because that's what it felt like.

With a sound like the world's largest telephone book being ripped in half, the doorway between our two dimensions tore open.

The force of it pushed us to the ground, sent us spiralling backwards, humans and non-humans alike.

When it was over, I looked up.

Whereas before, the similarities to a Stargate had been obvious and plentiful, here they ended as abruptly as a swan-dive onto a concrete sidewalk.

Instead of the shimmering wall of white I'd been expecting, inside the circle was a black hole. Just completely black — so awfully, terribly black it was almost painful to look at. It was the absence of light. All the universe's dark matter concentrated into one, eight-by-eight-foot space.

I turned my gaze away, unable to bear it any longer.

'HA-HA-HA-HA-HA!' cried a voice from somewhere up ahead of me.

I shifted my gaze.

Boot.

She was on her feet again, arms splayed, face pointed at the Not-Stargate, a look of absolute fucking insanity playing across it. Eyes so impossibly wide I was amazed they didn't simply up and fall right out of her head.

'BEHOLD! SHE OF MANY NAMES! THE MOTHER! THE R'IN! BELOVED KICKER OF ORPHANS!' She dropped to her knees in the snow, arms splayed. 'COME FORTH — NIDRETH!'

The black wall of nothingness danced and shimmered and twitched as something on the other side began to make its way through — a black canopy, pawed at from the opposite side by reaching hands.

A hand emerged.

Then a foot.

A leg.

The ripple-murmur of excitement from the non-humans around us ceased, as suddenly as hitting mute on a TV set. They all turned and looked at each other, Phonies and Gimp-beasts and Faceless Men alike, united in this moment through a mutual sense of utter confusion and bafflement.

Boot blinked, face now pinched tight, eyes squinted almost comically. 'But... I don't — *this isn't right*. This isn't what's supposed to happen. You're not —'

I followed my gaze back over to where she was looking.

I gasped.

Bear!

Now, in the interest of clarity, I should clarify the thing I was looking at was not a bear — at least, not in the usual sense of the term.

Big. Stocky. Maybe nine feet tall. Thick dark fur covered its body almost in its entirety, save for a small patch on its chest, where a cluster-fuck of what looked like inch-long nipples stood hard and erect in the freezing wind. Paws like shovels, long claws sticking out of them, looking like something out of the fucking cretaceous period. But really, it was the bear part that caught my attention.

It leaned back on its hind legs and clacked its jaws, being overly bear-like, and sending a fresh bout of fear-shit shooting out the back of me.

Then, just as I was beginning to think things couldn't possibly get any worse, from over its shoulder I saw something else beginning to make its way through the Not-Stargate.

I gasped again.

Two bears!

Wait—no. Not a bear. It was too small, for one thing. And pink. Just some kind of amorphous *blob*-thing, actually, like a giant, pulsating booger.

Other things were beginning to flood through the Not-Stargate now. Strange, awful things, things that defied description on account of how utterly strange and awful they were.

I'm not sure who fired first, or which particular strange and awful thing they were firing at. All I know is, it was like a starting pistol.

The hell-creatures charged us—humans and Phonies alike.

That was when everything went to shit.

FOURTEEN

GUNFIRE. SCREAMING. THE WHIP-splash of sprayed blood and tissue as pieces of people and creatures who were not people became spontaneously detached from said persons'/creatures' bodies.

It was like one of those scenes they always have in war movies where the poor soldiers are forced to charge right into the thick of it, even though that's probably a great way to get shot to death by Nazis. There's always explosions and gunfire, and at least one guy lying on the beach with his legs blown off, crying for his mommy or a fucking medic or whatever as the life quickly drains out of him like a hole punched in the side of a juice box. I mean, true, nobody was shooting at me, and I couldn't see any Nazis (at least, not yet).

But it was still very scary.

I stood there, frozen on the snow, unable to do anything but watch in horrid fascination as everything suddenly went to hell around me. Soldiers opened fire on Phonies as Phonies whipped their mouth-tentacles at other creatures, who in turn then clawed/stabbed/bit at the soldiers. It was a cyclical sort of affair, really.

A creature with long, spindly legs like a spider, only made out of what looked like bone, pounced on a soldier a few feet away from me, bone-legs punching holes in him with the frantic energy of a pneumatic drill.

I locked eyes with another creature through the chaos; this one tall, dressed in a black, tattered robe, with what looked to be — I shit you not — *two* faces on its head. Then it got closer and I saw that it was indeed two faces, though neither of which looked like his. They were like masks. Poor, shoddy masks, still pouring with blood. Seriously, I don't know who he thought he was fooling, but it wasn't very convincing.

He charged me.

I'd like to tell you this is the part where I suddenly snapped out of my paralysis, where I summoned all my gusto and performed some tasty-ass kung fu and kicked his dick off or whatever — but I didn't. I just stood there instead, completely motionless, snow collecting in my hair like dandruff.

The shaggy-looking face-burglar bore down on me, dagger-fingers raised high in the air, screaming like a man having just caught his testicles in a car door. Oh yeah, he had dagger-fingers too — did I mention that? Go figure.

He drew back his hands, now only feet away, still shrieking that god-awful sound —

VROOM.

There was a sudden flash of something hard and glowing right in front of my eyes.

Face-burglar stopped charging me.

He looked down at the ground instead.

I followed his gaze, turning just in time to witness Face-burglar's hands flop to the deck, dagger-fingers still extended and reaching for my neck.

For some reason I found this very confusing.

I blinked.

What the – ?

'HA-HA! YOU LIKE THAT, HMM?' cried a voice from directly beside me.

I turned.

Frankie.

He spun the futuristic battle-axe, the blade whish-whooshing in the air directly in front of him and nearly cutting his own goddamn head off. 'CONSIDER YOUSELF *HANDI*CAPPED, BITCH!'

I grabbed his arm. '*Come on!*'

I dragged him over behind another stack of copper tubing and bent low.

I peeked over the top.

It was fucking pandemonium out there. God, all those severed limbs. Like an explosion at a mannequin factory. All the while, creatures both big and small – and in increasingly disgusting variety – continued to pour out of the Not-Stargate by the dozen.

I leaned back around. 'We have to turn that machine off!'

Frankie nodded. 'I hear you. Let me just go clear you a path –'

I grabbed his arm again.

'*Would you quit with the Rambo shit already?* This is serious. How the hell are we going to get over there?'

He thought it over a moment. 'You're right, Dan. We're gonna need help on this one.' Before I knew what he was doing, he suddenly jumped to his feet. 'YO, G-MAN! SPARE A SECOND?'

I looked over to where he was shouting, saw Mr G battling with a multi-legged creature comprised of what looked to be human feet. Seriously, just feet everywhere.

'I'M A LITTLE BUSY RIGHT NOW!' he cried.

Frankie turned back to me. 'He says he's busy.' He thought about it. 'Also, that he hates you. I think it's a race-thing.'

I looked through the crowd for Espinosa. I couldn't see her. I wondered if she was dead—also, if anybody would notice if Frankie and I suddenly just went home, if we simply said *no thanks* to all this crazy bullshit and got our pale yet perfectly formed asses the hell out of there. Because that's what I felt like doing.

But then, if we left now, Boot and her gang would bring Nidreth or Yithyla or whatever the hell her name was through. Then Earth—and everybody on it—would be destroyed.

Whether I liked it or not, now might be our one and only chance to stop that from happening.

Fuck it.

'Cover me!'

I leapt up from the behind the stack of tubing, not really sure what I was doing but doing it anyway.

I ran. Frankie at my side, swinging the battle-axe that may or may not have been from the future in a fashion that would have been irresponsible had we not been hoping to cause as much bodily harm as possible. Random muzzle-flashes punctuated the night, bright and dazzling, even under the glare from the floodlights. Men screaming. Creatures hissing and shrieking and, in some cases, cursing.

We dodged thrashing limbs and tentacles and made a beeline for the generator, Frankie screaming gallantly as he swung the battle-axe around, drawing more attention than anything else.

I went to jump over a torso—

I slipped on the bloody sludge and went down face-first, burying my head straight up a dead soldier's ass.

I frantically pushed myself up —

A naked, cackling man ran past my field of vision, flaccid penis slapping furiously against his thighs.

Christ, war is hell.

'Dan!'

I shot a look back over my shoulder, saw Frankie wrestling with one of the Gimp-beasts, which had bitten onto the battle-axe's handle and was subsequently refusing to let go — and in general just being a total dick.

I made to go to them, but Frankie shook his head.

'No! Just turn it off! We're running out of time!'

'But — *what about you?'* I cried.

'I'll be fine! Just go! Hurry!' He turned his attention back to the Gimp-beast. *'All right, dick-bag — prepare to learn what your own junk tastes like!'*

I decided he would be fine.

Spinning on the spot, I continued on towards the generator, more gunfire popping all around me.

I finally reached it, yanked the lever —

Nothing.

It wouldn't budge.

I tried again.

Still nothing. It was like it had fused in place, or something.

Sudden noise from my right caused me to turn around.

Two Faceless Men, sprinting towards my position, faces, still, like poorly forged Picasso paintings.

I froze, remembering suddenly how vulnerable and exposed I was — even more so since Frankie had become indisposed. Hell, I didn't even have a weapon—which, looking back now, just seemed like one hell of an oversight.

Are you sure you don't have a weapon, Dan? Think hard now.

I blinked as the obvious occurred to me.

Hands pawing at my jacket, I pulled out Mr G's faux pistol.

I pointed it at one of the men and squeezed my finger in the place where the trigger would have been, not really expecting it to work —

And it didn't.

So that was fucking disappointing.

Then I remembered.

The magic words! You didn't say the magic words, asshole!

I raised it again.

'*Pew?*'

The man on the left immediately hit the dirt, gripping his balls and wailing.

Huh.

I turned on the other faceless fuck-bag.

'*Pew-pew-pew!*'

He flopped face-first onto the snow.

I stared down at the little pistol in my hand, amazed.

Well I'll be a sonofabitch…

'*Dan!*' cried Frankie.

Oh – right.

I turned back to the console, wondering if I should try shooting at it instead—

Something small and hard suddenly crashed into me, taking me off my feet and spilling me over onto the snow. The "gun" in my hand went flying up into the air.

Winded, I looked up.

I groaned.

236

It was Boot.

'*This is all your fault!*' she cried, her words barely audible through all the tentacles fighting for space in her mouth.

I blinked. '*What?* My *fault?*'

That just felt a little unfair.

'*This wasn't supposed to happen!*' she went on, hands at my throat, nails digging at my Adam's apple like she wanted to tear the fucking thing clean off—which she probably did. '*SHE was meant to come through!*'

I gasped as I was suddenly lifted off the snow.

'THIS IS ALL YOUR FAULT, KINGSLAYER!'

She began to carry me backwards, my shoes brushing the frozen ground as I fought to breathe.

Lights appeared in my vision, like a thousand exploding suns. It occurred to me I was about to pass out.

Then I realised where it was she was taking me, and—

Reality snapped suddenly back into view.

I stiffened.

The Not-Stargate! She's taking you towards the Not-Stargate, Dan!

I tried to speak, to plead. I didn't want to go through the Not-Stargate—for reasons I should not have to elaborate on at this point, and not just because that was where all the monsters came from.

She dragged me towards the wall of blackness.

So close, now. So close I could feel the *pull* of it, the bad gravity, attempting to suck me in and gobble me up whole like some hungry giant.

'Wait—!'

Sudden darkness enveloped me as my head was shoved suddenly through the doorway.

And then I saw... *things*. Awful, indescribable things, things I still dream about to this very day, the things that fuel my nightmares.

It was only for a second, but felt like much longer.

Then before I knew it I was being pulled back through the Not-Stargate, squinting against sudden, dazzling light in my face.

I blinked. I was very confused.

Then I heard a scream, and turned, realising the second my eyes fell on them why I was no longer being fed headfirst into Hell.

The Not-bear reared back on its hind legs, still with a clump of Boot's arm in its mouth. Seriously, I could see digits and everything.

The bear! The bear saved you!

Whether or not this was the case, I wasn't sure. I still wasn't going to be friends with it, though.

From the snow a few yards away, Boot glared furiously. '*You dick! You're supposed to kill* him!'

The bear turned to look at me.

The two of us locked eyes.

And then something passed between us. Some knowledge, of mutual respect and appreciation. The acknowledgement of one majestic beast towards another — or, you know, so I was *guessing*.

Ordinarily this is the part where it would descend upon me like fat kid on a Tootsie Roll, tear my body to ribbons like Hulk Hogan with a telephone book before shoving me hard and deep into its gullet.

Instead, it gave a subtle nod, before quickly turning and waddling off in the opposite direction, furry ass wagging in the snow.

I didn't wait around.

Seizing the opportunity, I sprinted over to where Boot lay spread-eagled on the snow and kicked her directly in the crotch.

Look, I'm not proud of it, okay? It's not like I *wanted* to kick her in the vagina or anything. But if we ever want true equality, these are the sorts of sacrifices that are going to have to be made. And besides, she may have just ended the world. She kind of deserved it.

Boot cried, 'OOF!' and rolled over on the snow, pawing at her lady parts with her one remaining arm.

She glared round at me. 'SERIOUSLY?!'

I grabbed her foot.

'Wait – what are you doing?'

I began to drag her towards the Not-Stargate. 'You want to meet your queen so bad?'

Her eyes quit glowing as it suddenly dawned on her exactly what it was I was about to do.

She thrashed.

'No – you can't! You mustn't! I am the King – !'

I snatched her up by the hood of her Korn hoodie, pulling her to her feet.

I spun her around.

'THEN GO BE WITH HER!'

I pushed her through the doorway.

Boot screamed, tentacles flying out to whip at me, but it was too late. She reached out with her one remaining arm, trying to grab something, anything, to keep from going through.

Then the darkness swallowed her, her scream cutting off instantly like a stereo after a power-cut.

Not waiting for a moment, I turned back to the crowd – who I noticed had all now stopped fighting and were staring at me, open-mouthed (or its equivalent), at the unthinkable thing I had just done to their kin – and, as in many cases, their leader.

'Frankie!'

But he was already on the move.

With a cry far more dramatic than was realistically necessary, he raised the battle-axe up high.

And then, as everybody standing atop Devil's Spire watched, he brought it down on the console upon which the lever resided.

There was a flash of light and shriek of metal as the futuristic battle-axe sunk through it, sparks flying fucking everywhere and reminding me, for some reason, of fireworks.

The hieroglyphs on the Not-Stargate went suddenly dark.

The high-pitched *whirring* from whichever machine currently powering it quickly faded.

I turned my attention back towards the black hole.

In the short few seconds before the thing blinked out of existence, I thought I saw rippling across its surface—like someone trying desperately to get through from the other side. An impression of hands—or, should I say, *a* hand—pawing at it, frantically trying to break back through.

Then, with a *snap* like a rubber band breaking—

The black hole vanished.

I turned back to the crowd.

Almost immediately, the remaining creatures began to disperse—Phonies and abominations alike—fleeing into the snowstorm. I didn't go after them. I know I probably should have. But what do you want me to say? I was exhausted.

I stepped back over to the others.

'Well,' I said, brushing down my jacket with my hands. 'Guess that's over.'

Mr G nodded. He looked like hell. There were blood-flecks all over his trench coat, and his hair was a mess. He also had what looked like footprints on his face for some reason. So that was weird.

'We did it. We won—*you* won, Kingslayer.'

'Yeah,' I said. I rocked.

From somewhere behind us, a woman's voice suddenly shouted, '*Umm — a little help here, please?*'

I stiffened.

Espinosa. Shit.

We hurried over to where she lay on the snow, pinned beneath one of the Gimp-beasts and looking very, very unhappy about it. Like Mr G, she was also covered in blood.

We freed her and pulled her to her feet.

'Are you okay?' asked Mr G.

She shot him a look like that was about the most stupid thing she'd ever heard, then sighed. 'Guess I'll live.' She turned towards me. '*Is it over? Did we win?*'

I nodded.

She scoffed. 'Well — I'll be damned.' She looked around at all the dead bodies littering the ground. 'Not sure how I'm going to explain this to my superiors, though...'

I frowned as a thought occurred to me.

'Hey, where's Frankie?'

It was then I heard it — a scratching, like metal on metal, coming from somewhere back over by the Not-Stargate.

I turned that way.

Frankie. At the iron lung-thing.

Gizmo!

Feet dancing over sprawled bodies and limbs, we hurried over to where he was standing, fingers pawing frantically at the lid.

'*Help me!*' he cried.

I grabbed the other end and heaved, but it was no good. My fingers were frozen, and the thing was locked down tight. No way we were getting it open.

From beside me, Mr G said, 'Get out of the way!' and gripped the lid in both hands.

The steel coffin-lid came away with an ungodly shriek, flying up into the air and vanishing into the wind.

Immediately, Frankie reached into the coffin, began pulling at plugs and bits of wiring as he fought desperately to free the little guy from his restraints.

He took Gizmo in his arms, cradling him like a baby, using his jacket to shield him from the wind and snow.

The little guy looked awful. Face all waxy and pale. He could barely keep his eyes open.

Frankie frowned. 'He's so cold.'

Mr G nodded. 'He's been drained of his life force. His essence. It's a miracle he's still alive.'

'*So what do we do? How do we save him?*'

Mr G hesitated.

I knew what he was thinking. Even though it wasn't his fault, Gizmo was a liability. As long as he was alive, there would be people trying to seek him out, to gain his power. And as long as that was the case, the people of Earth would never be safe. A wildcard if ever there was one.

Frankie shook his head. 'Uh-uh. No way. We're not just letting him *die*. The fuck's wrong with you?'

'I'm sorry,' said Mr G. 'I wish there was some other way.'

I looked up suddenly as a thought occurred to me.

'Actually, guys... I think I might have an idea.'

FIFTEEN

THEY MET US AT the turn-off, a good few hours later—a couple dozen of them, all dressed in matching fur coats and bobble-hats.

It was still snowing pretty hard by this point, though not nearly as hard as it had been—which was a good thing really, as we probably wouldn't have been able to make the journey at all, had the opposite been true.

We stepped out of the Impala and into the raging wind, Frankie still cradling Gizmo in his arms like a baby, having refused to let anybody else hold him the entire car journey. I'm not sure whether he thought we might suddenly throw him out the car window or something, or if he was simply savouring what little time he had left with the guy. Either way, he was not letting that little dude go for anything.

As we approached, one of the men stepped forward from the crowd. It was Nut-sack Face. On his shoulder sat a windswept A'doy, looking, unfortunately, the exact same amount of rabbit as the last time I'd seen him.

It had taken a lot of talking-around before he'd finally agreed to take Gizmo off of our hands. Mostly, I knew, because of their whole hands-off approach with regards to anything even slightly mankind-related. But after I had made the point that, had we *failed*, him and his little town would have been destroyed too, he had eventually come around to the opinion that he at the very least owed me one—a debt I was collecting now.

We shared a brief nod, before he turned his attention to Mr G.

'You have the Naoggrath?'

Mr G nodded. 'That's right.'

There was something pissy about the way he said it. It surprised me; I'd never heard him talk that way before. I mean, not to anyone *else*, anyway. But then, they *had* shunned him from the community, so I supposed that was about right.

'Bring it to me.'

Frankie went to step forward, but Mr G put out a hand.

'First I want your word. Your promise that you'll take good care of—' he cast a quick glance at the little bundle of fur poking out of Frankie's jacket, '—of *Gizmo*.'

A short pause.

A'doy nodded.

'Well. All right.'

Frankie carried Gizmo over to Nut-sack Face, shoulders hunched against the wind, me following closely behind.

Reluctantly, he handed him over.

'So long, little guy,' he said, his voice husky. 'Be seeing you.'

He sniffled and wiped his nose.

I turned back to A'doy. 'So. Guess you were right about that whole "chosen one" thing, after all.'

This was something I had thought about a lot during the drive over here. I mean, not to blow my own horn or anything, but I was basically like a superhero now. Like Superman, only less closest-homosexual and paraplegic. Batman, perhaps. I wondered if I should wear a cape from now on, if they were hard to make, and what exactly the charge for dry-cleaning on something like that was. It's important to always have clean clothes when you're famous.

A'doy and Nut-sack Face shared a glance.

A'doy cleared his throat. 'Actually, we, uh, may have exaggerated a little on that part...'

I stared at him. 'What do you mean, "exaggerated"?'

'I mean we made it up. All of it. We needed somebody to go stop Boot and her gang from opening a doorway into the Neverwas, so...'

I blinked. I couldn't believe what I was hearing.

'So, wait—I'm *not* the chosen one?'

And after I'd already decided on an outfit, too. Sonofabitch.

'Yeah. That's our bad.' He sighed and turned back to Nut-sack Face. '*Shall we?*'

And so off they went, waddling back down the road-that-wasn't-really-a-road — a gangbang of mutants and monsters and aliens — snow billowing down all around them in a fashion that would have been pretty fucking epic, had I not just found out I'd been essentially used as a pawn by a talking, sociopathic bunny rabbit.

Touché, you little furry asshole. Touché.

I turned back to Frankie. 'Come on. Let's get the hell out of here.'

SIXTEEN

IT WAS MORNING BY the time we finally made it back to the apartment.

My body feeling like several stacked grand pianos, we fell through the door, the two of us immediately making a slow, shuffling beeline for the couch.

We slumped into it with a mutual sigh, then simply sat there a while, staring at the blank television set, both wanting to turn it on but not having the energy, me wondering if I willed it hard enough it might simply turn itself on or whatever. I thought that would have been pretty neat.

'So,' said Frankie.

I nodded. 'So.'

'Saved the world again. Starting to become kind of a regular thing now, huh?'

'No, it isn't,' I said.

He chuckled to himself. 'Yeah—but seriously, you should consider going legit. You know, like on the books? You never know; you might even get paid next time.'

"Next time." You sonofabitch.

I looked over at the window. It had stopped snowing by this point, the sky now, for the most part, clear—which I thought was about right, given my track record with luck so far.

I turned back to Frankie. 'Listen, I need you to promise me something.'

A concerned look from Frankie. 'Sure, Dan. We're best friends. Just name it.'

'I need you to promise me you will not mention a word of this to Abby.'

'Eat a dick.'

'Frankie—'

'No way, Dan! I can't lie to Abby—*are you nuts*? Have you any idea what she'd do to me if she ever found out? She'd *castrate* me, Dan— and I don't mean like she'd "have a stern talking with me", or whatever. I mean she'd *literally* kick my dick into fucking scrambled egg.'

'That's... probably an exaggeration.'

He shook his head. 'Forget it, Dan. I'm not going to—'

He was interrupted from his raving by the sudden sound of a door slamming.

We both pounced to our feet, expecting more bad-guys—these ones perhaps with even *bigger, grosser* nipples—

It wasn't bad-guys.

'*What the hell is going on here?!*' said Abby, appearing suddenly into the room like an apparition, her little suitcase-thing dragging lifelessly behind her like the stiff, unmoving corpse of a vanquished enemy — which, to be honest, wouldn't have surprised me at all.

I stiffened. 'Oh, Abby! Hey!'

'Don't *hey* me — *why's the apartment trashed? And why are you both so dirty?*'

'Well —'

'*And is that blood?*' she said, pointing at my pants, which I noticed now for the first time were practically coated in the stuff.

I looked to where she was gesturing. 'What — *this*? Ha-ha. No, that's just...'

Oil? Tar? Paint? Quick — tell her it's paint, Dan!

'...ketchup.'

Balls.

'Ketchup?'

'Uh-huh.' I elbowed Frankie. 'Isn't that right?'

Abby swung her gaze around to look at him.

Frankie looked frantically back and forth between us, face pale and pleading, looking like a kid having just been asked by his soon-to-be-divorced parents which one of them he likes better.

He lasted exactly three seconds.

With a child-like cry, he collapsed to his knees on the carpet, hands clasped firmly over his balls, face drenched in an instant.

'*It was all Dan's idea!*' he cried, before curling up into the foetal position on the carpet, face in his hands and weeping hysterically, now a broken shell of a man.

I glared down at him.

Judas.

'Well?' said Abby.

So I told her about everything that had happened. About Lake Fairburn and the Men in Black. About Gizmo and Boot — and, *yes*, even

A'doy, the mischievous, talking bunny rabbit, who I was pretty sure now was actually a real, bona fide evil genius.

When I was finished, Abby stared at me. *'You punched a bear to death?'*

Okay, so I *may* have exaggerated a little on the details — *whatever.*

I shrugged. 'More or less...'

'That's the most retarded thing I've ever heard.'

I nodded. 'Imagine how the bear feels.' I frowned. 'But — wait. What are you doing back? I thought your dad was, well — you know.'

There was a moment's weighty pause.

Oh, no.

Abby didn't cry often — a byproduct of being a lethal killing machine, I supposed — but when she did, it was almost always a whole thing. It had long ago been established that, despite her kick-ass demeanour, Abby was in a lot of ways like an onion. She had *layers.* And at least one of these layers, if picked at hard enough, would result in tears.

She fell into my arms — a trembling mass of blonde hair — sobbing into the collar of my jacket, me feeling like an asshole, and not sure why.

Exactly how long we stayed like that, I'm not sure. Long enough for me to get soaked, put it that way.

The morning rolled onward.

INTERLUDE—PART 4

'BUT—*WAIT,*' SAID LAKE, leaning across the table towards me. His eyes were wild and staring, his brow creased furiously. He looked like a man battling a math puzzle he knew he'd never solve, but who continued to battle it anyway, because it simply wasn't in his nature to give up. So that was probably very noble. *'What happened then?'*

I blinked. *'Then?'*

'What happened to all the—' he swallowed, '—"*monsters*"? The ones that came out of the doorway? Where did they all go?'

'I don't know.'

I mean, what was I, the fucking *monster police*?

'You don't know? A small army of Hell-demons floods through onto our plane of existence—*and you just let them go*?!'

He was getting pretty loud now, his voice a little below a shriek.

Throughout the course of our conversation he'd grown more and more invested, urging me on whenever I slowed down or tried to take a break or whatever. In the beginning I'd assumed it had been some sort of therapy tactic; some throw-him-in-the-deep-end manoeuvre I was unfamiliar with, because I wasn't a psychiatrist.

Now I wasn't so sure.

'Well, I—'

He pounced to his feet, thrusting an accusatory finger across the table. '*Have you any idea how irresponsible that was?!*'

I stared. I mean, *sure*, I guessed he had a point.

I held up my hands. 'Doctor, if you'll just calm down, I—'

'They could be anywhere...' he said, his eyes scanning the corners, head whipping left and right in almost comical fashion. 'Right now — *right at this very moment!*'

He had his fingers in his hair now, running them back and forth across his scalp in a fashion that in no small way reminded me of a crazy person — an observation that, despite the sudden nose-dive my therapy session had apparently just taken, I still took time to find more than a little ironic.

'*I — I have to get out of here!*'

He began shedding clothes.

He whipped off his tie and shirt, before letting both drop to the ground with a muted ruffle.

Then came his pants.

I threw my hands in front of my face. '*Dude!*'

'*Quick — run, Daniel!*'

He barrel-rolled over his desk, dick and balls flapping all over the damn place, then sprinted to the door, his smooth, hairless ass the last thing I saw before he vanished down the hall, a pale, shrieking blur.

Somewhere not too far away I heard the sound of a door opening, then closing.

I waited until I could no longer hear the sound of his panicked screaming. Then, with a long sigh, I slowly pushed myself up from my chair and went home.

EPILOGUE

'SO HOW DID YOUR first therapy session go?' said Frankie.

It was the morning after my meeting with Dr Lake. We were sitting on the couch, watching an old *Little House on the Prairie* rerun. A half-circle of refrigerated pizza sat on the coffee table before us, so old it probably still remembered what Jesus looked like.

'I think I gave my therapist a nervous breakdown,' I said.

'Ha. Figures.' He took another bite of his pizza, pulled it out and looked at it strangely a moment, before shrugging and popping it back into his mouth. 'How's Abby doing?'

I sighed.

Abby.

Turns out her father had indeed passed away, just as presumed. There had been tears. Cursing. Lots of random and spontaneous threats of dick-punches—not that I thought she really *meant* this last, or anything. But hey, everybody has a process.

It had taken several weeks before she was able to forgive me for not "including" her in the whole "Gizmo" thing—or what I had since come to think of as Mine and Frankie's Week of Extreme Retardation. But she was coming around.

'She's okay. I mean, we still have a long way to go. But she'll get there.'

'Well. That's good.'

I nodded. It was.

I turned and looked out the window at the snow.

I had thought a lot about all that had happened during the few weeks following the whole thing in Merlot, what it might mean for Future Dan, and his anus.

So turns out I wasn't the fabled "chosen one" as A'doy and his asshole friends had so deviously misled me to believe—something I was still feeling pretty raw over, if I'm honest. I mean, *sure*, it meant less danger—which was good—but I'd always thought it would have been cool to know what owning a utility belt felt like. Now I guessed I'd never know.

As for the Phonies, I still wasn't sure what the hell those fuckers really were, if they were aliens or multi-dimensional beings or what. Although A'doy had indeed informed us of their origins back in the church-museum, considering that "other" big thing he'd lied about, it would have been foolish of me to take him at his word. That, and he was kind of a dick. So there was that to consider, too.

I turned my attention back to Frankie. 'Hey, do you want to—?'

Before I could finish, from the space just above the coffee table in front of me, a brilliant light began to form.

There was a crackle of electricity, a flash of condensed lightning, before, with a sound like a man farting loudly into a steel drum, from the air less than three feet away from our faces, a shape began to form.

Frankie and I shared a glance.

What the dick?

We turned our attention back to the sphere of light — what looked more like a wormhole, now that I looked at it — turning just in time to witness a head poke itself through.

It was the head of a man — or rather, what one might look like if run through an industrial-sized clothes-press; all long and elongated, with a big, pointed chin, whiskers poking off it either side like a cat.

'Dan Pratt!' it said, an unmistakable urgency in its voice. 'My name is U'tahlalala, and I have travelled much distance to see you. Our planet is under attack. We need your help. Only you, the Kingslayer, can rid us of —'

I turned to Frankie. 'Care to do the honours?'

'With pleasure.'

Popping the pizza slice into his mouth, he promptly leaned forward and pushed the man's head back through the hole.

'*Wait!*' said the man, googly eyes widening before, with another deafening fart-sound, both he and the hole he appeared from vanished back into the ether from whence they came.

Frankie fell back into the couch and immediately resumed munching pizza. He looked at the TV and groaned. 'Let's watch something else. This is boring — besides, I bet she's not even really blind.'

I glanced at my watch. 'Can't. Got to go get balloons for the party.'

He shrugged. 'Suit yourself.'

I began to make my way over to the door, when Frankie called after me.

'Oh, hey, get me some Pop Rocks when you're out? It's, uh... for my Grammy. Yeah, she loves Pop Rocks. She's such a slut. Seriously, it's embarrassing.'

I groaned and reached for my jacket.

***

Evening came, and it was time for the party, so I put on some clean clothes and started pretending like I wanted to be there.

This was my usual routine for parties. I walked through the apartment, one of those little plastic cups in my hand, nodding smiles to people I passed whom I only vaguely recognised, even though I didn't really want them to be there. I dodged arms and elbows. Winced at how loud the music was, because even when letting your hair down, it's still important to be considerate of the neighbours.

Through some miracle or another, I eventually found myself in the living room, which I was disheartened to discover was just as lively and bustling with people as the rest of the apartment.

People in Christmas cardigans laughed as festive-themed jokes about Santa and his sack were tossed wildly back and forth across the living room like a goddamn midget in a gangbang, yucking it up like it was about the funniest thing they'd ever heard, despite probably having heard the exact same joke — or one just like it — only the Christmas before. Other people with party blowers hanging out of their mouths like cigarettes drunkenly professed their New Year's resolutions to anyone who would hear them, despite knowing full well they had no intention whatsoever of keeping them, but who felt seemingly compelled to tell everyone just the same.

Amongst those on the couch sat a similarly cardigan-laden Frankie, a child's electric piano in his lap, that he looked to be showing to some girl from Abby's work (*Leanne? Lorraine?*), whom I only vaguely remembered because of that fucking lazy eye she had.

He tapped a ditty out on the keys, and she laughed — though I couldn't hear exactly what was played. Christ, that eye, though.

It seemed everybody was having a great time but me.

Sighing, I shot a look around for Abby —

There was a crash and a yelp as the door to the apartment suddenly flew open.

I spun around on instinct, butthole tensing reflexively like in those perilous moments right before a prostate exam, turning just in time to witness a heavily armed Chuck Norris storm his way into my apartment, guns hanging from seemingly every appendage.

'*Okay, everyone! Don't panic! I'm — !*'

His eyes fell on Frankie sitting on the couch and he gasped.

'*Frankie?!*'

Frankie turned to him. 'Oh. Hi, Chuck. What's up?'

Chuck waddled over, face a mask of concern. 'Is everything okay? I got your message, and I thought —'

Frankie laughed. 'Oh yeah — *that*. Yeah, it's cool. Dan and I took care of it.'

Chuck let out a deep sigh. His moustache quivered. 'God, I was so worried!' He collapsed into Frankie's arms, tears streaming down his face in torrents.

Frankie patted his back. 'There, there. It's okay. You're okay, big guy.'

I turned my attention back to the party, finding Abby standing by the TV with Eric — whose face I noticed, unfortunately, still resembled that of a criminally abused ham.

'Hey!' she said as I approached. 'Where'd you go? I've been looking all over for you.' I glanced over her shoulder at Eric, who waved cheerily.

Ugh.

I turned my attention back to Abby. 'Oh, you know. Just, uh...'

Yeah, Dan — where did *you go? Tell her. Tell her how you were cowering in a ball on your bed, wondering how anyone could be in a party mood, considering what's coming, how if they knew they'd probably all go throw themselves into traffic or a volcano or something –*

'*Dan?*'

Abby was looking at me strangely.

I cleared my throat. 'I'm fine. Think I'm just gonna go get some fresh air.'

I let myself out and quietly made my way up to the roof.

It was a place I'd started coming a lot, recently. In the evenings, mostly, watching the sun sink into the horizon, how it would make the sky bleed, right before it dipped out of view. I'm not sure what it was about the roof that appealed to me. The quiet, sure – but if I'm honest it was really the solitude I sought. You don't have to pretend like you're not scared to death when there's nobody around to witness you shitting your pants.

I stared out at the horizon, the sun slowly making its way down into the Earth –

'*Not enjoying the party?*' said a voice suddenly from behind me, scaring me half to death.

I recognised it at once.

Mr G.

He was standing propped against the wall by the exit, one foot resting on it like he wasn't even trying to be cool. I saw he'd gone and gotten himself a new trench coat – this one a fancy dark number, instead of the simple beige I'd grown accustomed to. I had to admit, it looked good on him. But then, what clothing didn't when you looked the equivalent of this generation's James Dean.

'How long have you been standing there?' I said.

'Long enough to know that something is bothering you, Kingslayer.' He pushed himself off the wall and stepped towards me. '*Speak.* Tell me what's on your mind.'

I thought it over a moment, before finally letting out a long sigh.

'Back at Devil's Spire,' I said. 'When Boot pushed my head through the Doorway. I saw... *things.*'

Fierce frown from G-man. Like his eyebrows were waging war on his nose. 'What did you see?'

What did I see, you ask? How about cars on fire? Buildings turned to rubble. Literal *mountains of human bones and skeletons. So high. So terribly, terribly high. And monsters, big ones and little ones, scurrying about and being monster-like, all whilst a choir of agonised screams played in the background.*

And above it all, tall as a skyscraper and blotting out the sun, "She" had loomed.

And in that brief moment as our eyes had met, I'd heard a voice in my head — a voice like glass breaking, brakes grinding, children screaming.

SOON.

I shuddered at the memory. 'I'm not sure, exactly. But... I think it was the future.'

This seemed to concern Mr G very much.

He frowned. 'The Neverwas is still very much a place of mystery — even to those of us that are from there.'

'That's not very helpful.'

'I know — I was just saying.'

We watched the sunset a moment.

I turned back to him. 'So — you're a Phony, huh?'

He nodded. 'Last time I checked.'

'How's that work, exactly? Shouldn't you be off pillaging people's bodies or whatever?' Not that I was complaining or anything. I'm just saying, I was curious.

He scoffed. 'Whilst A'doy may indeed be a devious little cocksucker, he is right about some things. There are those of us who wish nothing more than to coexist with humans. For O'tsaris like myself, for instance, we are forbidden from taking a host without that host's full consent — usually via written agreement.'

'An agreement?' I said. *'You mean like a prenuptial?'*

'Don't make this weird.'

'Oh — sorry.' I looked out at the horizon again, that endless procession of lights. 'So what will you do now? What's next for you?'

He shrugged. 'A lot of things came spilling out of that doorway. They'll need someone out there looking for them. Guess I'm as good a guy for the job as any.'

'Yeah.'

Well good luck with that.

He rested a hand on my shoulder. 'Listen, I know you feel the hand you've been dealt is a harsh one — and it is. No denying it. And I don't know whether you're really the chosen one or not. But if you ever need me, I'll be there.'

For a moment I thought he was gonna give me a special phone or radio or something, like the one that goes directly to the president's office — which would have been freaking cool, but he didn't.

'But how will I know how to find —?' I began, but paused when, turning around, I saw the guy was nowhere to be seen.

I scoffed.

That is one mysterious motherfucker.

Just then, the door to the roof went again.

'All right,' said Abby, marching across the roof towards me. 'That's it. You better tell me what's up with you before I start punching dicks. What's wrong with you?'

'Nothing. I'm fine.'

'No, Dan, you're *not*. You've been acting weird since... well, since all that weird stuff happened.' She thought about it. 'That *other* weird stuff, I mean. *Spill.*'

'Honestly, I'm fine. Just feeling a little nauseous from all that grinding going on downstairs. I mean, Christ, did you see Doug?'

By the look of pure horror that flashed over her face, I could tell that she had.

Now, I know it might seem like kind of a dick move on my part, lying to Abby like that. But it was for her own protection. Even if she was both smarter and braver than I was, unburdening all of my problems on her just wasn't cool. You didn't do that to the people you loved. Even if not doing so made you fucking miserable. They say love is sacrifice, and never had that been more true than in my current situation.

But I had made my decision.

She sighed. 'Well, if you're *sure* you're okay —'

'I'm not sure. I'm drowning here, Abby. It's like I can't breathe. Like there's a pillow over my face, one made of *shit* —

A shit-pillow!

—and every snatched gasp of air I manage is slowly poisoning me because of the sheer volume of shit-covered shitting *shit* in it.'

I took a deep breath.

Of course, on the other hand, nobody likes a martyr...

She pointed a threatening finger at me. 'Talk.'

I did.

When I was finished, a heavy silence descended upon us — which, if I'm honest, did nothing to lessen my sense of dread. Christ, I was fucking doomed.

'Well?' I said, after a moment. '*Aren't you going to say something?*' Not to be an ass or anything, but if she'd come here to comfort me, she was doing a pretty piss-poor job. She was being kind of a dick, frankly.

She thought it over. 'Look, I'm not going to say that what you saw was... *wrong*... that it wasn't the "future". I have no idea what waits in store for us.' She took my face in her hands, turned me to face her. 'But whatever it is — *we'll face it together*. Do you hear me? You're not alone, Dan. Even if it sometimes feels like you are.'

And suddenly, just like that, I *did* feel better.

Because Abby was right. So maybe we couldn't see the future. *So what?* We'd stopped invasion attempts before. We could do it again — which was aiming pretty fucking high, true, but at least it was better than the doom-themed spiral of futility I'd been stuck in these past few weeks.

I began to tell Abby this —

I looked down.

'What are you doing...?!' I said.

She was on her knees — one knee, to be exact. In her hand was a box, its lid open.

I gasped.

'OH NO YOU DIDN'T. YOU DID NOT JUST STEAL MY THUNDER LIKE THAT.'

She smirked. 'Shouldn't have taken so long then, should you?'

Some stuff happened after that. Things were said. Declarations of some variety or another were made. There might have been tears — but then again, maybe there weren't. Guess we'll just have to leave that part to your imagination.

We stood there holding each other, snow falling lightly down around us, watching as the sun finally started to dip itself behind the horizon.

No, we couldn't know what kinds of awful things might be waiting for us further on down the line.

But one thing was for sure, whatever it was, we would face it together.

'Dan?' said Abby, tilting her head to look up at me, eyes bright and staring in the dimming light.

'*Hmm?*'

'Merry Christmas.'

DID YOU ENJOY THIS BOOK?

If so, let the author know!

Visit him at his website: www.richardlangridgeauthor.com.

JOIN THE RESISTANCE!

Subscribe to the Dan and Frankie newsletter to receive updates on all the latest Dan and Frankie news, as well as the occasional free gift!

Visit www.richardlangridgeauthor.com and subscribe today!

ABOUT THE AUTHOR

Richard Langridge is a novelist, musician, and notorious cheese lover. He currently lives in the United Kingdom with his fiancée Victoria, and their son Harry. He once rescued a litter of puppies from a burning building and is prone to telling outrageous lies. He also likes to refer to himself in third person. He does not know why.

When not writing about nonsense, you can usually find him over at his blog, www.richardlangridgeauthor.com

ACKNOWLEDGEMENTS

A book is like a baby.

They're both tiny—that's the first thing. You can put them in a bag, tuck them under your armpit or maybe in a pocket, providing you're wearing balloon pants, and you're a crazy person. Getting them from one place to another is always a breeze. Logistically speaking, they're pretty much even.

They have similar gestation periods—that's the other thing. Getting them out into the world is always a bloody and traumatic experience, regardless of what the other mothers might have told you beforehand, or how many drugs you're on.

And, just as with labour, getting this book out into the world simply would not have been possible without the help and support from several lovely people gently coaxing it out of my metaphorical vagina—all of whom I'd like to thank now.

Firstly, to Charli Vince, for once again knocking it out of the park with this cover. I mean, seriously, just look at it. Holy crap.

If the "marketing folk" are correct, covers play a huge role in whether or not a person decides to pick up a book. In a lot of ways, covers are the candy we authors use to lure all you unwitting fools

into the back of our blacked-out panel vans—which I guess technically makes her kind of my accomplice. I dunno. Either way, you can find more of her work over at: www.charlivince.com

To my good friend and fellow author Sam Cox, for being my writing buddy on this adventure, and for pretending not to question our friendship all those times I overused nipple metaphors. You're a terrible liar.

To all my many, many beta readers, of whom there are simply too many to mention, and whose cookies I swear I will one day get to them. No, I swear. For really realsies this time. Promise.

To my parents, for not acting too disappointed in my life choices, even though we all know better, and for never stopping me from watching all those ridiculous movies as a kid—which in hindsight probably makes you terrible parents. I mean, holy crap, *Jaws*? Really? I WAS FOUR, MUM.

A wet, slippery thank you to the 'ol ball-and-chain; my beautiful little Jasmine flower, Victoria, for her love and support, and for continuing to put up with my crap even though let's face it we both know you can do way better.

And finally, to my special little guy, Harry, for filling my days with joy/misery, and for being *literally* the coolest person I've ever met, little or otherwise.

You get it from me.

Printed in Great Britain
by Amazon